William M. (William Mumford) Baker

The Virginians in Texas

A sStory for Young old Folks and Old Young Folks

William M. (William Mumford) Baker

The Virginians in Texas
A sStory for Young old Folks and Old Young Folks

ISBN/EAN: 9783744773133

Printed in Europe, USA, Canada, Australia, Japan

Cover: Foto ©Andreas Hilbeck / pixelio.de

More available books at **www.hansebooks.com**

THE VIRGINIANS IN TEXAS

A Story

For Young Old Folks and Old Young Folks

BY

WILLIAM M. BAKER

AUTHOR OF "INSIDE" "THE NEW TIMOTHY" "CARTER QUARTERMAN" "MOSE EVANS"
"A YEAR WORTH LIVING" &c.

NEW YORK
HARPER & BROTHERS, PUBLISHERS
FRANKLIN SQUARE
1878

TO

MY NAME-BOY, W. M. B., JR.

My Dear Willie:

This book was my first attempt, written when I was little more than a boy myself. As to that, I hope I may remain, in some respects, a boy as long as I live—if it be to the age of Methuselah; yes, and in the other world too—a boy forever.

You have read this story over and over in the pages of *Harper's Monthly*, and tell me that you prefer it to any other of my books. Very well, here it is; I make you a present of it. If other people like it half so well as you do, I shall be satisfied. You are proud of Texas. That the great State of your birth may some day be proud of you is the hope of

YOUR LOVING FATHER.

THE VIRGINIANS IN TEXAS.

CHAPTER I.

MOVING TO TEXAS.

THIS gentleman whom we see riding towards us along this forest road is Mr. Morton McRobert, late of Virginia. He wears, you see, a broad-brimmed woollen hat to protect him from the sun, and because no amount of crushing in travelling will injure it. As he rides nearer to us you can see enough of his face under the rim of his hat to read therein cheerfulness, sincerity, and quiet determination. You know that he is not going to church by the copperas-colored clothes he wears—worn for hard service, and not for show. The horse he rides is a good one, as you notice—strong, spirited, with small, sharp-pointed ears in incessant motion. Black Bob is his name.

But let horse and rider pass on, for we hear the sound of coming wheels behind him, and we want to see who it is. And while the sound comes nearer along the winding of the sandy road among the trees, just a word or two about Mr. McRobert. It would have been in strict accordance with Texas usage if we had stopped him when we had first met him and proceeded thus:

"Good-morning, sir."

"Good-morning," he would have replied.

"Moving, I reckon?"

"Yes, sir."

"What state are you from?"

"Virginia."

Then if you happened to be from Virginia too, you would instantly ask, "Ah, indeed! What county?" And if you were from the same or bordering counties, there would be no telling when the conversation would end—not until you had ascertained the degree of your relationship to him, if it took three hours; for all the great-grandparents of Virginians were second cousins at the very least. If you were not from Virginia, you would only ask, taking less interest in him, "I say, stranger, what did you leave for?"

Nor in the early days of Texas would a mover to the state have been astonished, scarce displeased, at the question. Many came there then on account of frauds or murders committed elsewhere. Of these some continued their evil courses in their new home, and soon perished by intemperance or the bowie-knife. But very many turned over a new leaf altogether, refunded ultimately all they owed, and lived many a long year afterwards, prosperous in cattle and lands, respected and happy. Criminals rarely fly to Texas these days. They are more certainly caught and carried back than if they had concealed themselves in the cellars of their own homes. Emigration to Texas now is at the rate of two hundred and fifty thousand a year, and the population is rising into millions.

If Mr. McRobert had been one of the refugees from justice, in answer to any such question he would have said, "Oh, well, yes, I had a difficulty in the neighborhood where I lived." It would not have been prudent for you to have pressed the topic beyond this; but, if the new-comer had conversed further about it, he would have assured you that, whatever the trouble was, it was *he* who had been shamefully wronged, which was strange, as the word "difficulty" embraced everything—theft, forgery, assassination.

However, I hardly think any one would have questioned Mr. McRobert as closely as was usual in the case of strangers. It is astonishing how much of his character, good or bad, a man carries in his face; and there was an aspect of dignity and self-respect in the countenance and bearing of this gentleman that would have repressed all impertinence. If he had answered your inquiries, however, he would have said that he had been a wealthy planter in Virginia. I do not think he would have detailed to any one the manner in which he had been swindled out of his property by the base treachery of a man named Watkins, whom he had greatly esteemed and trusted. This was a part of his past experience which he never alluded to, hardly even in his own family; and of which he thought even as little as possible. It is not necessary to enter into any detail just here. The result was, that he had been rapidly reduced from wealth to almost poverty.

His coming to Texas happened in this way: Years before, his brother Frank, warm-hearted but wayward, had gone to Texas, had fought in all its early wars with Indians and Mexicans, had settled there, and had become extravagantly attached to the country. Remaining, so far as was known, unmarried, all he seemed to care for was Texas and his brother Morton's family. "A letter from Uncle Frank!" by any one returning from the post-office was an announcement always hailed with special pleasure.

Now, it so happened that, very soon after his heavy loss, such a letter arrived.

That morning Mr. McRobert had risen from a night of sleepless anxiety as to the future. At family worship he had besought divine direction as to his plans; and it was when the family were at breakfast that Hark, the black man, brought in the letter in a huge brown envelope, and laid it on the table. It really seemed a providence, a direct reply to prayer, a flash of light upon a dark spot.

In this way:

Uncle Frank had often urged his brother to move to Texas. In this letter, though he had heard nothing of his brother's loss, he pressed the same thing with more force than before. In addition he made a special offer. He had "located"—that is, had picked out and legally secured—a league of fine land on the Colorado River, which he offered to his brother as a free gift in case he would move to Texas. To show how much he was in earnest, whole-souled Uncle Frank had actually enclosed the patent to the land, with its broad red seal, the transfer endorsed on the back of the parchment.

Madison, the eldest boy, read the letter aloud. It was full of descriptions of the health, fertility, beauty, prosperity of Texas, and urgent were Uncle Frank's entreaties that the family would come out. He spoke very disrespectfully of Old Virginia in comparison with the "New Dominion," as he styled Texas. He offered, from his large herds, to give his brother a "start," as he called it, of cows and horses; to help him build a cabin; urged upon him "anything and everything" if he would only come out. No one of the family had ever had such an idea. Texas? As well move to Kamtchatka! But the first thought of father and mother was that it seemed a providence! Just as they were cut to the soul by the treachery of a friend, here were the warm heart and hand of a brother; just as their estate had slipped from them and they knew not what to do, another and much larger estate lay there upon the table among the breakfast things in that parchment, if they would have it! Here was their Father in heaven, with his left hand afflicting them in Virginia, but with his right hand, at the same instant, touching the heart and prompting the hand of Uncle Frank far away in Texas; and all to bring about, as I think we will see, the greater good and happiness of the family than if he had permitted events to roll on in their usual channel. Christians read in their own experience as distinctly as in Scripture that "all things work together for good to them that love God."

The same loving hand that laid that letter on the table that morning touched, at the same instant, the heart of the family to accept the offer. When Madison had finished reading the letter it was a settled matter that they would remove to Texas. No one said so, but all felt that it was. William was twelve years old—two years younger than Madison—and he expressed the feeling of the whole table when, at last, he burst out, the first to break the silence, "Oh, I am so glad we are going to Texas!" Bessie did not say anything, of course, as she was not yet four years old; but whatever delighted "Brother Will" and Josie delighted her.

One person, however, did speak about it—in fact, speak about nothing else henceforth—and that was Rohamma, the one negro woman left to the family. She had just brought in a plate of hot batter-cakes, and did not wait to hear anything said after the letter was read. Hurrying into the kitchen, she caught Hark, her husband, somewhat roughly by the shoulder, and exclaimed,

"All done now! we gwine to Texas, you nigger! What you bring dat letter for?"

Her opinion of the matter 'Markable, too, well knew long before night. This was her boy whom she had insisted on naming Remarkable, but the first syllable of his name had got worn off, so to speak, by constant use, and, having no one else to express herself upon, a more thoroughly spanked negro child was not in all Virginia. For some days after she waited at table with solemn, silent protest on her face. In addition to her perpetual bewailment of the matter over her wash-tub and ovens, she ventured once, and only once, to utter her sentiments. They broke from her in spite of herself one day when engaged with her mistress in packing.

Poor Rohamma! Texas was to her Indians and Mexicans, wild beasts, "varmints," and poor white folks, and all that was horrible to imagine. She would almost rather have died than go. And, the fact is, so felt her mistress too, although she endeavored to conceal it. Rohamma did not look at her "Miss 'Manda" as she expressed her horror and protest in reference to Texas. But when she had finished her mistress turned to her from the trunk over which she was kneeling, and said, quietly,

"Rohamma, we are going to Texas; that is settled. But if you don't want to go, very well; your Mass Morton will leave you and Hark and 'Markable. Colonel Jones is anxious to buy you all. You needn't go if you don't want to." For all this took place before the Civil War and the emancipation of the slaves.

The "girl" glanced up at the pale anxious face and tearful eyes of he mistress, laid down the folded sheets she was handling, and burst into tears; they had been babies together—had never been apart.

"Law! Miss 'Manda," she sobbed, "you know I won't stay. Texas is dreffful; but if the fam'ly must go, I goes too!"

A long, long time it took; weeks of confusion and getting-ready and leave-taking. It was only at the last day that Uncle George made his appearance on the scene. A wealthy planter, and living in an adjoining county, he had held himself hitherto aloof from his brother in his misfortune. When he found him actually starting for Texas, this brother, driven partly by feeling and a great deal more by what people would say—for, to the neighborhood, going to Texas was the falling down a tremendous precipice—endeavored to interpose. It was too late.

"But, at least, don't take the children with you to such a country," he urged. "It's no place for them, at any rate. Leave them on my place for a time, anyhow; they'll be at home with their cousins there. You are certain to come back to Virginia. Don't take them. Amanda had better stay too. If you must go, Morton, go by yourself first and see how you like the country."

No; Mr. McRobert's mind was now made up. The offer, which once would have been gladly accepted, was made too late. As to his wife, when misfortune befalls, nothing short of death can tear a true woman such as she was from a husband. And so, before the neighbors could fairly believe it, the McRobert family were gone.

They could have gone by sea to New Orleans, and so to Galveston; but Mrs. McRobert had a peculiar horror of the sea, and the journey was made overland.

All this time Mr. McRobert has ridden on past us, and we are waiting to see what follows him. Here they come toiling along in the deep sand. An open barouche first, drawn by a pair of strong mules. That is right. Never take horses to draw on a long journey; mules are far the best on every account. That is Madison you see on the front seat driving. Bessie is beside him. She insisted on sitting there, rather than by her mother on the back seat, that she might see everything. Let the carriage roll by. Next comes a wagon with four mules. That is Hark walking and driving. The wagon is strong, blue, covered with canvas, and packed with trunks and camping things. Rohamma and 'Markable are riding inside; they walk sometimes, but ride when tired. After the wagon comes William, on his white pony; "Slow" he calls him, just because he thinks he is the fastest pony, when put at it, that ever trotted. There is yet another boy. He is seated beside his mother, and it is almost impossible to say what the round-headed and thoughtful child is named. His father calls him Dodles, Madison rarely speaks of him except as Doodle-bug, Willie alludes to him as Doady, his mother as Josie. He takes little interest in anything except machinery, concerning which he is considered an authority. Although only nine years old, the household agree that he is to be a distinguished engineer and inventor.

And this is the order of travel ever since they left Virginia, and now here they are entering, after several weeks of travel, upon the soil, at last, of Western Texas. Mr. McRobert rides before to buy corn, or to fix upon a good camping-place for the night, or to have the ferry-boat ready when a river is to be crossed. Will rides behind to pick up anything that may be dropped from the carriage or wagon, and to bring up the rear generally. 'Markable by himself, or Rohamma with Bessie, in walking, are very apt to loiter behind, and Will's business is to keep them up. Sometimes Madison changes with Will or with his father. Mrs. McRobert often walks, or even rides on horseback or in the wagon for a change.

Twenty miles a day is all they aim to make; sometimes it is less, sometimes more than this, as the camping-places happen to fit. Grass for the animals, wood for the camp-fire, water for cooking and drinking, are the requisites. Arrived at such a spot about sundown, the carriage and wagon are arranged to the windward side, both to escape danger from the sparks and to keep off the wind. The animals are unharnessed and fed with corn, and afterwards well rubbed down by

Hark, and tethered out to graze—all night if they will. Meanwhile Mr. McRobert and Madison have taken the tent out of the wagon and put it up—on sloping ground, if possible, in case it should rain. Then a huge log is cut and rolled to the mouth of the tent, and a fire built against it by 'Markable.

All this time Will has attended to his pony, Slow, and assisted his mother. As to Rohamma, by the time all are ready for it, she has supper on the fire. The fare is far coarser than was ever placed on their table in Virginia; yet, appetite? not one but eats with a relish never known before; not one but seems many pounds fatter since starting. Two members of the family enjoy it especially — Duke and Snap — the one Madison's big mastiff, the other Will's pet terrier. They were trotting under the wagon when we first met the family, and this is the reason we did not see them before.

But they are tired enough when supper is over; so Mr. McRobert reads a passage from his pocket Bible, and commends the little group to God's unsleeping care during the night. Then to bed. The boys always lodge in the tent, their parents in the wagon; while the servants sleep upon the ground on their blankets, with their feet to the fire, the soundest of all. Notwithstanding their travel, Duke and Snap seem to be up and around all night, seeing that all is right. Often enough Hark is roused by their furious barking to drive off some intruding hog or cow. Once or twice he found that they had treed an opossum near the camp, and next morning it was broiling on the coals for all who would partake.

By early dawn all are up and dressed, refreshed by their sleep in the open air, the sweetest of all sleep. A rapid breakfast, a quick stowing-away of everything, a crack of Hark's whip, and soon the smouldering camp-fire remains the only relic of the family's home for a night. At noon there is a short stop for an hour or so, for a hasty snack, seated upon the grass beside the grazing mules.

On Saturday afternoons an early halt is always made, the camp fixed with more care than usual, and the Sabbath spent in rest. Pleasant Sabbaths they were too, upon which all looked back, long after, with pleasure, as they had anticipated them during the travel of the week with joy. The animals are well rubbed and fed, and permitted to graze all day. In the morning there is the singing of sweet, familiar hymns beneath the forest trees, the elder children memorizing hymns or verses from Scripture, or reading as they lie upon the clean grass. None enjoyed the day more than the servants — singing together their camp-meeting songs, or carding their heads with wool-cards, or sleeping soundly beneath the wagon. It was a time of enjoyment, of rest to all: even Duke and Snap appreciated it, lying at their ease in the sun.

And so day succeeded day, and week followed week. Every day something new. Now the harness would break in some severe tug uphill; or a swingle-tree would snap in two; or a particularly bad stretch of road would occur where all would have to walk; or it would rain; or a halt had to be made at the roadside shop while mending was done; or a village was passed through, where small purchases had to be made and innumerable questions had to be answered.

It was on the 3d day of March the family left Loiterwater, the name of their place in Virginia; and on the night of the 6th of May Mr. McRobert told them at supper that by that time next day they might reach the Colorado River, somewhere near their future home. When morning came, all were up before light, and an exciting time it was, as, indeed, it had been for a week past.

The whole aspect of the country since they had crossed the Brazos was entirely unlike anything they had ever before seen. Only occasionally would they pass through a belt of post-oaks or a bottom of pecan-trees. For the most part, the hard, smooth road wound over the rollings of the prairie. Bessie fairly screamed with joy when she beheld the vast expanse as splendid with innumerable flowers as the sky is with stars, chiefly blue and red, set off in deep green grass. A buoyancy of spirits, an excitement, a positive exhilaration, possessed every one. The pure, clear air was inhaled like the drinking of wine. As Mr. and Mrs. McRobert said to one another, the singular feeling experienced was more like a return of the exquisite joy of childhood than anything else; and even the children thought their parents seemed younger, happier, and handsomer than they had ever known

them. Madison could hardly attend to his driving. Will was almost wild, darting now to the right, now to the left of the road, to gather some particularly bright flowers for Bessie; Josie enjoying it all the more, even if he said less.

When the first herd of deer was seen grazing off to the left, even Madison shouted till he was almost hoarse. But when a rabbit jumped up almost from under the hoofs of the team, ran a few steps, and then stopped and sat looking at them with such droll ears, nearly a foot long, even Duke and Snap were too much astonished to pursue. As to Will, off he shot after it on Slow, calling on the dogs until recalled from the hopeless chase by his father. And so on all day; for there was too much eagerness to stop to dine.

About the middle of the afternoon a range of blue hills hemmed them in upon the left, one peak towering above the rest, and at their base was a dense valley of timber, through which they could catch now and then the silver gleam of the Colorado. But the attention of the family was now diverted by seeing a horseman galloping towards them across the prairie from the mountains. He was a singular, alarming object. A heavy wool hat came down almost entirely over his bearded face; a buckskin suit heavily fringed; a gun before him on the saddle, where hung a coil of rope; a wild, rough pony under him, completed his appearance. And it increased their alarm when they saw him gallop right up to Mr. Morton on the road before them in the distance, rein up his horse, leap off, unhook the coil of rope from the pommel of the saddle and throw it on the ground, then actually seize hold upon and tear him from his saddle! They were terrified lest they should see the gleam of a scalping-knife in his hand, and Madison sprang out of the carriage and ran to defend his father. In the midst of the consternation of the family, little Bessie, who had been looking eagerly on, lisped out, "I expetht thath my Uncle Frank!" The alarm was changed to joy; and from every lip rang the cry, "Oh, Uncle Frank! Uncle Frank!"

CHAPTER II.

GETTING A LITTLE FIXED.

It was Uncle Frank sure enough! He had received his brother's letter announcing their coming, and for two weeks past he had been watching out for them with his spy-glass from the top of Pilot Knob, for that was the name of the lofty peak they had seen. By dark he had them safe and sound inside his house, a large and rambling sort of log cabin on the other side of the Colorado. "Harkal," he called it, meaning thereby the Spanish "*jacal*" —the Mexican name for a "cabin."

The children long remembered this as the most exciting night of their lives. They could not realize it. Only a little while ago in Virginia, which now seemed far, far away; now in Texas, and actually seated under Uncle Frank's roof, around the huge fireplace. They could hardly talk for looking around. There were the rough log walls, with near a dozen guns of various sorts supported on wooden pegs along them; while all kinds of twisted powder-horns, and shot-pouches made out of spotted skins, hung beside. Then there was the queer "puncheon" floor and the odd wooden chairs and stools; singular-shaped gourds hung by a thong around the middle with a cob stuck in the mouth; spears with curious iron heads, which they afterwards learned were to "jig" fish with; nets to trap partridges; large knives in skin sheaths; and dozens of other things new to them.

They were interested, too, in Francisco, their uncle's Mexican servant-boy, who was blowing at the coffee-pot on the hearth and baking flat cakes, which Uncle Frank called "tor-teyas"—a name which they afterwards found was spelled *tortillas*. He was the first Mexican they had ever seen, and they eyed him closely. He seemed to hold himself almost sullenly aloof from them too, and Mrs. McRobert noticed that his black eyes followed his master wherever he went, like those of a dog, loving and wistful.

Above all, there was Uncle Frank. Such a beard, and such a dress, and so radiant with joy and welcome. They were almost afraid of him, he looked so much like a bear; all, at least, except Bessie, and she had climbed upon his knees as soon as he sat down, and, with a child's (and, above all, a girl-child's) instinctive knowledge of character, loved him dearly from the start. Henceforth papa and mamma might almost bid good-bye to her—she was "Uncle Frank's girl."

Such cups and saucers there were, too, when they sat down to table—no two cups or plates or dishes alike. And the broiled venison—shot that day specially for them, Uncle Frank said—the great dish of wild honey beside it, the nice fresh butter, the buttermilk in a big wash-pitcher, and the hot, crisp tortillas—the children, and their parents too, never made so hearty a meal. Only they could hardly eat for talking—asking and answering a hundred questions. Bessie kept silent, watching Uncle Frank. She saw him drink one cup of coffee and then another. But when Francisco brought the coffee-pot, boiling from the fire, to fill his cup a third time, she could hold in no longer, and cried out,

"Oh, Uncle Frank, you'll be thick; you drinkth too *muth* coffee!"

All laughed, and Uncle Frank said, "Why, Bess, coffee is what I live on. People in Texas drink coffee all day when they can get it. The pot's always on the hearth, and it's never cold when anybody's on the ranch. *Ranch* means 'here, at home.'"

In fact, all were happy; but no one more so than their host. He seemed overflowing with joy. When they first sat down to table, his brother had said, "If you please, Frank," and had asked a blessing.

"That's the first time a blessing has ever been asked in this house," said Uncle Frank. "It seems like Virginia itself. Don't you remember, Morton, how father used always to ask blessing in your very words, and to return thanks too? And mother, when father was away at Richmond, would always put her hands together and say blessing in his place? How it all comes back to me! I have been mighty wild, I know. Never mind, that's all past; I take another trail from to-night."

And so after supper it was at Uncle Frank's own request that his brother read a chapter and offered a prayer. He thanked God for having led them safely through their journey; for permitting them to meet after so many years. He entreated his blessing upon them in the new life they were entering upon. There were tears in more eyes than one when they arose from their knees. But even then Madison could not but notice the astonished look of Francisco, standing by the door. No wonder. It was the first time the Mexican had ever seen Protestant worship, and it was something entirely new to him.

Bright and early next morning the children were up and out. The broad landscape, the sparkling air, the wind blowing as if they were out at sea—all was new and exhilarating. There was Francisco too, just starting off with a coil of singular-looking rope on one arm and a bucket on the other. The children answered his smiling and yet reluctant "*Buenos dias!*" with the same salutation, only in English—"Good-morning!"

2

"Why, what is this?" said Will, touching, as they walked with Francisco, the rope—a hide cut into strips.

"Lariat," replied the Mexican. "That," continued he, pointing to another rope hanging on the branch of a mesquit-tree they were passing, and made of hair nicely twisted together—"that *cabris.*"

"But what are you going to do with your lariat?"

By this time they had reached a rude rail pen, in which were near a dozen calves. Without replying, Francisco let down the bars and admitted one of the impatient cows standing without. But before the calf could reach its mother a noose, thrown by the skilful Francisco, was around its neck, and the other end of the lariat run around a tree in the pen. The calf was permitted to suck for a minute or so, then the tightened rope held it struggling nearer the tree, while Francisco, first pouring water from the bucket over his hands, proceeded to milk. Only about a quart was obtained, and the same process had to be gone through with all the cows before the bucket was filled.

"I say, Francisco, you must teach me how to throw the lariat," said Madison, as they walked towards the house.

The Mexican laughed and nodded. Notwithstanding his black eyes and hair and swarthy color, and outlandish, broad-brimmed, high-crowned black hat, the children felt far more at ease in regard to him than they had done the night before.

"See here," said Francisco; and, handing the milk-bucket to Madison, he pointed to a broken-off limb projecting from a mesquit-tree some thirty feet off, and with a swift hurl of his hand the noosed end of the lariat was around it in a moment, while the other end remained in his grasp. "You try," he continued; and, running to the tree, he disengaged the lariat, coiled it again, and placed it in the hand of his companion.

Madison *did* try his best, but at the first throw the noose did not reach half-way to the tree. At the next it went that far, but did not come within five feet of the tree even, falling to one side. At the next throw the whole lariat flew out of his hand far over the top of the tree, amid the hearty laughter of all.

"Never mind—try every day—learn at last. This one the smartest," he added, nodding his head at Josie, who was standing soberly by, as they proceeded to the house; and the boys both resolved that learn they would, if effort and patience could accomplish it. Meanwhile they began to look up somewhat to the Mexican, who seemed about the age of Madison. But they did not dream of half he could do, or, alas! of what he was, as they were one day to learn.

"Now," said Uncle Frank, as they sat at table after breakfast, "what I propose is this: while sister Amanda and Bessie and Will and Doady, Josie, Dodles, Doodle-bug—what *is* his name?—rest themselves, suppose, Morton, that you and Madison take a ride with me—not on horseback, but in the boat; it's down at the bank, not a hundred yards from the house. We can look around a little. What do you say?"

Mr. McRobert and Madison willingly consented. After seeing that their animals had been securely tethered out to graze on the rich mesquit grass growing abundantly around, and of which they seemed to eat greedily, and yielding to the earnest entreaty of Will to go with them, they started. Uncle Frank first said a few words to Francisco, who nodded and said, "Si, si, señor," with a profusion of singular gestures with his fingers which struck Will as particularly funny.

"What did he say see, see, for, uncle, and twist his fingers so for?" inquired he, as they walked on.

"Oh, si, si, is Spanish for 'yes, yes;' and as to his fingers, Mexicans talk with them — five tongues on each hand and one in their mouth," replied his uncle. "You'll understand it all, Will, after a while."

In a few moments the whole party were embarked in the skiff and out upon the broad, clear river. It was a large, strong-built boat, nicely painted, the name *Dolores* written on the stern and on each side of the prow.

"Who was Dolores, uncle?" asked Will as they glided along.

"Not now — I'll tell you some of these days. Pshaw! why did I forget it!" replied his uncle, a little hastily, and there was a dark shadow across his face and a something in his tone that made all regret that the question had been asked.

"Ah, stop! I liked to have forgotten," he said. Laying his oars down, he took a tin cup from under the seat, dipped it in the river, washed it well, then filled it with water, and handed it to his brother.

"Thank you, I'm not thirsty," said Mr. McRobert.

"Never mind, please drink; and you, Madison, and you too, Will. That's right. That'll do."

"But why did you want us to drink?" asked his brother.

"I'll tell you to-night. Steer, will you, if you please; there's a paddle in the bottom, Morton. I want to go down stream."

As they sped rapidly along under the vigorous strokes of their uncle's oars the children exclaimed every moment with delight at the transparency of the water and the beauty of the scenery. A flock of wild-ducks flew so close over their heads that they could see the beautiful green of their necks and the very black of their eyes.

"Oh, if I only had a gun here!" said Madison.

"Yes, and knew how to hit," added Will.

"I'll see that you both learn to do that well enough before long," said their uncle. "I have got a good rifle for you at the harkal, Madison, and a double-barrel shot-gun for you, Will. I can't think what made me forget to give them to you before we left."

"Oh, uncle! thank you, thank you!" said both the delighted boys in a breath.

"It's often been with me, No deer, no supper. Mrs. Necessity was the old lady that taught me how to shoot," said their uncle. "And now

I think I can hit in less than ten yards of a doe's foreshoulder when I try hard. Throw us a little more into the bank, Morton—that's it."

"Oh, see—yonder's another river!" exclaimed both of the boys, for the thick undergrowth of the river-bank parted suddenly as they sped down the river, and revealed a beautiful stream almost as wide as the Colorado, on which they floated, of bluer water, flowing into the Colorado from among dense forest trees drooping over on each side.

"That? that isn't a river," said their uncle; "that's a spring-branch. The head of it is only a quarter of a mile or so up, out of the side of that high hill you see there."

"Who ever heard of such a spring?" said their father, amid the exclamation of the boys; "it seems a hundred times too much water to come from a dozen springs! What is its name?"

"The San Hieronymo. Everything is a *San*-Something in this country. That means *Saint*. There is the San Gabriel, the San Marcos—beautiful streams not sixty miles from here—San Pedro Springs, San Antonio River, and town too. Then there's the Brazos River; its full name was *Brazos de Dios*—the arms of God. There's the Trinity River too. Corpus Christi is the name of a town on the Gulf. And so of a hundred other streams or towns. However little religion the old Spaniards had in their hearts and hands, they had plenty of it, in this way, on their tongues. The names—the Trinity, for instance—shock one at first in

such common use. You soon get accustomed to it, and think of it only as a river. Besides, the old names are giving way to new ones as Americans come in."

"Some of the names in Texas can hardly be an improvement upon the old," said his brother. "Let me see; we crossed Muddy and Brushy and Dry Creeks, I remember."

"And through the towns of Bucksnort and Scrougeabout and Hog-eye, you remember, papa?" cried Madison.

"Yes, and mamma bought a doll for Bessie in Split-skull. And Hark told me," continued Will, "that he heard talk of a place called Lickskillet."

"There are names worse than those," interrupted his uncle. "But never mind that now. I want to turn into the San Hieronymo. Catch those willows, Madison, and pull us along. 'Hold on to the willows! Grab a root!'—you'll know what those phrases mean first time you are adrift out here on the river when it is booming. That's it. Now look out you don't grab a rattlesnake!"

Thus saying, the Texan rowed the boat up the windings of the beautiful tributary until the party landed at last upon a rock towering some hundreds of feet above the whole region. From where they stood the country lay open before them, as in a picture.

"Now here's a view I wanted you to look at, Morton," said his brother; and, so saying, he led them to a mesquit-tree rooted in a rift of the rock on which they stood, and stuck this map upon it by the two pins, refer-

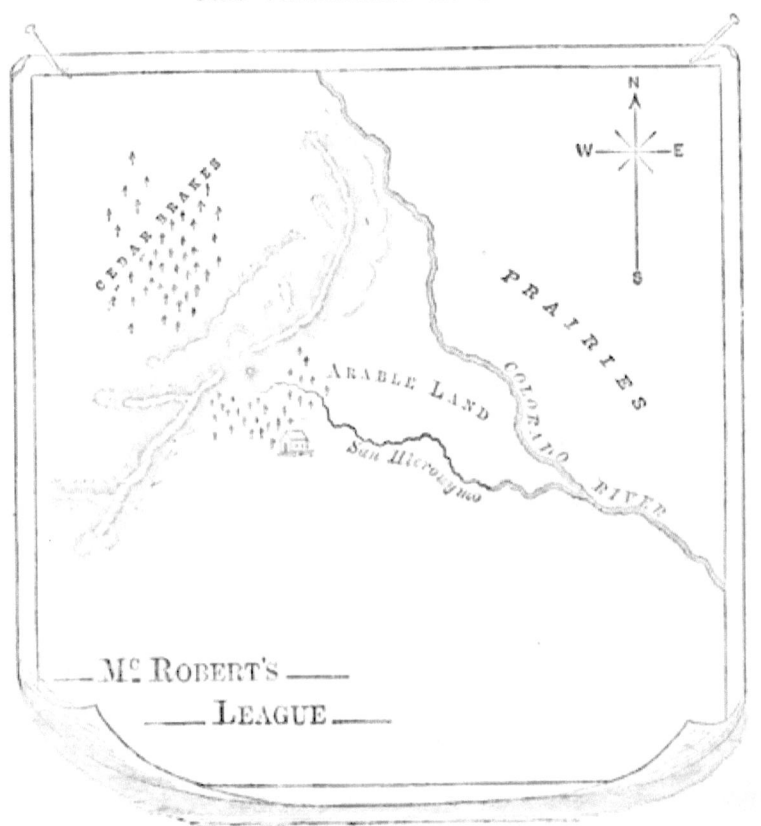

McRobert's ___
___League___

ring to it and then to the country lying at their feet, as he explained. "You see," he added, "where the San Hieronymo enters the Colorado, below us as we stand. You can trace it along by its timber. This high point is about a mile from the river. Where you see that thick grove of big live-oaks on our left is where the San Hieronymo bursts up from under the hills; they are big enough to call mountains in a new country. They'll grow, you know;" but they saw he was joking. "It is," he added, "a splendid building-place this—plenty of water, wood, and rock for building; besides being high and shady.

The mountain is just right to keep off the northers, while the south is open to let in the summer breeze up the valley. Back of the grove you see the country rolls up the mountains into the cedar brakes; cedar enough there to fence in all Texas. Coming on down from that, and between the creek and the river, is open prairie, rich as cream, ready and anxious for the plough, good for wheat, corn, cotton—anything. Come on farther down; that thick pecan forest is all river bottom. There's a little tract of land worth looking at—one or two miles river front, stretching I don't know how many miles back! Well, what do you think of your land?"

"*My* land! you do not mean to say—"

"Yes, it is," said his brother Frank, interrupting him; "that's *your* league. It's more than a league: it's a league and a *labor*—four thousand six hundred acres in one body."

"My dear brother," said Mr. McRobert, after a moment's silence, and in a faltering voice, "how can I thank you? I assure you—"

"Thanks!" said his brother, impetuously. "When I ran away to Texas, and George and all were dead against me as a good-for-nothing scamp, didn't you stand up for me with father and the rest? And you can't have forgotten that five hundred you mailed me when I was so hard-up after the fight at San Jacinto. That is the league Texas gave me because I was in that fight. I bought the next league to it on the other side of the San Hieronymo with part of the money you sent me, improved it, and got a stock of cattle with the rest. So you may well regard it as your land—bought with your own dollars; only this is a better league for you than the one my ranch is on. And if you *do* owe me anything, you have more than paid it up by coming out to Texas to live beside me."

"And you had not heard about the conduct of Watkins when you wrote?" asked his brother.

"Oh! couldn't I pick him off his horse with a rifle beautifully if he was at all in range!" replied the Texan. "But no, I didn't hear of it till your last letter. Only Hark, Rohamma, and 'Markable left out of near one hundred hands! However, since it's brought you to Texas, I don't object."

"It was hard at first," said his brother; "but I have no bitter feelings towards the man. I ought not to have endorsed for him. However, I did the best I could under the circumstances. I am not a fatalist, but I am satisfied it will all be right in the end—I am satisfied of it," he repeated, warmly. "There's no such thing as chance in my religion; it is Providence—a wise and loving and special Providence—I believe in. Each day I am to do all I can, according to the very best of my judgment at the time; and I am sure that it will all be right in the end, and *feel* sure of it."

During this time the party had descended to the San Hieronymo, entered the boat, and pushed off.

"I don't at all fancy rowing all the way back home up-stream," said the younger brother, when they had reached its junction with the river. "We'll land a little farther up, and ride home. I see Francisco is there with the horses."

Climbing up the bank, at which they speedily arrived, they left the boat to be rowed back by Francisco, while they mounted the horses he had brought. There were Black Bob and Slow for Mr. Morton McRobert and Will, and two mustangs for Madison and his uncle. The boys now, for the first time, noticed closely the Texan fittings for the animals. The bridles were particularly strong, with immense curb-bits, Uncle Frank's bridle being heavily plated with silver stars, with which his saddle also was plentifully adorned.

"I got the bridle and saddle at San Jacinto," said Uncle Frank, as they rode homewards. "It belonged to one of the Mexican officers killed there."

"But what do people use such big wooden stirrups and such great spurs for?" asked Madison.

"Oh, the stirrups and saddle and rider go together," replied his uncle. "You are obliged to have such stirrups and mud-leathers in going through chaparral after stock, or your legs would be badly torn. The saddle is deep, with such a high pommel—horn, we call it—so that a man can keep his seat when his mustang pitches, or when he has roped anything. As to spurs, they must be severe to manage these vicious horses with. Mine are not larger than a dollar. I have seen them as large as a saucer, and jingling with bells."

Thus conversing, they wound their way through a forest of pecans, live-oaks, wild plum, hackberry, prickly ash, and other trees, gay with the foliage and flowers of the season. Passing up the river bottom on the other side of the San Hieronymo, the boys asking and the uncle answering a hundred questions, they were soon home again. Not long after they arrived, the active Francisco came up from the bank of the river, accompanied by Hark bearing a bucket of river-water for cooking. Taking a gourdful of it in his hand,

their host entered the house, and offered it to Mrs. McRobert, who thanked him and drank a little.

"Now, Bessie," said her uncle to his little niece, as she climbed into his lap, "take a good drink from this gourd; it's nice cool water, and I'll catch a horned frog for you, first I see."

Bessie complied, saying, "A frog, uncle. Who wants a *frog?*" and her uncle handed the gourd back to Hark. When it was refilled he gave it to Josie, who drank more deeply than any.

"But why on earth did you make us all drink Colorado water for, uncle?" burst forth Will.

"Simply because when once you have drunk Colorado water, nowhere else can you ever feel at home again as long as you live but in Texas. You may laugh," he continued, "but it's a solemn fact, never known to fail."

These last words were not lost on Hark, as he passed out of the door with the bucket. He had drunk at the river himself, that could not be undone. There was only one course left. In two minutes 'Markable had, under compulsion, swallowed a gourdful.

"What you make de chile drink for, man? He no want it!" inquired the unsuspecting Rohamma, who stood near by, hanging out her washing.

"Drink some y'rself and I tell you," replied her husband. But it was not until after long entreaty that she would consent, and then suspiciously; and, after much prying in the gourd, she permitted a small quantity to pass her lips. Almost before she had done so her eye caught the triumphant look of her husband, and she hesitated suspiciously and inquiringly in the act of swallowing.

"Too late now, gal!" cried he. "Yah! yah! yah! Mass Frank say, when folks once drunk Colorado water dey nebber can lebe Texas—nebber, nebber again!"

With a look of horror and disgust, the woman spat out the water on the ground as if it were poison; spat and spat again, wiping her lips energetically with her apron.

"I nebber swallered a drop. But I nebber forgive you, nebber—you see if I do. Lib in dis here Texas? Nebber see ole Virginny again? I'd raffer die right here, now right off! Texas! Eugh!" with utter disgust. But as she spoke a shade of dismay suddenly deepened the darkness of her face. She had forgotten. That very morning, on the river bank, washing, she had taken one, two, three hearty drinks. It was too late!

"Well," she groaned, "de will above be done! Anyhow, I ha'n't long to lib, I hope," and, with a load on her heart, she turned into the log kitchen to prepare dinner for the hungry husband.

Poor Rohamma! Many a heart besides yours has yearned in Texas after its old home. Woman, especially, recoils from the life of the frontier. Bravely has many a young wife, just brought to Texas by her husband in pursuit of fortune, struggled between her love for him and her desperate yearning back to her kindred and the scenes and companions of her girlhood in the old states. Bitter tears wept in a husband's absence have been stoutly chased away before his return by determined smiles — summer showers driven away by the shining of the sun. Far more painful is it when, in the turns of fortune, the aged mother is brought to Texas, leaving all her heart among the graves and the friends of her lifetime. It is only young trees that bear transplanting to a new soil. And yet, strange to say, let bride or matron or any other settler in Texas return to the old states, I know not why it is, whether the *glamour* of the West is on them, or whether the witchery *was* in the water they drank, their old home is home to them no longer. Old friends, old haunts, old occupations, have lost their charm; there is a sense of uneasiness. The yearning to get back to the West becomes a craving, a passion. Once back again in Texas, nothing more is said of returning to the old states. It is singular, but it is the invariable fact. Texans call it "the mustang feeling." The most sensible theory is this: Adam and Eve lived before the Fall in a fresh, new world. An old, settled state of things is utterly unlike that. The yearning back to the West, when once resided in, is the sleeping Adam-and-Eve feeling yet in the bones, an instinctive yearning and longing backwards towards Eden.

CHAPTER III.

AN EXCURSION AND AN ACCIDENT.

It was Saturday when the party made the little voyage of discovery just mentioned. The rest of the afternoon was spent in getting all things ready for a quiet Sabbath. But before they went to rest that night, after full discussion, it was determined, bright and early on Monday morning, to go to the tract in a body and select a building spot.

Mr. McRobert, like a sensible man, always consulted with his wife in all his plans. Even the children were freely admitted, on all proper occasions, to express themselves; but the father remained the executive, with full veto power too. And herein was found the secret of 'the singularly strong attachment of the members of the family to each other; and the joyful, hearty, and intelligent interest taken by all, even by Bessie—as far as that is concerned, even by the servants—in all the family plans.

The Sabbath came, and was spent, as the McRoberts always spent their Sabbaths—except that they had no church to go to as in Virginia, and so had to make a church for the day of Uncle Frank's harkal. As usual, all, even the servants, were scrupulously clean and arrayed in their best. At breakfast, Uncle Frank could not suppress an exclamation of surprise and pleasure at the "Sunday appearance," as he called it, of all. As to little Bessie, in her red dress, and morocco shoes, and neat little collar, and rosy shining face, and smoothly parted hair, and demure look, she seemed ten times sweeter than ever.

"Well, this does look like Virginia!" exclaimed their host. "It's the first time I've seen Sunday in Texas for years."

Immediately after breakfast he disappeared into his own room. When he reappeared, you would hardly have known him. He had shaved—at least a little—and scissored his luxuriant beard that he left, and hair, and had changed his check-shirt for one of linen, and had donned a broadcloth suit, fished up from the forgotten depths of his trunk. Francisco had blacked his boots for him—the first time the Mexican had ever done such a thing—under Hark's instruction. Handsome, sincere, genial in appearance before, he now seemed even more so—a little sunburnt, that was all. Bessie fairly danced around him, clapping her hands with glee.

"Well, yes, I do feel more like a Virginian and a gentleman," said he. "Texas is the thing! all we have got to do is to Virginianize it a little."

The day was largely spent in conversation, all agreeing that the more they talked, only that much the more they found to talk about.

After an early breakfast on Monday morning the entire party repaired, in the carriage and on horseback, to the spring-head of the San Hieronymo. If nature had arranged the whole place just to be a home, it could not have been better done. In truth, the God of nature, their heavenly Father, *had* arranged the place at the creation of the world in love to this family — knowing that it would, when its day came, settle just there. And in this he showed no more forethought and affection for this particular family than he has for all who fear and love him. In no sense was Mr. McRobert other than a strong-minded, sensible man; yet that thought flashed upon him as he walked with his family over the place.

There was the high summit upon which Uncle Frank had pointed out the country the day the two boys and their father had been with him there, which commanded a view of the river and the valley open far to the south, and at the base of this, and crowned with magnificent live-oaks, there was a level acre or so, the very spot for a house. Off, not sixty yards to the left, was the spring—a monster spring. It gushed out right from under the mountain cold and clear, sixty-two feet across, and from ten to twenty feet deep. As the children stood on the rocky banks they could see the very bottom, and fish of all sizes float-ing leisurely far down, it was so transparent. It was not a spring, in fact—it was rather a river flowing under the mountain and breaking out there. For drinking, for washing clothes, for fishing, what could be more convenient? and for bathing, you could hardly hold yourself on the bank from jumping in. Then there was the mountain towering up on the north side, under which the house beside the spring could nestle like a chicken under a hen, while the northers were whistling over all the world besides; the open prairie for their cattle and for cultivation lying to the east.

"Now, the first thing to be done," said Uncle Frank, as the whole party sat down together on the clean rock near the spring, breathless from rambling about, and exclaiming with wonder and delight—"the first thing to be done here I found in the Bible yesterday. I'm sorry to say it's the first time I have opened my Bible for a long time — one mother put in my trunk when I came to Texas; but I happened on this yesterday, and it's sound sense as well as Scripture: 'Prepare thy work without, and make it fit for thyself in the field; and afterwards build thine house.' Yes, you must fix for planting first, and then build. Now, it happens first-rate—I've had a Dutchman up in the cedar brake for I don't know how many months cutting rails. I paid him in land. Brother Morton, you and I and Madison must take the wagon and mules up there to-morrow and begin hauling rails."

"But how about the ploughing?" inquired his brother.

"Oh, I have had another Dutchman

breaking up the prairie all last winter, poor fellow! I paid *him* in cattle; but he was snake-bit, and died before he could get them up. But Hark will have to plough it over again with a long bull-tongue. I have oxen out on grass that we can get up to do that while we are hauling rails."

"How long will it take us?" asked his brother.

"Not long; it's down-hill all the way from the brake. You won't need but a small patch, for garden things and a little corn—almost too late even for that. What with your building and fixing and fencing, it will be full next winter before you will be ready to put in anything like a crop. You ought to have been here six months ago; you ought, in fact, to have come here years ago, when I did."

"People use cedar altogether for fencing here, do they not?" inquired his brother.

"Hereabout they do. Once fence your land well with cedar, and that work's done for your lifetime. Your fence may catch fire and burn up from the prairie, but it can never rot. Some people plant osage orange—*bois d'arc* ('bow dark') they call it—for a hedge. Farther west they throw up a ridge by digging a deep ditch, and plant prickly pears thick on top of the ridge. Others wattle in with brush and posts. But cedar is far best when you can get it. Compensation of nature, as philosophers call it: wood is tolerably scarce here, but then it lasts forever, what you have. What do you think of it, Dodles?" he asked of his little nephew, who came up from the water as he spoke.

"Me? I think it is a splendid place to make a flutter-wheel mill, uncle. I'm going," he added, "to make one to-morrow," at which they laughed, it was so like the boy to say it.

"What a singular species of cactus!" exclaimed Mrs. McRobert, who had rambled off to one side; "it is as large and round as one's head; and what a beautiful cream-colored blossom it has! And here is another kind still, all in little lobes, a flower at the end of each, growing right out of the rocks!"

"That is the Turk's-head cactus," said Uncle Frank, as all hurried to the spot. "You'll find plenty of it hereabout. The switch-cactus grows only in the sandy river bottom; it can be trained to run twenty feet long, not thicker than your finger. It is singular," he continued, "how everything in this country has thorns. There's the mesquit-tree—nothing but thorns. Yonder is a chaparral bush—every twig and every leaf covered with thorns. A little later it's loaded with delicious currants. The plan is to put a sheet on the ground under it, and beat off the fruit into the sheet with a stick."

"They have given out lately," said his brother, "that the gum of the mesquit has all the properties of gum-arabic, and far better for medicinal use."

"I'm glad to hear it," said the Texan. "A grove of them looks more like a deserted apple-orchard in winter than anything else. They make a hot fire, and that's all the use I've had of them. But I was talking of thorns. The farther west you go, the worse it is. The very grass is covered with thorns. As to the plate-cactus, it grows as large as a house almost—many plates twenty inches across. When range is poor, stock-keepers rake them on a fire and burn off the prickles so that the cattle can eat them. Cattle often are choked to death trying to eat them with thorns still on. As to their beautiful red pears, three of them are certain to give a man a chill. They split open the plates and use them for poultices, sometimes, I believe. Nothing's made in vain, I suppose. The very frogs have thorns all over the back and head. Here is one I put in my pocket for Bessie. Oh, you needn't be afraid of it; it's clean, and as harmless as can be. The children are hardly ever without them in their pockets or bosoms, and you can pick them up any hour of the day anywhere. They say they live on ants and other vermin. But what use their horns are, I can't imagine; *some* use, you may be certain."

"What do you call that, uncle?" said Madison, as they passed through a belt of prairie on their way home, pointing to a singular-looking sort of tree.

"Thorns again, you see," replied his uncle. "We call that the Spanish bayonet. It's one of the aloe species. You see it's like the trunk of a tree, with ten thousand spikes like, only larger than, bayonets, growing out on every side from the ground up. I'd just as lief be speared by a ranchero at once as thrown from a mustang against them. The points are keener than a needle. I knew a lady who had one growing in the yard, who put a spool on the end of every bayonet, to keep her children from being hurt.

The tree was odd-enough-looking before."

"And what use is it, uncle?" asked Will.

"Why, I suppose if any one was to plant them close together, they could make an awful fence. But if you noticed, as we passed it, a long, blue sheath had shot up a yard above the circle of bayonets. Soon that sheath will burst open into a hundred pure white blooms. It's the grandest flower in the world—perfumes the whole prairie. The magnificent flower, standing white and gorgeous above all the bayonets, and growing out from the bayonets, always reminds me of happiness after trouble."

"Or heaven after earth," added his sister. "But I did not think you were so romantic, Frank."

"Do you see those flowers?" asked the Texan, stopping with the party, and waving his hand towards the prairie, that rolled from his feet away off north and east to the horizon, brilliant, actually dazzling to the eye, as the sun shone upon it, with flowers. "Once in riding over that prairie to the San Gabriel, my horse fell lame just as I started. I was obliged to go, so I walked leading him. Just for the curiosity of it, I began, as I walked, to pick and count the different kinds of flowers I passed. I went on to a hundred and twenty-three, and stopped it, tired out. This," he added, taking a small five-leaved flower out of the hand of Bessie, which was loaded, as well as her apron, with flowers—"this is the Texas star; it always bends to the north; you had better look at it well, boys, in case you get lost—the compass flower some people call it. It's about the only flower whose name I know. But the cattle are rapidly destroying the flowers: they are all disappearing as emigration comes in."

"Speaking of emigration," said his brother, "I have been told that there are kinds of animals that keep in advance of emigration."

"Yes," replied his brother; "soon as an Indian sees a bee, he knows it's time for him to be leaving. It's the same with squirrels. I have seen them crossing the Brazos westward in shoals. They had a story that they kept a ferryman there busy a week ferrying them over—a flat-boat load every time. Same with quails—they were never known till white people began to come to the country."

"I do believe this is hoarhound," said Mrs. McRobert, stopping by the edge of a thick vegetation near the yard.

"Yes," said Uncle Frank, "they say it comes in with settlement too. There's enough of it—and sage too—growing around here to doctor a city. The castor-oil plant, too — *Palma Christi*, as it is called. I had not improved this place a year before it was growing twenty feet high all around the yard and the stables. Nature must think there's going to be lots of children raised here, I thought, when I first saw it, with plenty of green watermelons to make them sick. Then there's the cockle-burr too. Texas never heard of such a thing until it began to be ploughed. It seemed seed sown at the fall, only waiting for man to come to spring right up and make good the curse, 'Thorns also and this-tles shall it bring forth. In the sweat of thy face shalt thou eat bread.' There's the milk-weed, too, and the old Virginia Jamestown weed that has sprung up here since the Indians left, and I don't know what all."

But here the speaker was interrupted by the screams of Rohamma, running from the house towards them: "Oh, Mass Morton! oh, Miss 'Manda! snake-bit! snake-bit! Mass Will snake-bit! Oh! but didn't I *tell* everybody we oughtn't to come here!"

Sure enough, Will was not with the party. Going on ahead of them to the house, he had been searching for bait for fishing among some old logs in the field beyond, and now made his appearance with Rohamma, holding out his bleeding hand. Quite a scene of consternation followed, in the midst of which Will explained that in thrusting his hand under a log to roll it over for grubs, he had felt a severe pain in his finger, and as he drew it out a ground rattlesnake had attempted to glide away — which, however, with the aid of 'Markable, he had killed. 'Markable himself was lamed for the time by a violent blow from a pair of tongs in the hands of Rohamma, endeavoring to aid in killing the reptile. Even before Will reached them the wound had turned blue, and the arm had begun to swell—sure sign of the virulent poison. He bore it like a man, but was as ashy-pale as his frightened mother; while little Bess made the air vocal with her cries. Meanwhile Uncle Frank had darted into the house, and now returned with one of the gourds which had been hanging in the house, and a tin cup.

" Here, Will !" he said, pressing the full cup on the boy, "drink this—drink all of it, as fast as you can !"

"But what is it, uncle?" inquired Will.

"You never mind what it is," replied his uncle. "It's whiskey. I've put some sugar in it—drink! drink! Never be afraid; it won't hurt you. Pour out another cup for him, Madison; drink it too! Never mind how it burns your throat !"

"Your hartshorn, Amanda! Where is it?" asked her husband; and in a few moments a rag wet with hartshorn was applied to the wound, for the fang of the snake had passed entirely through the base of the middle finger of the left hand, making a hole on each side.

"Have you any brandy?" asked Mr. McRobert.

"Only some brandy fruit," replied his wife.

"The very thing!" said Uncle Frank; and in a few moments Robamma had produced and opened the jar.

Under the urgency of all Will ate, nothing loath, peach after peach; swallowing down, with many a wry face, the whiskey pressed upon him continually by his uncle. He had already swallowed enough to intoxicate a grown man, yet it did not affect him in the least.

"Now if he were a whiskey-drinker, this remedy wouldn't do the least good," said his uncle; "but, as it is, he's safe now."

Sure enough, in a few hours his trouble seemed over. For three days he could not use his hand or arm easily; but this soon passed off, and in time his adventure was forgotten. Brandy peaches, however, he declared he had eaten enough of to last him the rest of his life—he could never be induced to eat one again—and of whiskey he had a special abhorrence.

"One day," said Uncle Frank, as they sat at dinner, "I had what you, Morton, would call, I suppose, a special providence happen to me. I was riding through the thickest part of the Yegua Bottom—*yay-wah* he pronounced it. I had often gone the road before—knew it as well as I do the way to San Hieronymo Spring, but I got lost. As I stumbled about in the forest, I chanced upon a faint trail, and followed it up till it led me to a little cabin in the deepest part of the woods. Before I could get to the door a woman heard my horse's hoofs, and came running out as if she was crazy.

"'Thank God! thank God!' she said. 'What is good for a snakebite, mister? Get off, quick! What is good for a snake-bite? My boy's bit, my boy's bit! What is good for it? Quick, mister, quick!'

"I jumped off, went in, found a little four-year-old boy, lying on the bed, badly bitten just above the ankle-joint. There he lay, the wound blue, the leg dreadfully swollen. The father was off to the Port with the wagon; nobody there but that poor mother with her only child. What with fright and what with ignorance, she didn't know what on earth to do. If you believe me, the poor creature had put on a pot full of wild hoarhound, and was boiling *that* to make him drink; it was the only thing like medicine she had or could guess at. It's well I came, and just then too; in two hours he would have been far enough gone beyond the best doctor that ever lived. I had a flask of whiskey in my saddle-bags, and kept the mouth of it between his lips, the end tilted up, while his mother was tying a rag full of wet salt to the wound; and that was about the only thing she *did* have. In a little time my flask was empty, and Charley, as she called him, was safe and sound asleep. I had hard work to get away from that woman. 'I had given up everything,' she said, 'and was just praying to God to help me when I heard you coming. How did you happen to be passing such an out-of-the-way place as this, and just in the nick of time? It was God that sent you. Oh, bless him, bless him, bless him!' she exclaimed, looking upwards, her hands clasped and her eyes streaming with tears. She made me stay till she could cook something for me, then put me in the road, and off I rode, and I do believe to this day she almost believes I was an angel sent that way—a queer sort of angel, with a beard, a pair of revolvers, and a flask of whiskey! However, I was mighty glad I happened to lose my road."

"And you remember Steuben Brown you were telling me about yesterday, uncle?" said Madison.

"How was that?" inquired his father.

"Oh, it is only a little matter that happened a few years ago down the river," said the Texan. "Mr. Brown was out a little, looking up some hogs he had, and Steuben with him—Steuben was just about the age of Will here. On a sudden the Indians were on them. Brown had his boy on the horse before him. He put spurs to his animal, and might have got off safe, but he was looking around at the Comanches as he loped off, and a limb of one of these live-oaks struck him full in the breast. The Indians had riddled him with arrows before he could even begin to try to get up."

"But about Steuben, uncle?" interrupted Will.

"Well, he wasn't hurt. In double-quick time the Indians had caught the horse, and off they went. As soon as they struck the prairie, they made the little fellow run before them, his father's scalp hanging round his neck, the blood trickling down. Whenever he would halt, an Indian would prick him on with a spear. At night they would give him only what they threw away to eat, treating the child worse than a white man ever treats a dog. A day or two after starting, one of them pounded some rock into fine bits. Taking a handful of the pieces, he stripped off Steuben's shoes and stockings, rolled up his breeches, and rubbed the flint into the child's legs and feet till they were all one sore. This was to keep him from escaping. They were pushing on for Santa Fé; but just before they got there, the poor little fellow dropped, gave out. They thought he was as good as dead, and left him lying where he fell, half in, half out of a water-hole in the prairie. It chanced—it happened—it providenced, if you say so—that a company of traders, going from Santa

Fé, turned considerably out of their road to water just at that hole. He was so small, and in a dead faint, lying there stark-naked, starved, and cut to pieces from head to foot, they never would have noticed him if they had not come right to the hole to water. As it was, in four months he was in his mother's arms, alive and well. That is what you people call a special providence, is it not?"

"Every providence is a special providence," replied his brother. "If Charley had died there alone by himself with his mother, or if Steuben had died before the traders came, it would have been equally the providence, the special providence, of God. He has special love and care in afflicting us as in blessing us. The way is to see him in *everything*; when we are prospered, to rejoice in it as from *him*; when we are afflicted, to submit cheerfully to it, as equally from the same all-wise and loving Friend."

"I must tell you a little thing about Will, Frank," said Mrs. McRobert—Will had before this gone out. "One day his father took him out hunting, when he was only four years old. They went some distance in the woods. His father told him to stand still by a certain tree, while he went off to get a shot at some doves. But the birds flew up, or something, and his father had to go still farther on. Will became alarmed, and began to call; but his father—not to frighten the birds—would not answer. At last he ceased to call, and his father, coming back, saw the little fellow on his knees, on the ground, his hands clasped above his head, exclaiming, 'O God, please bring pa back! please bring pa back!' His earthly father having failed him, he had turned to his heavenly."

"This morning," her husband said, "I came upon Will before we started. He was making a great noise in the yard, dancing and jumping. 'Why, what are you doing, Will?' said I. 'Oh,' he replied, 'I'm so happy! and I'm only laughing with my legs!'"

"Bessie's my pet!" said her uncle. "Wonder if *she* ever said a smart thing in her life?"

"All her smartness is to come yet, uncle," replied Madison. "But this morning Hark killed the hog you told him to before breakfast. Just before we sat down to table, Bessie came out to where I was staking out Slow, and said, 'Bubber, oh, Bubber! I thaw a gotht to-day!' 'A ghost!' said I, 'what was it?' 'Oh, it wath the gotht of the hog Hark killed; Rohamma wath cooking ith gotht.'"

"However," said Mr. McRobert, rising, "we have no more time to hear about the children. Suppose we ride this afternoon up into the cedar brake."

"You were telling about the Indians, Frank," his wife said, as they left: "you do not think there are any Indians *now*?"

"Well, yes," he replied, "there are a few, yes—only a few." But it was plain he did not wish to say more, for he added, "They are so gentlemanly, they would not hurt the feelings of a lady—oh no, not for the world." He said it so solemnly, however, that it was plain he was joking, and the lady became quite silent as they went.

CHAPTER IV.

MADISON'S FIRST SHOT.—THE HONEY HUNT.

A WORLD of work there was to do, but for it there were plenty of willing hearts and hands. A garden to be ploughed, fenced, planted, kept clean; a log-house, sixteen feet square, to be put up for Hark, Rohamma, and 'Markable; a larger house built for the family of cedar logs, consisting of two rooms, each twenty feet square, with a ten-foot hall between, all under one roof, with a gallery ten feet broad running along the whole length of the house on the south side. Then there were chimneys to erect, stables to put up, a hundred other things to do—enough to fill, brimful, every hour of every day for years to come.

Now, the fact is, the McRobert family had not been the earliest risers in all Virginia. Far from it. The sun had generally shown himself high and long before the parents made their appearance, for they loved to linger long around the fireside at night, hearing music, reading, engaging in conversation, and making it in a good many ways quite late before going to bed. Madison and Will, too, unless there was something like a rabbit hunt in the wind, or a sliding upon snow fallen during the night, were apt to be the last up—hardly well awake at a late breakfast. Bessie was the earliest riser of all. Up from her warm nest in the little crib by her parents' bed at early dawn, she was out with the rest of the birds, singing more sweetly than any of them. This invariably awoke Josie, who was too apt to be indignant at her for awakening first, seeing that it took him longer to dress than all the rest. It was impossible to sleep soundly after he had got up, and gone to arguing with her about it; so that if it had not been for her it is impossible to tell when the family *would* have risen.

As for the servants—catch them up long before the master and mistress? Not exactly. Around their fires till midnight, talking and cooking and eating by turns—discussing all events upon their own plantation and all the plantations for ten miles around—it was late before they slept. If it had not been for Watkins, the overseer, not a soul would have even looked out until "sun up." But there was no late rising with *him*—he was wide awake before three, up and out. He took their very business away from the chanticleers of the whole neighborhood. His awakening powers were not exactly like those of Bessie in the house, but far more effective. Sharp as a razor, and as cold and thin too, if Watkins ever woke late in the morning from that eventful day when, at three o'clock A.M. to a second, he first opened his eyes upon the hills of Vermont, then people generally are mistaken. If he slept at all, it was like a razor, the blade turned down in the handle—cold, keen, even between the sheets—ready for use any instant. Mr. McRobert, his employer, did not find *him* too late a riser. The precise reverse.

But when Mr. Watkins had succeeded at last in swindling them out of all they possessed, and the family had left their old home, they left something behind them besides "old Virginia." The parents, at least, silently resolved—without a word even to each other about it—to begin a new life with a new home. And all the circumstances conspired happily to this under the new skies. In the first place, they had been so very busy all day—hard at work at a thousand things—that they were too tired to sit up late. An early supper, a little reading and conversation, family worship—and the household was sound asleep before ten. Then there was so much to do towards their new home—something left with reluctance the night before—that day-break found all the family astir. The boys sprang from their beds first, with more eagerness than they ever did to hunt or to slide or to fish; their work now was something far more important and interesting to them. And as every member of the household had his own or her own particular world of work to do, it was the same with all.

It was as much as Mrs. McRobert could do to keep her family in clothing. Though their attire was of the strongest material, many a rent made by mesquit thorns had to be mended. Unused to work, it would have gone hard with her had it not been for her increased health and strength. The children—and her husband most of all—were astonished and delighted at the fresh bloom in her cheeks, and the new light in her eyes, and the unwonted elasticity of her step. And so it was with her husband. With both of them this going to a young country was like going back to their youth—to the days when they were first married; they were beginning life afresh, only a great deal wiser and happier even than before. Had they remained in Virginia after the loss of their property, it would have been in a reduced, humiliated condition. Everything they saw would have reminded them of the past. With every one they met the conversation would have unavoidably turned upon their change in life, with all its painful incidents and results. The disaster would have weighed upon them, a heavy burden for life.

As it was, in coming to Texas they threw the whole matter off their shoulders, almost off their very memory—left it all behind them in Virginia. No scenes, no circumstances, no persons here to remind them of the past. Everything was new, fresh, animating—appealing continually to them for ever-fresh exertion. It was indeed an excellent idea that led them from Virginia to Texas. Even if they had lost none of their property, the removal would have been a wise one for the wonderful effects it wrought in them, as we shall see. It is by the loss of earth we gain heaven at last; and, as it turned out, their loss was the greatest possible blessing—the lever which raised the whole family, in every sense of the word, bodily, intellectually, spiritually, to a higher level by far than they would otherwise have known. It was the kindness of their Father in heaven—a Father who delights to bless his children in unexpected ways, and by events and means which seem least likely of all.

May passed in hard work: by the end of it the large garden had been fenced, planted, and gave promise of a luxuriant and abundant supply of vegetables. The negro house, too, had been neatly finished, and the logs hauled, hewn, notched, and ready for the larger house. All looked anxiously forward to its completion. It was a good mile to Uncle Frank's, up the river; besides, they wanted to be in their own home. We see with what joy the birds build their nests; what a glad flying-about, and eager twittering, and enthusiastic energy they throw into the matter from dawn till dusk. Men possess the same instinct. People who inherit fine houses, all built to their hands, have no idea what an enjoyment they miss in not having to select a site from the hands of Nature, and clear it up, and plan and build according to one's own fancy, or, rather, two's own fancy, for half the pleasure is in the discussion between husband and wife, the deferring to each other, and suggesting, and proposing.

Since Adam and Eve left Eden hand in hand, the sweetest of all food is that which a young couple eat when they sit down for the first time in their own house, though it be of logs, and at their own table, though it be only a goods-box; and the sweetest slumber known since Adam and Eve left their couch of roses in Paradise is that which such a pair enjoy when they lie down at night for the first time under their own roof, even though the stars twinkle through it everywhere. When there are, as in this case, children to take the same eager interest in building a home, the gladness is that much the noisier as well as greater.

The family had made their home all this time at Uncle Frank's ranch, but on the 26th of June the house was all finished. Early that morning the moving began. The night before, Hark had unfortunately left his axe up in the cedar brake; and while all else were busy packing and starting off for the new place, as Hark could not be spared, Madison had to leave immediately after breakfast for the brake to bring in the axe.

"I do declare, it's too bad," he said, as he mounted Slow. "I wouldn't have missed going with them this morning for anything, and here I have to ride alone 'way up into that dreary brake. However, I'll take my rifle along; who knows but I might get a crack at a squirrel?"

Now, ever since Madison obtained his rifle, he had been practising with it at a mark behind the house of afternoons, when matters more important had been attended to. So far he had never killed anything, though he had wasted any quantity of bullets in trying.

"I'll tell you what we'll do, Slow, old fellow!" said he to his horse, as they entered the brake, after a ride of a mile or two. "Behind that clump of bushes yonder is Plum Spring. It's early in the morning yet; who knows but I might find a turkey, or a squirrel, or something at the water? I'll tie you here anyhow, creep up, and see. A squirrel of my own shooting to carry home for our first dinner in the new house—wouldn't it be grand!"

So saying, he alighted, tied his pony to a bush, motioned Duke, who now came breathless after him from the house, to lie down by the horse; then, taking his rifle, he crept cautiously up towards the spring. Arrived within fifty yards of it, he peeped carefully through the brush, and the rifle actually fell from his hands, while the sudden beating of his heart was really painful. No wonder. There stood a noble buck right before him, drinking! It had arrived just as he did, was drinking eagerly, as if very thirsty. The wind, too, was from it towards Madison, so that it could not detect the boy by scent.

For nearly two minutes Madison sat looking at the buck, without even a thought of his rifle. He was even shaking in every limb with the "buck ague," that old hunters so laugh at in new beginners.

Suddenly the thought flashed upon him, "Oh, if I only could kill it, wouldn't it be grand! I'd give a million of dollars! What would they say? I'll try, anyhow. I know I'll miss; but I'll have a shot, anyhow."

With shaking hand he picked up his rifle, and ran it through a forked bush that happened there, just the thing. Then, taking a long aim at the side of the buck—for it stood broadside to him—he shut his eyes, and fired. The next instant he tried to jump up with a hurrah of mad excitement on his lips; but he was so weakened by the sight that he could not at first utter a syllable or stir from the spot. The instant he fired the buck had sprung straight up in the air—it seemed ten feet high to Madison—and then had fallen almost in its very tracks, shot through the heart. In a few moments the boy was standing on him, weak and almost delirious with excitement and joy. He whistled to Duke, ran towards his horse, then ran back lest the deer should disappear before he could return. Finally, he untied the pony and led him, snorting and shying, to the spot. Then he tied him firmly to a sapling, as near the buck as possible, and let him get a little accustomed to it. Next he thought about the axe, untied the pony again, galloped on him a few hundred yards to where it was left, got it, hurried back, tied Slow as before, and attempted to raise the hind-legs of the buck upon the saddle, so as to draw it up on the back of the horse. Hard work it was, and the perspiration streamed from every pore.

At last he succeeded: the buck was balanced in the saddle, and

Madison walked beside, steadying it by the immense antlers with his left hand, while he held the reins and supported the rifle and axe upon his shoulder with the right. And thus, slowly and safely, he made his way along the road by which they had hauled rails to the new place.

It seemed as if he would never get there; but he did so at length, and there were all the family just arrived. His heart beating fast, and prouder than Alexander the Great after a battle, he was among them before they knew he was near. You can imagine the sensation he made, the shouts of surprise, the questions! The hero sat down from sheer exhaustion, while Uncle Frank and Will took the buck off the pony, and hung it by the hind-hoofs to the limb of a tree near the house. But his proudest moment was when Uncle Frank, after walking round and round it as it hung, looking at it with his head on one side, said, as he sharpened his knife on his palm before proceeding to flay it, " Well, Madison, you'll do; I never saw a finer buck, nor made a better shot in my life."

Madison had only one request to make. " Mother," said he, " can't Rohamma cook some of it for our first dinner?—My having to go for that axe was not so bad at last," he continued, to himself, as he walked into the house to wash his hands and change his bloody clothes. " Pa says things always turn out best—and I believe they do."

From that day Will, Dodles, and all the rest, too, looked upon Madison as being much more of a man.

"Oh! it was all accident my hitting it," he said; but he thought a good deal more of himself for it, notwithstanding. Many a deer did he afterwards supply their table with, but no shot so triumphant as that: it remained one of the sweetest joys of his life.

For some days Uncle Frank remained with them to help arrange matters. The children were almost wild. "Oh, but don't it *smell* good!" Josie exclaimed of their new abode, as they stood for a moment in the hall, and they all inhaled the odor of the cedar logs, of which the house was built, with fresh delight.

"Hah, but not better than the cypress clapboards do!" cried Will. "You come smell and see!" Whereupon they raced into the yard, to test the superior fragrance of the cypress shingles, clean and white and aromatic, which covered the roof; and so they raced in and out, up and down, round and round, till bedtime.

"I noticed bee signs a month or two ago down the river," Uncle Frank said, next morning at breakfast. "The sun is just rising; we have plenty of time. Now you've got venison enough, suppose we try for some honey, too, to set up housekeeping with? Shall I take Madison and Will with me? We needn't be gone long."

No sooner proposed than agreed to. In a few minutes they were off, loaded down with axes, and as many buckets as they could hang about their horses. Riding south, down to the river, they alighted, at Uncle Frank's request, near a sandy flat and tied their animals.

Their uncle then coolly took his seat on a log beside the river, crossed his legs, and fanned himself with his hat.

"But where's the honey?" said Will, looking around.

"Don't be in a hurry; it's coming," he replied, continuing to fan himself, while the boys looked at him with astonishment, and then burst into a laugh, supposing him to be joking. But he fanned on until they had subsided into astonishment again. "Don't you see there?" said their uncle, at last, pointing to the moist sand. "There they are, sure enough."

Following the direction of his finger, the boys observed two or three bees on the sand, apparently sucking up the moisture.

"Now," said Uncle Frank, suddenly mounting his horse, "you stay here with the buckets and things until I come back or you hear me call."

He spoke with his eyes fastened on the bees, and as he spoke one of them rose from the sand, circled round and round in the air, then darted straight off into the forest, the Texan hard after it, his eyes fastened upon it, and driving the spurs into his horse. In a moment he was out of sight.

"It would take sharper eyes than mine to follow a bee on horseback," said Will.

"There's no telling what one can do till they try," answered Madison, gravely, with a thought of yesterday's shot. "I suppose," he continued, "it's easier to do it because, when the bee starts, he goes straight —makes a bee-line, they call it—for home. If he was to fly crooked, nobody could follow him."

"I hope we won't have to wait long," said Will. And they did not; for in a few minutes they heard their uncle's "Hoop-pee!" sounding in the distance—a shrill cry on the upper keys of the voice, which can be heard amazingly far, owing to its sharpness —just as a pointed arrow or a conical Minié bullet flies farther than a blunt stick or a slug. In a minute the boys were on their animals, with all their things, and in a short time had reached their uncle. They found him seated on a log.

"Now, boys," he said, "take the three horses and tie them 'way off yonder a hundred yards. If the bees get at them, we'll have more dancing in our fandango than is agreeable. Leave the things here. We've managed to kill two birds with one stone this morning," he continued, as the boys returned. "We'll attend to this one first;" and he pointed to a swarm of bees clustered in a thick knot upon a log near by. At his direction the boys rapidly collected wood for a fire, in the midst of which he flashed some powder, setting it into a blaze. Upon this they heaped leaves, so as to make a dense smoke.

"But what are we going to take them home in?" asked Madison.

"Always have your saddle-blanket made into a bag," replied Uncle Frank, producing his own, and opening its mouth; "it's just as easy, and there's no telling what use you may have for it when out hunting."

So saying, he picked up some long

switches which he had cut, and, bending each into a circle, held by its ends wrapped together, he placed them in the bag till it could stand on its mouth like a sort of small balloon. He then produced a bit of bark with honey on it, and rubbed the inside of the bag-box well with the honey.

"Now, Madison," he said, "I want you to take hold of this string at the upper end of our hive. Hold it over the swarm, and drop it, easy, down upon them. I'll guide the mouth of the bag on them myself. Don't be afraid of a sting or so."

Slowly and cautiously the thing was done, and the swarm safe inside the bag. Uncle Frank then cautiously worked the mouth of the bag together.

"But it will never do to tie up the mouth, uncle; they'll die for want of air," said Madison.

"Cut slits in the bag," said Will.

"And let the air in and them out," replied his uncle. "No, sir, give me your hat—it's straw, coarse-plaited—the very thing," and in a few minutes he had managed to slip the crown of the hat in, and had tied the mouth of the bag firmly around it over the hat-band.

"There's a good bag of bees for your mother, boys," said their uncle. "Tie the end-string to that swinging branch, Madison, so that the brim of the hat will rest on the ground. That's it. Now for the honey."

"Where on earth did you get it from?" asked Madison.

"Do you see the hole about the size of a dollar in that cottonwood?" said their uncle, pointing to a spot on the side of a huge tree, some ten feet from the ground; "and do you see this long stick?—that's the where and the how."

"But how did you reach up there? Rode up to it on horseback, of course?"

"Guessed right; and I had to ride away fast enough when I drew out the stick with the honey.

"But now for good, hard work," continued the Texan. "Off with your coat, Madison; make a big fire, Will; have plenty of leaves ready by it to make a smoke. Now for the axes: it's soft wood—hollow at that."

Soon the woods rang with the sound of the axes.

"Look out, Duke! out of the way!" cried Madison, as he dashed his axe into the side opposite his uncle. But it was a good hour's work, with many a panting, perspiring pause, before the tree gave sign of falling; especially as, in spite of all their uncle could say, the boys would work too furiously, in their eagerness to get at the honey.

"Leaves, leaves, Will! — pile on leaves!" cried his uncle, as the tree at last came down with a thundering crash.

In an instant, Duke and Snap both were into the boughs of the fallen tree, expecting to catch a possum, at least. They acknowledged their mistake with loud yells, as they dashed out again, with a swarm of exasperated bees after them, which seemed to fill the whole foliage.

As to the boys, following their uncle, they fled towards the horses for dear life. It was some minutes before they ventured back, and even then they were safe only in the thickest of the smoke. Gradually their uncle managed to drag the fire till it was against the trunk of the tree, near the hole. Then, mounting the trunk, he began cutting a deep, long notch at the hole, and another seven feet above.

Then, as Will and Madison enveloped him in smoke by fresh leaves, he managed with a few sturdy blows to split out the piece, near two feet broad, between the notches. As he did so, he dropped his axe and ran, the boys after him. Venturing back after a while, they saw, their eyes smarting with smoke, a sight worth seeing. The side of the hollow split off revealed in the huge trunk layer on layer of the finest honey, enough to fill barrels instead of buckets. But at this moment they were startled by a yell in the bushes near by, and, to their amazement, Josie came tearing out, brushing with both hands, and as hard as he could, at his bare head, around which was a perfect halo of bees. He had followed them unseen, being a quiet, silent, but very determined boy, and it took some time to rid him of the bees, rub some salt his uncle had brought on purpose over his wounds, tie up his head—for he had left his hat in his hurry—with a handkerchief, and finish scolding him for coming. But the honey was the best cure for stings and scolding.

"Eat as much as you like, boys," said their uncle, handing each a comb as large as a dinner-plate, and taking an enormous bite out of another himself. "It's about dinner-time, and this is our only dinner. It can't hurt you."

I am afraid to say how much they *did* eat; but having satisfied themselves, and a little over, they proceeded to fill their buckets. As to Uncle Frank, his hands were full, carrying the bag of bees.

"Oh, uncle, it's such a pity to leave so much honey!" cried Will, after they had filled all their buckets and were starting.

"It won't be lost, Will," replied his uncle; "and look here, boys," he said, as they went, "I want you to understand one thing. There was once a poor, starved sewing-woman who was taken from her attic in a city to the seashore. 'Thank God,' she said, when she saw the ocean, 'that for once in my life I see enough of something.' So it is in Texas; there is *enough* of everything! Look here, if the French who came to Texas had brought France with them, and the Irish had brought Ireland with them, they could have put them both in the area of Texas easy, with room enough over to pack in two or three Rhode Islands besides to hold France and Ireland steady. Plenty of wind in Texas; land, sunshine, health, work, happiness, everything—plenty, plenty as the sky above us! Oh, as to that honey? The bees will carry it off to some other place near by, which we will hunt up some of these days. Besides, a gentleman in black will be along to-night who is desperately fond of honey. Who knows but what somebody may fix to collect him too? Never mind that now; come along!"

The boys were too tired, satiated with honey, and occupied in balancing, as they rode, their buckets, one before each of them, heavy and overflowing, upon the horn of his saddle, to ask more questions, and they were soon at home. Josie's face was so swollen that nobody could scold him, as he trudged home behind them on foot; they had to laugh. But little he cared; the fun more than paid for it all.

The honey was gladly received by Mrs. McRobert. Hark soon had a box made, into which the swarm was transferred. It was the beginning of a long range of hives, the descendants, in course of time, of that swarm.

"Now," said Mr. McRobert, as he glanced at the boys, grimy with perspiration and smoke, and sticky from head to foot with honey, "I think the best thing you can do, when you get cool, is to take a good bath in the San Hieronymo."

"With *plenty* of soap!" Josie managed to add, through his swollen lips, as he obeyed his father.

CHAPTER V.

THE WILD MAN OF THE WOODS.—THE STORY OF TEXAS.

"You had your adventures to-day, all of you," said Mrs. McRobert at tea that night; "yet, though I remained close at home, I'll warrant I had the strangest adventure of all."

"What was it?" was the exclamation of everybody.

"I was alone all the morning," said Mrs. McRobert. "You, Frank, and Madison, and Will—the very dogs with you—were out after the honey. Mr. McRobert had Hark with him out in the field; Rohamma had taken Bessie and 'Markable with her down to her washing on the spring. I was sitting alone in the house sewing. Seeing a shadow on the floor, I looked up, and came as near fainting as I ever did in my life."

"Was it a bear, ma?" asked the excited Will.

"A gotht, wasn't it?" said Bessie.

"It was a man," said their mother, "and such a man! His face was covered with a beard that seemed to reach to his very waist. His clothes, all tattered, hung about him in rags."

"Black—broadcloth, in fact, were they not?" asked Uncle Frank.

"Yes, and I could not help noticing it even in my fright. He held his hat in his hand, instead of having it on his head in the house, like one used to good society. In fact, by his manner and all, he seemed to be a gentleman who had been lost in the mountains for weeks."

"But what did he want?" asked her husband.

"Well, although I was terribly alarmed at first—being alone—his manner reassured me. 'I beg pardon, madam,' he said, with a bow, 'for coming so abruptly upon you. I must, indeed, be an alarming object, as I see by your fright. Excuse me, but could I have a drink of water?'"

"The very same!" ejaculated her brother-in-law.

"I thought it strange," continued Mrs. McRobert, "that he should come to the house for water when there was the spring outside the gate. I suppose I showed this in my face, for he immediately went on, 'The truth is, madam, I am exceedingly hungry; I believe I am starving.'"

"It's the very same man I saw once," interrupted her brother-in-law. "I came upon him suddenly in the woods near this a month ago. One of my oxen had died a day before of something or other, and, if you believe me, that man had actually driven away the buzzards, had cut out some of the flesh, and was cooking it on a little fire when I came on him. The moment he heard my step, without even waiting to look around, he jumped and ran for his life. I didn't want to shoot him, you know; and before I knew what to make of it he was out of sight."

"Oh, mother," said Madison, "don't you remember Rohamma coming up so frightened from the calf-pen one night, saying she saw a man there trying to milk one of the cows into his hat?"

"Yes," replied his mother, "but I thought at the time it was only one of her fancies—she is so bitterly opposed to Texas. I told her not to say a word more about it."

"Hark was telling me of having seen such a man in the cedar brake," said Mr. McRobert. "Now I recollect, Hark said he came on him early one morning fast asleep in a kind of nest he had made of cedar bark."

"I wonder if it could have been his knife I picked up that day on the flat rock at the spring! You know how we wondered about it. Here it is," continued Madison—"such a beautiful pearl-handled knife! And here is C. R. on the silver of it. I never noticed it before."

"But you have not told us all," said his father, now deeply interested.

"There is little more to tell," replied his wife. "I supplied him amply with everything I could lay my hands on in the safe, wrapped up in a towel. I did not know what to say. 'A thousand thanks, madam,' he said, as he turned to go. 'If you will do me one favor more, I will be under the greatest obligations; and that is, please do not mention to any one my visit.' I managed to say that was impossible; I must inform you all as soon as you returned. He hesitated a moment, with his hat in his hand, as if to say something; then thanked me again, made a bow, and was gone. It all seems like a dream to me. I was glad enough to see you return."

"Who can it be?" mused her husband. "He may watch to see us leave the place, and come again when you are alone!"

"I am not afraid of him. I am so much stronger than I used to be in Virginia—am no longer nervous at all," replied his wife. "It would be well always to leave Duke at home. We women know some things by instinct. I'm not at all afraid of him —only sorry. I'm satisfied he would not attempt to hurt me, or any one. He looks scared, like a chased rabbit. All he seems to wish is to keep out of sight. It was only for food that he came to the house."

"It can't be a Texan," said her brother-in-law, "or he could kill what he wanted to eat in the woods. But perhaps he hasn't got a gun; that's strange. Black broadcloth, too. Hunters don't wear *that* among the chaparral. I can't make it out at all."

"A great many singular people come to Texas," said Mr. McRobert, in conclusion.

"Watkins told me one day that it was the Botany Bay of the world," said Madison. "And he said, Uncle Frank, that when the Texans took Texas from Mexico, it was the grandest piece of rascality the world ever saw."

"He was the sharp overseer that did the swindling, wasn't he?" asked his uncle.

"Yes," replied his nephew; "but a good many people in Virginia thought so. Uncle George said so the day before we left. I remember hearing Mr. Hudson say so over and over again at the Court-house when he was running for Congress, just before Texas was annexed. How was it, uncle? Can't you tell us all about it? It's an hour before bedtime yet."

"Yes, Frank, we would all like to hear," said his brother, as they rose from the table and took their seats about the room. "In fact, I have not read much on the subject. Up to the day we got your League letter, Texas seemed as far away from us as the moon."

"We must remember, however, that it is a Texan that is telling us," said Mrs. McRobert, with a smile, as she took up her sewing.

"Well," replied Uncle Frank, taking the big rocking-chair, "let me sit down here, for a backwoodsman has always to be moving, even when he is sitting still. Get on your night-gown, Bessie, and get in my lap; I'll talk you to sleep. The battle of San Jacinto happened in this way—"

"Oh no, Frank, go back of that; begin at the beginning," said his brother.

"It won't take long to tell you all the facts, even beginning at the start," said Uncle Frank. "All Mexico and Texas were once the realm of a people about whom we know almost nothing — a civilized, prosperous people. Where they came from, and where they went to, too, for that matter, nobody knows. Some year in the first quarter of the sixteenth century, Cortez conquered Mexico, and added it to the Spanish kingdom. Spain, like a fool, appointed only Spaniards governors, and all other offices, too, were filled only by people sent out. This enraged the native residents of mixed Spanish and Mexican blood. When Napoleon invaded Spain, Mexico set up for itself, and never would go back under rule of the mother country, but started a sort of make-believe republic, patterned after the United States — on paper. Now, as to Texas—"

"What does 'Texas' mean, uncle?" asked Will.

"Texas, or ' *Tejas,*' is Spanish for wigwams. Well," continued the Texan, "La Salle, a Frenchman, was the first European on Texas soil, landing in 1685. During many a long year after there was a continual quarrel between France and Spain for possession of the soil, with many an insurrection of the Indian inhabitants against both. For a hundred and fifty years Texas has been the scene of wars and adventures of all sorts, and for thousands of years before that, for what we know. Now for the history of *our* Texas. In 1821, Moses Austin, a Connecticut man, obtained from Mexico permission to colonize three hundred families in Texas. Dying soon after, he left his son, Stephen F. Austin, to carry out his plans. He did so, and Texas and Coahuila were recognized as forming one state of the United States of Mexico, under the Federal Constitution of 1824."

"What was the difference," asked his brother, "between that Constitution and the Federal Constitution of *our* United States?"

"Just this," replied the Texan: "the Mexican Constitution did not recognize the right of trial by jury; made Roman Catholicism the only religion of the people; made Congress, instead of the courts, the highest interpreter of the laws; permitted the President to command the armies of the republic; and failed to define the rights of the several states of the confederacy."

"The first settlers of the country, then, were all Roman Catholics, or became suddenly so on arriving?" asked his brother.

"Well, they all thought that no government had the right to require any such test, and therefore paid no attention to it. It was in 1827 that the Constitution of the State of Texas and Coahuila was adopted, and sworn to by the officers and people of the state.

Certainly there was no robbery of Mexico by unprincipled men from the United States, so far. The colonists settled the country by the express encouragement of and grants from Mexico, grants continued for years, and confirmed again and again by successive administrations. One of the first things that began to alarm Mexico was the effort made by the United States to buy Texas from it. No less than three such attempts were made by the United States between 1825 and 1829. The fact is, Texas was really a part of the territory purchased by the United States from Napoleon, under the general name of Louisiana, and ought never to have been given up to Spain."

"I never knew that before," said his brother.

"It's none the less true," continued the Texan.

"Once alarmed about Texas, Mexico began a long series of tyrannical acts towards it. Meanwhile, revolution followed revolution in Mexico, until, in 1835, Santa Anna abolished the state legislatures, overthrew the whole fabric of the government, assumed despotic power. Talk of the thirteen colonies cutting loose from England! Texas had a hundred times greater cause for separating from Mexico! Texans *would* have been slaves indeed if they had done anything less. At a convention of the people at our Washington, March 2, 1836, Texas was declared an independent republic. On April 21, following, the battle of San Jacinto — the Yorktown of Texas — was fought and won, and Texas was free! That's the whole story."

"Tell us, uncle, do tell us something about San Jacinto," said Madison. "You were there, you know."

"I'll make a short story of it, then. You see, it was on Sunday, March 6, that the Alamo, in San Antonio, was stormed, and all the garrison butchered. The Mexicans, under Santa Anna, were sixteen to one of the Texans, and they lost in the fight three times the whole number of Texans engaged. It was the noblest fight in the world. Travis and Crocket and the rest, refusing to retreat or surrender, held out so long as a grain of powder or a bullet was left; then, taking to their knives and clubbing their muskets, they fought till they were actually stifled — overwhelmed, suffocated — by the Mexicans pouring in shoals over the walls upon them. Sunday, March 27, Fannin's command, which had surrendered at Goliad under promise of quarter, were butchered in cold blood by order of Santa Anna. I knew two young fellows there, mere boys: when they were being marched out to be shot, they waved their hats above their heads, and died with 'Hurrah for Texas!' on their lips; three hundred and thirty men butchered in cold blood. This was the way Santa Anna invaded Texas from the west.

"You may suppose the country was alarmed. Men, women, and children abandoned everything, and fled eastward, swarming along all the roads; crossing the rivers, one hardly knows how; cold, hungry, ragged, worn to death with fright and fatigue. The whole country was emptying itself eastward before the Mexicans, burning up the houses and towns behind them as they left, to leave as little as possible for the yellow rascals. Those were terrible days, I tell you.

"All this time the only army Texas had in the field was under Houston, and that was retreating eastward, too, to make a better stand. At last the army — seven hundred and eighty-three strong—came face to face with the Mexicans on the prairie of San Jacinto. Old Sam—Houston, I mean—commanded us, while Santa Anna was general of the Mexicans.

"There was some little skirmishing, on the 20th of April, 1836, remember; the morning of the 21st, however, dawned clear and bright on the two armies. About nine o'clock, who should come along but General Cos, with reinforcements for Santa Anna, making the enemy some sixteen hundred strong. It didn't make any difference; they were bound to be whipped. On account of the bloody massacres by the Mexicans, there was such a feeling in our men that they were ready and eager for fight, certain to whip at 'that; they would have been that much more hungry for a fight if it had to be with fifty thousand men. I remember it all as if it were yesterday.

"There was a small *mot*—that is, grove of trees—between our camp and them, behind which, about two-o'clock, we formed our lines. Deaf Smith—he couldn't hear, but he could *do* tremendously; our head scout he was—had just come in, after cutting down the bridge over the bayou, the only way they had to escape after the fight, as there were deep sea-marshes all around them. The fact is, Santa Anna, coward and bully as he was, felt sure the victory was his. After a hearty dinner, he lay down to take his *siesta*, as they call it. They were such fools as to know nothing at all about the foe they had to deal with—only *Mexicans*, they were, you know. We were wide-awake, I assure you. I never felt so bright and happy in my life. Our cannon, the 'twin-sisters,' began the work by being run within two hundred yards of the 'Greasers,' where it poured grape and canister thick and fast into the Mexicans.

"The first roar of the cannon was like dropping a live coal in a powder-magazine. Such a shout along our lines, 'Remember the Alamo! Remember Goliad!'

"Just then the Mexicans fired into us.

"We held our fire, wrathful as we were, till within pistol-shot; then poured it in—every Texan aiming at his man—such a volley as swept their breastworks almost bare.

"But we did not stop to see. On we went over the breastworks, right on top. In fifteen minutes it was all over—the Mexicans flying like sheep, the Texans after them. They didn't even have time to fire their loaded cannon.

"Before it was dark, there were six hundred and thirty Mexicans killed, two hundred and eight wounded, and seven hundred and thirty taken prisoners. The whole prairie was a perfect wreck—guns, camp equipages, dead and dying Mexicans—while we had only eight killed and twenty-five wounded.

"Oh, well, next morning five of us were out by dawn to see what was to be seen. After we got out from the camp, Sylvester—one of us—was about shooting a deer that he saw, when he noticed a Mexican trying to steal along. Sylvester shouted to us; and, when we rode up to him, he threw himself on the ground and covered himself with his blanket. He lay there, like a worm at our feet. I told him to get up, but he only uncovered his face.

"I had to order him to get up, I don't know how many times. When he did, he came fawning towards Sylvester like a whipped dog, shook hands with him, and then kissed Syl's hand, and it was none of the cleanest either.

"We asked the poor trembling thing who he was. He was only a private soldier, he said. I had noticed some studs in his shirt-bosom too fine for any common Mexican. When I pointed to these, the poor fellow actually burst out crying, the tears running down his dirty cheeks. With his soiled face, and tangled hair and whiskers, and crouching, pitiful, whining way, I would just as soon have thought of killing a sick baby.

"He was too frightened to walk or even stand, so I helped him on my horse, and carried him into camp. As I led him past where the Mexican prisoners were guarded, they looked as if they could not believe their own eyes, and kept exclaiming, '*El Presidente!*'

"Sure enough, it was Santa Anna."

"And did they kill him and all the prisoners, uncle?" asked Will, with breathless interest.

"No, no," replied his uncle, "that's the difference between Mexicans and Texans. Every kindness was shown to them all. As to Santa Anna, it would have been a blessing, to his own country especially, if he had been killed in the fight."

"But why do Mexicans regard him as such a great man?" asked Mrs. McRobert.

"Only because he is the greatest man they have," replied the Texan. "A sun-perch not larger than your hand is a whale among minnows, you know."

"What sort of people are the Mexicans, uncle?" inquired Madison.

"I have lived among them a long time now," replied his uncle. "Some Mexicans were among the noblest patriots of our Revolution; yet an ignorant, lazy, treacherous, cruel, cowardly set they often are; there are noble exceptions, of course. I am speaking of the lowest class of Mexicans, and I hope they really are better than I think them: an old Texan may be prejudiced. No wonder, they are mongrels—a mixture of Indian, Negro, and Spanish. They are more like what I have read of the Hindoos than anything else. Give a Mexican his blanket and his mustang, his tortillas and a handful or two of red peppers, a fandango now and then and a game cock, a pack of cards and a bottle of brandy, and he wishes nothing else on earth.

"The government—or, rather, the misgovernment—of their own country is in the hands of a few men. The mass of the people are like sheep, knowing and caring for nothing whatever beyond their little daily personal wants. I said there were exceptions. I am speaking of the majority of them."

"But what makes all the difference between them and us, uncle?" said Madison.

"Oh, we are of a totally different stock and blood. Our ancestry and training have been altogether superior. Besides, their climate is a voluptuous, enervating one. They have never had motive enough to rouse them. Their government is only a revolution and a tyranny alternately. They don't read or think—never expand themselves by *exertion*. Above all, they are cursed with a religion which would drag down any people, if once fastened firmly on them: it has been their religion from the start, and it has kept them down."

"I was in Francisco's cabin, one day," said Will, "and he had stuck up some red, glaring pictures of the Virgin Mary, and a little queer crucifix in one corner. As for me, I've no contempt, only pity, for them."

"Yes, to have such things in their cabins, and to go to church and to confessional, and to pay their priests, is about the whole of their religion. It restrains them in nothing, and it teaches them nothing. Their having that, instead of no religion at all, is someway a providence, I suppose. I'm an old Texan, however—maybe prejudiced."

"It is strange," said Mr. McRobert, "that we send missionaries far away to the Hindoos and Chinese, and no one seems even to have thought of sending the Bible to these at our doors. You are too harsh upon them; how can they help being exactly what they are?"

"It would do no good," replied his brother. "Other people have some spirit in their religion — the Irish Catholics, for instance: they feel warmly for it, will argue and fight for it; but Mexicans are sluggish and indifferent. To do anything with one of them is like trying to do something with a man made of straw or sand. He will nod his head and say, '*Sí, sí, señor!*' to everything you say, and neither understand nor care any more about it. There is nothing in a Mexican to get hold of—they don't seem to have a bone in their body."

"But they improve as Americans mix in with them, do they not?" inquired his brother.

"About as much as water does with fire," replied the Texan. "No, they yield, give place, die off, but never rise. It's the old story of Indian and white man—the one race melts away like snow before the other. Mexico is worth annexing just in proportion as it becomes Americanized, and no faster. As if Mexico was not yielding before the superior race fast enough, it is, in addition, everlastingly at war in itself, tearing itself to pieces, bleeding itself to death: there is a steady decrease all the time. Before long the whole country will come under the Stars and Stripes—will sink under our flag of itself, without any taking on our part, in sheer self-exhaustion. And a magnificent country it is, except for its population; that's the only bad part of the country, the population. There are mines of all kinds of ores in abundance, the most beautiful scenery, the most fertile soil, the most healthful and delicious climate, in the world; it is far ahead of any state in the Union. I'm glad to see Texas peopling so fast with emigration. It is like filling up a reservoir until the time comes to let it pour over Mexico. Our plan is to do nothing now, nothing wrong against Mexico; a wrong-doing always kicks back on the wrong-doer like a dirty musket —only to wait. Filibustering is the very thing we ought not to do; it only throws things back. We've only to wait—wait's the word—and Mexico is ours; all quietly, naturally, inevitably, of its own accord, as the only thing it can possibly do; ours, fairly, lawfully ours; with nobody in the world to say a word against it. But, dear me," said the Texan, rising from his rocking-chair, "how I have been talking! Where shall I lay Bessie? sound asleep an hour ago."

Since Uncle Frank spoke, revolutions under Miramon, Comonfort, Maximilian, Juarez, Lerdo, Diaz, have gone on grinding Mexico to powder between them, like corn between the stones of a tremendous grist-mill. This grinding has been accompanied, as though fitted into it with cog-wheels, by the workings of the Civil War between the North and South of our own country; for all things—the very turning of the globe on its axis, too—hasten that

"One far-off divine event
To which the whole creation moves."

In 1849, Dr. Daniel Baker, a Presbyterian missionary, preached the first Protestant sermon on the banks of the Rio Grande, which separates Texas from Mexico. At his suggestion an excellent lady, Miss Rankin, first from Brownsville and then from Monterey, circulated the Bible all through Mexico; for, in the course of political events directed of Heaven towards the same end, the property of the Roman Catholic Church, which had been enormous, had been confiscated meanwhile, their religious orders broken up and driven from the country. As a result, there are to-day Protestant churches flourishing all over Mexico, the massacre of these in some places merely hastening their growth; and very soon Mexico, like the rest of the world, will be thoroughly christianized. Even Uncle Frank would not have dared to hope for results so wonderful.

And he only added, after laying Bessie down, "I must be up early and go to our honey tree. If I am not mistaken, we'll get something there to-morrow out of the hollow we laid open, not as sweet, may be, but a good deal heavier than the honey. Good-night."

CHAPTER VI.

A DOUBLE ADVENTURE.

BEFORE breakfast was over, Uncle Frank, who had gone home the night before, appeared at San Hieronymo—as the new place had come to be called—his rifle in his hand, his belt displaying two revolvers and a huge bowie-knife — evidently armed and equipped for fighting, if need be, as well as hunting.

"I want you to go with me this time, Morton," he said to his brother; "I'm satisfied there's something more at the bee tree worth bringing."

But his brother resisted all his entreaties. He was not fond of hunting at any time. Besides, he wished to get thoroughly settled first in his new home, and a vast deal remained yet to be done. As to the Texan, it was impossible for him to confine himself to work; there was not excitement enough in it for him.

"I suppose, then, I must take Madison," he said. "I don't like to, however."

"I'm sorry to hear you say so, uncle," said his nephew, who had acquired a passion for hunting since his exploit with the buck, and who was always eager to go along.

"You will see," replied his uncle, "why I don't want to take you before night. However, come along — only you must mind exactly what I say."

"Oh, take me, too, uncle," cried Will and Josie in the same breath.

"No, sir!" replied the Texan, in a decided tone.

It took but a few moments for Madison to get ready. In addition to his rifle, his uncle made him add a butcher-knife to his arms. The dogs were tied to prevent their following. In a short time they had ridden down the river to the edge of the forest. Instead, however, of going direct to the bee tree, the Texan plunged into a dense bottom thicket.

"I want to go to the tree roundabout, on account of the wind," he said.

"What wind, uncle?" asked Madison; "and what are we hunting?"

"You'll find out soon enough; only watch out, make no noise, and do exactly as I tell you," replied his uncle.

But their road was obstructed in a way they had not thought of.

"What tracks are these?" inquired Madison, suddenly stopping and pointing to the ground. "It must be some of our pigs. I didn't know they came as far from the house as this."

"Oh, pshaw!" said his uncle, as soon as he saw the tracks; "why didn't I think of it? We must turn right back. Come quick!"

But while his uncle was speaking, Madison had discovered, but a few feet before them, the animal that made the tracks. Seeing it was a wild animal, with an "Oh, uncle, look there!" Madison raised his rifle and fired.

"Oh my! what did you do that for!" exclaimed the Texan. "Drop your rifle, and up into that sapling, quick! Here they are!—quick! quick!" and the uncle himself sprang for the nearest tree and clambered up, his companion doing the same into another near at hand.

But he was not fast enough. Before he was half-way up he felt something hook into his shoe and pull. He held on to a limb he had seized with all his might; and the string of his shoe breaking, it was torn off as he scrambled up.

Seated at last in a fork of the tree, some eight feet from the ground, he did not know whether to be frightened or to laugh heartily. The whole ground below was swarming with scores of a small animal. It resembled a hog, especially in the tusks and head. The body, however, tapered off behind, and was singularly striped with black.

With bristles up and furious snapping of the tusks, the creatures crowded around the trees in which the hunters had taken refuge, eager for battle, their little eyes sparkling with rage. But the boy could not refrain from laughing aloud when he looked up at his uncle. There he sat in the small tree into which he had scrambled, and which was bending and swaying with his weight, a look of the utmost alarm and concern upon his face. Madison had supposed that his uncle would not have taken to a tree even from a lion, and this sudden terror and his ludicrous position amused him beyond measure, though he himself took good care to hold on tight all the time.

"What are they, uncle? What are we going to do? When are they going away?" he asked, at length.

"They are peccaries—Mexican hogs; we are going to stay where we are until they leave—unless we wish to be cut to bits by their lancet tusks—

and when that will be I cannot say," his uncle replied, not in the best humor. "There is no use of attempting to kill them all; besides, I have only enough powder and balls for the bee tree."

There was no help for it but patience. Once or twice Madison attempted, holding firmly with his left hand to a limb, to slash at them with his knife in his right hand, but it only made them more furious, and he began to be alarmed lest they might tear down the tree in which he was lodged. At times he could not but laugh; but after an hour spent in this way, he began to think it was not so funny as it might be, after all, for the creatures showed no intention of leaving whatever.

"They certainly are the spryest things, to be hogs, that I ever saw," said the uncle, at length. "I had a tame one once, and when it was feeding I have tried a hundred times to pull it by the tail, but always, before I could get my hand on it, it had its snout there instead."

Another hour passed; the animals still crowded around their saplings, trying at times, with undiminished rage, to get at the hunters, their little eyes flashing at them as if they said, "You big fellows, what cowards you are! We dare you to come down!" How much longer the hunters might have had to remain it was impossible to say, had not relief suddenly come from a most unexpected quarter. All at once the creatures stopped and began to sniff—then suddenly dashed away with wild grunts, and were out of sight in a moment.

"Hush!" said the uncle, "be perfectly still; draw yourself up a little into the tree, but don't breathe hardly. Yes, I thought so—here he comes!"

As he said this, an enormous black bear made his appearance from towards the river, and passed deliberately within fifty feet of them. To Madison the animal seemed, among the bushes, of gigantic proportions; and he trembled, his sapling shaking under him, with excitement.

"It's not the peccaries he is after," said the Texan, sliding down his tree when the bear had got well past, and motioning to his nephew to follow him. "Just as I thought; it's the honey. He's been there last night, has been to the river to drink, and is going back. Nothing in the world a bear likes so much as honey! Now, Madison," he continued, "I think you had better go to where we have tied the horses and return home; it's a dangerous job for a boy like you to be in, and I'm bound to fix his flint for him before I leave."

Madison by this time had regained his rifle, and long and hard did he plead: "You let me start with you, you know, uncle," he urged.

"Yes, I know, but I've thought better of it; go home, Madison—go home; some other time you shall try it with me," was his uncle's only reply.

Very discontentedly the boy went to his horse, while his uncle plunged into the forest.

Mounting, and riding slowly along the river bank, the young Texan reached the spot from which they had trailed the bee to its hive. A sudden thought struck the boy, and he drew rein and stopped to consider.

"Uncle don't want me to go with his consent," he reasoned to himself, "for then he would blame himself if I got hurt. But suppose I go *without* his consent, he can't blame himself then; he can say he told me to go home. Here's the track of our horses to and from the bee tree. I'll go a little ways, anyhow, and see. Besides, if I might get hurt, so might he, and I ought to be near to help."

This reasoning did not satisfy his conscience at all; but the passion for hunting had seized upon him since killing the buck, and, both in men and in animals, there is no instinct or passion stronger when once aroused. Many a quiet student or business man does not dream of possessing such a dormant passion, until some success in sport starts him for life with eagerness in a path never before thought of. Let the gravest clergyman alive get fairly on the trail of an antelope, a stag, a big buffalo, and he will dash head-foremost after it, tearing his clothes to ribbons through the woods, smashing his spectacles, yelling and blood-thirsty, losing not his hat only, but his grammar, dignity, and decorum. Even fishing—in some respects the meanest, least interesting form of hunting, except when sharks or whales are the game—often becomes a mania. The exciting elements of both chance and skill unite, in hunting, to give zest to it; and it is better to indulge with fishing-tackle and rifle than with lottery-tickets and cards.

In a few minutes the excited boy had hidden his horse, and, rifle in hand, was cautiously approaching the bee tree. Every few moments he would stop to listen for his uncle, and then creep nearer and nearer. At last he could see the tree, lying as they had felled it, although the opening was out of sight, hidden by the brush. Still he heard and saw nothing of his uncle.

"I wonder what can keep him," thought he. "I'll tell you what you had better do," he said to himself; "you just climb this cottonwood here; you'll be safe there, and can see everything, too."

No sooner said than done. This time he carried his rifle up with him, as he rapidly but silently ascended to the first fork.

He was hardly seated before he heard in the distance the crack of a rifle.

"Why, that's uncle, now!" he said to himself, and he began to descend. "No, I won't," he continued, resuming his seat; "it might be somebody else; anyhow, I'll wait awhile and see."

So saying, he glanced towards the opening in the bee tree, now full in view, and saw a good deal more than he had bargained for.

The stump of the tree was towards him; the top of the fallen monarch of the forest from him; the chasm in its side not more than sixty feet from where he sat. The bear was actually inside the opening. Having eaten all it could from the outside, it had squeezed itself in, and, with its body half up the hollow, was greedily devouring its favorite food. Thus it was that it had not heard or smelled the approach of the boy. The delicious food, and the honey daubed all over its head and nose, and the bees swarming fast and furious around, had made it oblivious, in its bear's paradise, to everything else in the world.

Madison had seen bears in shows, but this was the first he had ever seen loose in its native forests, and the difference is very great. He was startled, but not terrified. In the first place, he was safely up a tree; in the second place, he was expecting his uncle every moment. For half an hour he sat looking on, in a stupor from excess of excitement, when he again heard the sharp crack of a rifle, more distant than before. He knew it must be his uncle; it was in the direction in which he had left him: besides, there was no one else in the forest, that he knew of.

For some time before this, it had occurred to him that it would be a glorious thing if he could only kill the bear—ten times greater than the killing of the buck. He had dismissed the idea, however, as impossible. "My ball couldn't hurt him much through all that wool and fat," he thought; "if I only had a fair crack at his head, it would be different."

But now it suddenly came to him, "Suppose uncle is off after other game, he may not come here at all; and when he goes home and finds I'm not there, how will he or anybody know where to look? And who can tell how long that bear will stay there eating?"

This put a new face on the matter. Slowly the idea dawned on him of actually attempting to kill the animal. But it was a long time before he could resolve upon the step. At last he thought, "It'll do no hurt to try; anyhow, I'm safe up here." Saying this to himself, he took aim—resting his rifle in the fork of a small branch —at the centre of the animal's back, and fired.

As the sound rang on the air, the bear gave a desperate plunge backwards out of the hollow of the tree; but the plunge was so violent that it was carried down along the trunk into the hollow below the cut. Madison could now see that its whole head was coated thickly with honey and wax; the wool so plastered thereby over its eyes that it was blind for the time. The slit made in the tree was narrow also; it must have been with difficulty that it had forced itself in. Now, gorged and swollen with eating, it was no easy matter to get out.

In a little while, too, the young Texan could guess, at least, that the ball had broken its back. For ten minutes it was writhing, struggling, and turning itself, a huge black mass of honey and wool, before it occurred to Madison to load again. This he did as rapidly as possible. By this time the bear had got its head and fore-shoulders out of the log, and was trying, evidently in great pain, to get the rest of its body out. Again the crack of the rifle woke the forest echoes, but the ball struck the earth to one side.

Another convulsive struggle of the bear. Full half of its body was out, and it stopped an instant, panting, when another ball from the tree struck it on the head, and the monster lay, half in and half out of the tree, motionless.

But the young Texan, though he was half crazy with delight, had no idea of descending from his nest. "There's no telling what might happen," he said to himself. In a few minutes he heard a rustling beneath him, and could detect among the bushes his uncle creeping cautiously up, his rifle in hand, cocked, ready to fire. The boy felt strongly disposed to call out, but he was ashamed at having disobeyed his uncle, and was silent for the moment. Meanwhile, his uncle had reached the very tree he was in, and, peering from behind it, had caught sight of the bear, and levelled his rifle to fire. The next instant he lowered it from his shoulder with a puzzled expression, then let it fall into the hollow of his arm. He saw that the animal was dead. Walking forward — cautiously at first—he finally punched it with the end of his rifle, exclaiming:

"Well! who in cre-a-tion—?"

This was more than Madison could stand, and, sliding rapidly down the tree, he approached the astonished Texan.

"Oh, uncle," he exclaimed, "I'm so sorry! I ought to have gone home. Please forgive me. I won't do so any more. I was only up there waiting for you to come."

His uncle only replied by taking a seat beside the bear on the tree, paying no attention to the enraged bees swarming around him, looking steadily at Madison.

"And it was you who shot it? I heard shots, but never dreamed it was *you*," he said, at length, after regarding him a while in silence.

"Yes, uncle, I'm very sorry; I waited a long time for you first, and I won't do it again. Are you angry with me?"

"Angry with you!" said his uncle, with sudden energy. "Angry with you! I guess *not!* But how was it?"

Madison then gave him a full account of the whole matter, to which his uncle listened with grave and even respectful attention. It was evident to the boy that his uncle thought a vast deal more than ever of him, and his heart bounded within him.

"Now, Madison," he said at length, "off with your coat, roll up your sleeves, out with your knife; we must get to work."

In a short time they had dragged the bear — and hard work it was — away from the bees, flayed it, disembowelled it, then cut up the huge carcass, tied it up in the skin, laid it on the stronger of the two horses which Madison had brought up for the purpose, and were slowly on their way home.

"It was a panther I got after," said the uncle, as they went. "Or, rather, it was a panther got after me. I had two good shots at him too. It's the second time we've had a pitched fight. I'll tell you about it. You know my Dutchman up in the cedar brake — Hoogenboom? Well, he has a wife and a cabinful of white-headed children 'way up among the mountains. One cold day last winter the Dutchman had gone over to New

Braunsfeld. I happened to be in the wagon, Francisco driving the oxen, going towards the cabin. When we were within a quarter of a mile of it, we heard the most awful screams.

"I was sure it was Indians. My rifle had been left behind—never leave it behind you, Madison, even when you go to bed—at least, when you go out; you'll be certain to be sorry for it before you get back. I ran on, however, telling Francisco to come on with the wagon. When I got to the cabin, there was the woman and all her children outside, yelling like forty. They were at dinner, when all at once a panther lighted right in the centre of the table, making a beautiful smash of plates and things. The smell of the fried pork had drawn it, and it had jumped in through the open door. In half a minute the woman and her children were outside. Before she had done telling, Francisco had stopped the team in front of the cabin. None of us had anything except a pair of tongs the woman had brought out in her hurry.

"While we were consulting what to do, the panther climbed up the chimney and made a jump from the roof at Francisco, who was riding on one of the oxen, knocking him off between the yoke on to the wagon-tongue.

"I snatched the tongs and jumped on the animal, and began pounding it the best I could; but it managed to slip out, and was gone like a shot. I knew it this morning by its having one eye knocked out with the tongs. I dare say we will meet again, and next time—never mind!"

.

CHAPTER VII.

CONTAINING WHAT WILL BE FOUND IN IT.

Yes, Madison *was* remarkably successful for so young a beginner. Uncle Frank was delighted. He was a boy after his own heart. But his father rather shook his head. He was glad to see his son bold, active, fearless, energetic; but he feared he might acquire too great a passion for hunting, to the neglect of other and more important things. So, with the full consent of his mother—the empress of the household—his father issued his decree. Save in rare cases, from Monday morning to Friday night was to be given to labor and study; Saturday only was to be devoted to hunting.

As a great deal had yet to be done, study for the present was confined to one good lesson well learned and recited to Mrs. McRobert before breakfast. All day was then given to work. After an early supper Madison read aloud, or instructed his younger brother. It is astonishing how fast the boys came on in their studies, for of all teachers in the world a child's own parents are the best—when they are at all qualified to be really parents.

By the end of July the garden was overflowing with the reward of all the toil. The boys had learned the art of raising watermelons by planting the seed in soil which had been dug up to the depth of near three feet. This permitted the roots to draw moisture from far below, even when the earth was all dry and burned on the surface. Subsoiling this is called, and it is the secret of raising a good crop of anything, and especially in a country subject to such droughts as Texas. In Virginia the boys had never entered the garden save to eat its fruits; but now almost everything in it was the result of their own toil, and they enjoyed it ten times as much. And so with all the family—there was a larger, deeper sense of enjoyment than they had ever known. They had now an object, an interest, in life, and enjoyed a vigor and a pleasure unimagined before.

Ever since reaching Texas Madison had paid special attention to writing, with the almost exclusive purpose of being able to write back to his favorite cousin, Charley—a son of his uncle George. Thus he wrote, about the end of August:

"My Dear Cousin,—I was glad to get your letter. I am sorry to know that things are so dull with you back there in dear 'Ole Virginny,' as Rohamma calls it. You don't get out of bed till the breakfast bell? Why, we are up and busy by five o'clock every morning. It is the best part of the day—it is so cool and fresh and clear. 'I don't think the world could have looked more beautiful in Eden to Adam and Eve than it does now,' I heard ma say to pa yesterday before breakfast. You don't know how fresh and young ma and pa are both getting to be. You know pa used to be almost all day in the house at home, reading papers and things, complaining of being a little sick; and ma about the same. Now it is very little of the time pa is in out of the open air, and they have not either of them been sick at all. We are all glad we came to Texas—glad, glad. We do not have so many fine things indoors; but we look more out of doors for our happiness now, and out of doors it is grand, I tell you! The pure air, the splendid scenery, the spring, the river, the prairie, to say nothing of our stock and our corn! What we have inside our houses, you know, is man's work; it is God's work that lies outside, and there is so much more of it, and I like it best.

"But I want to tell you about my learning how to swim. I have told you before all about our magnificent spring. It is a stream gushing up from under the mountain, near seventy feet broad and twenty feet deep in places—all in solid white rock. If you stand on the edge, you can see any quantity of fishes swimming about—the little ones near the top, the larger ones, as long as your arm, at the bottom. And then the water is so deliciously cold these hot days to bathe in. We have got the very place to bathe in too—fifty yards from the house, out of sight, behind a heap of rock and a willow grove. It is solid rock; but it shelves in so gradually! You remember how afraid I always was of the water. Uncle Frank laughed at me so much about it that I waded far out, but I couldn't swim. I tried my best over and over again, but it was no use. One day Uncle Frank said it was all nonsense; so he took me before I could help myself twenty feet from shore out into ten feet water. 'Now,' he said, 'wait till you get your breath. Be quiet—don't be flurried. I'm going to let you go here—you must swim to shore.' 'But I don't know how to swim,' I said, and I almost cried, and begged and held on like an eel. He kept me till I had got quiet again; then, sure enough, he suddenly left me to myself out there in ten feet water. Would you believe it, Charley, I actually swam ashore. I had to do it, you know, or go to the bottom! You can't tell how glad I was to find I really could swim. Since then I have been practising every morning—am not at all afraid. Will has not learned yet; but I guess he soon will, if Uncle Frank can only catch him. Old Doodle-bug—Josie, you know—he swam the first time he went in; he is the smartest of us all, you know. Duke can swim; and if it is nature to him to do so, I don't see why it should not be nature to us too, if only one would not be so frightened at first.

"I wish you were here. Every morning now I am out at the bathing-place as the sun rises. There is a flat, clean edge of rock just over a place twenty feet deep. When I have got off my clothes there, I whistle Duke to me, then plunge off head-foremost as deep as I can drive myself down, down into the pure, clear water—Duke head-foremost, too, after me. Such a kicking and splashing, and laughing and shouting—it is the best fun in the world! Pa lets me stay in only ten minutes; it is too exhilarating—it weakens one when one stays in longer than that. I come out all aglow—so happy and so hungry! and so stout and strong after breakfast!

"But I am making my letter too long, especially as I write so often. Pa says this is the best way to write compositions—writing a real letter to some one. But I hear Uncle Frank in the yard. To-day is Saturday—my hunting-day—and I must close. Love to all, from your affectionate cousin,   MADISON."

And it was well that Uncle Frank did come just then. Bessie was stooping over the ground playing with something when he entered the yard. As soon as she saw him,

"Oh, uncle, uncle!" she said, "do come here, hereth thuth a long caterpillar. I've been turning it over and over with a little thtick; it's got forty eleven legs—do come!"

Her uncle approached, gave one glance over her shoulder, and the next instant had snatched her almost across the yard. It was a centipede

near ten inches long. It *did* look like a huge caterpillar, only flatter, its body made up of flat shells, like a string of chestnuts touching each other, yellow and hard. There were two long feelers extending from beside its jaws, and no less than fifty legs on each side, long and hard, with cruel hooks on them.

"It's a mercy I came," said the Texan, holding down the squirming thing to the ground under the end of his rifle, as the mother ran out and took the terrified child from the ground. "Bessie was playing with it with a stick not three inches long; if it had seized on her hand, I don't see how we could have saved her. The miserable thing not only seizes on with its jaws, but it buries all of its hundred claws in the flesh, too—never lets go, and sends venom in through each claw. It would have to be cut off with a knife, and each separate claw actually dug out."

"Hold on, uncle!" cried Will; "don't crush it. I'll have a bottle in a moment!"

And in a few minutes he had run into the house and returned with a wide-mouthed soda glass jar six inches high. By a little management the reptile was driven in, the jar filled with whiskey and tightly corked up.

"Died drunk!" said Uncle Frank, as the centipede ceased to writhe in the jar. "And see what a purple it has turned! But what's your idea, Will?"

"Oh, I'm making a museum," answered Will. "Don't you remember that nice gentleman—a Swiss, pa called him—who stayed with us the other night. He had a long green tin case slung on his back, and such a queer knapsack. Studer, that was his name. He is collecting all sorts of bugs and flowers and things. I promised to save everything of the sort for him till he came back. Come and see what I've got, uncle!"

Accordingly, Will led him into his room. He had got Madison to make him a neat shelf along the wall, and on it were a row of bottles, given him by the Swiss naturalist. In one were half a dozen lizards of all sorts, —blue, green, yellow, striped, spotted —with tails four inches long.

"Hard work I had to catch these swift-jacks," said Will, "they run so fast. They flash through the grass like lightning in a cloud. I've only caught these, and you know there's a dozen other kinds."

"Where did you get this?" asked his uncle, taking up another jar containing a singular reptile. It was a sort of worm, near an inch in diameter, of a dun color, with jaws and short legs, loathsome to look on beyond expression, about three inches long, something of a leech, centipede, caterpillar, and snake, all in one.

"I found that by the corn-crib," said Will. "But what is it, uncle?"

"I don't know," replied the Texan. "I asked Studer, and he don't know; he says that it is altogether new to science. Nobody knows whether it can bite or not, but I declare I'd rather risk a centipede. This is the second I ever saw. Suppose we name it after you, the *Lacerta Gulielmi*—you

see I remember some of my school Latin—in English, Will's grub. But how did you catch this tarantula without crushing it?"

"It was so strange, uncle, I must tell you about it. One day," continued Will, "I was going out to the prairie to drive up the cows. As I was walking along the path, I saw this fellow taking his walk. See, his body is as big as a partridge-egg, all covered with black hair. Just look at his horrid red jaws; and his legs so stout and so hairy he could hardly lie under a big saucer. He looks the king of all the spiders—and I expect he is — their great-grandfather, at least. When he saw me, do you think, he didn't actually stop, and then come jumping at me, his mouth wide open! How he jumped! I didn't have any stick, and I was afraid of him, I tell you! Just then I noticed a wasp flying round and round him. The tarantula began to run for his hole, when the wasp struck him — bang! Oh, how mad he was! He reared himself up on his hind-legs, threw his fore-legs in the air, and clashed them together, working his ugly red jaws all the time. But the wasp only flew round and round until he saw his chance, then popped him again on the back, knocking him clean over. I stood there and watched the fight, I don't know how long. At last the tarantula tumbled over, and the wasp circled round till he was satisfied he was dead, then flew straight off about his business. I gave a hurrah for Captain Wasp, ran home, got my jar, and soon had Colonel Tarantula corked up. Did you ever know anybody to be killed by a bite of one of them, uncle?" asked Will, in conclusion.

"I've known many persons to be bitten by tarantulas and centipedes, but they were always doctored in time," replied his uncle. "A centipede crawled once over Francisco's leg when he was lying fast asleep: the prints of the claws are there still, and often pain him, although he knew nothing about it till he woke.

"Once," continued the Texan, turning to the others who had now come into the room, "I was out with the Rangers Indian-fighting. We had captured a wigwam full of squaws and pappooses. One morning I saw a little copper-colored rascal, about Josie's age, dig a centipede out of a hole, roast it on the coals, and eat it, just as we used to roast a pig's tail at hog-killing time—don't you remember, Morton?—and eat it."

"Will had a little adventure of the kind the other day," said Mrs. McRobert. "He had washed his face in the basin, and, with his eyes shut to keep out the soap, he applied the towel to his face, then dropped it with a scream, for a scorpion had fastened on his nose. It was on the towel, but he did not see it. I was dreadfully alarmed at first, but applied ammonia to it, and it was well before night."

"Oh, it didn't hurt more than a wasp sting," said Will; "not half as bad as a hornet."

"But it's the ants that are the worst," said his father; "there is a large bed of the red ants by the garden gate. I have been fighting them, as the boys call it, for weeks. First I poured down boiling water every day or two; then I blew them up by pouring powder into the hole as far as it would run; then I tried some potassium Mr. Studer gave me. I would place the lumps in the mouth of the hole, moistened with water, and every ant that walked over it dropped down dead, killed by the fumes. But they are there still: I do not see that I have diminished them in the least."

"And I've a nest in my yard," said his brother, "that I've fought for years. I've tried all the things you speak of; and I once mixed a quantity of turpentine and castor-oil, poured that down, and set it on fire: it burned as far as it had run. Next, I tried to blow sulphur-smoke down. By-the-bye, I knew a man who was himself killed by the fumes in trying that. Then I would sink a big jar in the path to and from the hole, the edge of the mouth on a level with the earth. Quarts on quarts I caught that way, but it didn't even thin them that I could see. Old Texans say the only way to break up a nest is to dig it entirely out. But then, they say, that the ants always carry their holes down till they come to water. I knew a gentleman who dug his well through an ant-nest on this account—seventy feet down he traced the hole, and didn't come to water at last. Then, again, I knew another man who had an ant-bed in the centre of his yard. He dug down six feet, and came to the central nest. There were the queen ants—the grandmothers of millions—near as big as a wasp, with wings too, and any quantity of eggs —a barrelful, which he burned: he dug it, and left a spring of abundant water instead. He told me that there were avenues running from it to fifty ant-nests hundreds of feet around in every direction, and that all the rest of the ants turned claws up, dead—all over the yard for an acre around—of broken hearts, when the citadel had been stormed, and their revered parents killed."

"It is the brown ant, the cutting ant, that does the mischief," said Mrs. McRobert. "They stripped our largest China-tree in one night of all its leaves; some were busy cutting, while others below were carrying away the leaves as they fell. If any of us prove to be sluggards here, it certainly will not be for want of going to the ant and considering her ways."

"You must not start me to talking about ants," her brother-in-law replied. "Some of them keep a certain kind of seed-grass carefully weeded, and gather in the seeds when ripe; that is, they make their negroes do it."

"Negroes? You are joking, uncle!" Josie exclaimed.

"No, I am not. I have seen the red ants attack a nest," his uncle replied, "of the black ants, kill the old ones, and return home, every ant with a negro ant-baby on its back. Often I have watched a long procession of these working ants carrying leaves or grain to their holes. At certain regular intervals, all along, the master-ants stood as overseers. Whenever the workers came near an overseer, I have noticed how they would hurry up, and then slacken off after they got past. Many a time I have seen an overseer-ant go for a poor worker that was tugging slowly along under his heavy load, cuff him, kick him, knock him down. When a nest is dug up, you are certain to find a beetle in it. Old Texans say that the ants keep it to worship as a god, but *that* I don't vouch for."

"And not one single insect or reptile but has its own particular end to accomplish in the world," said Morton McRobert.

"But what possible good do mosquitoes and horse-flies do?" asked his brother.

"There is no telling," was the reply; "the millions of insect life may consume things in earth and atmosphere which are in some way necessary, yet which would make the globe uninhabitable if not kept in bounds. As to the horse-flies, you well know that they actually drive the cattle up home—herd them from the prairies for their owners in summer—doing the work of thousands of herdsmen: change the name, call them winged herdsmen, and you will think more of these native-born Texans. Mosquitoes hover over damp places, and many an ague and yellow fever do they actually eat up in the bud, in its germs in the air; that is, if we only knew it. I can't tell what each separate star is made for, or for what each idiot is permitted; but I do know that all things are created and ordered by One infinitely wise and good."

"Don't you remember, pa," interrupted Madison, "the lines you made me get by heart:

'That nothing walks with aimless feet;
   That not one life shall be destroyed,
   Or cast as rubbish to the void,
When God hath made the pile complete;

'That not a worm is cloven in vain;
   That not a moth with vain desire
   Is shrivelled in a fruitless fire,
   Or but subserves another's gain.'"

"Yes," said his father; "that, in some way, no event, great or small, but is permitted by our Father in heaven. Only feel this — a sense of our Father—our Father always on his throne — our Father superintending everything and every event during each successive instant, and having him for our dearest, nearest friend, how it elevates and strengthens one all the time; as much—more, in fact —in adversity than in prosperity. To know, love, fear, serve, rejoice in such a friend all the time is the sum and substance of my religion!"

All this time Uncle Frank seemed to be busy examining a horned frog which Will had bottled up among his curiosities. He said nothing, but his brother's words made an impression on him, especially as they were spoken in the most natural manner.

"However," said Mrs. McRobert, after a pause, "if you are going up in the cedar brake, it is time to be off— it is nearly eight o'clock."

For some time, Mr. McRobert had a man cutting rails up the river, and constructing a raft with them for the purpose of floating them down to the mouth of the San Hieronymo. There Hark, was to be ready, with boat and ropes, to secure the raft, which was to be towed up the San Hieronymo, and then hauled to the prairie they were in course of fencing. Hark had already been despatched to the spot to make ready, and the two gentlemen, accompanied by Madison and Will, started for the brake. As it was his hunting-day, Madison and his uncle both took their rifles. On arriving at the spot, some two miles up the river, they found the raft still swinging against the bank, held by its ropes.

"I see some of our cows have been about here," said Madison, pointing to tracks in the soft edge of the river beside the raft.

It would have been well had all looked closer at the tracks, as well as at the ropes which held the raft.

"Friends and fellow-citizens!" said Uncle Frank, who was standing on a stump, "I've a proposition to make before we start the raft. It's very early. Hark has to bail out his boat and get his ropes ready for us below. They're out of venison at my ranch and at the house, too. Suppose we step up a mile or two to Plum Spring and kill a deer. I can feel in this trigger-finger that one is on his way there this moment for a drink. We can soon have it here, throw it upon the raft, and then float away for home."

Exacting a promise from his brother and Madison that they would return within two hours at the furthest, Mr. Morton McRobert yielded his consent, remaining behind with Will. After they had been gone a few moments, Mr. McRobert gave his son a charge on no account to leave the spot, and strolled off up the river to dig up a rare specimen of cactus, which he had promised to transplant into the front yard for his wife.

As he left, Will drew his fishing-line from his pocket, tied the end to a convenient stick, baited his hook with a grub—which he got by rolling an old log over—and began to fish in a deep pool beside the raft. It was a lovely morning, the water reflecting the calm blue sky above. In the distance could be heard the singular cry of the great gray owl of Texas, while the tree lizards were still keeping up their morning concert. Nothing could be more still and peaceful. Already Will had caught several fine gasper-goos, a splendid variety of trout, and was glancing about for his father, to whom he was anxious to display them, when he heard a noise behind him. Looking back, he saw that it was only a cow—somewhat smaller, of a dun color unusual to cows—and was about resuming his sport, when he saw that the cow, on catching sight of him, had stopped and was angrily shaking her head. Then it suddenly occurred to the boy that it might be one of the wild cows of which he had often heard Francisco speak. These are cattle that have run wild for many years, or are descended from domestic cattle, but have themselves never been tamed. They are regarded as among the most dangerous of all wild animals with which the woods of Texas abound. Even the most fearless hunter dreads to meet them upon an open prairie; for, especially when wounded, they are savagely furious. Now, it so happened that the ropes with which the raft was secured to the bank had been kept in an old brine-barrel in the smoke-house, and were saturated with salt. For several days the animal had visited the spot, and had chewed at the ropes until they were almost in two in several places; but no one had noticed it. She was now returning to the spot, when she caught sight of the boy.

In an instant Snap, Will's terrier, had dashed at her. Had it not been for this, she might have turned and gone her way. As it was, provoked by the assault, she rushed right at the boy over the body of his dog. There was only one chance for Will, and that was the raft. With a loud cry for his father, the boy sprang with all his might from the log, on which he was standing, upon the floating raft. The current already bore strongly against it; in a short time it would have broken loose of itself. The jar of the boy's feet was the last grain of pressure needed; and, as he struck upon the raft, the weakened rope that held it to the bank parted, and it began to float slowly away.

The wild cow, too, reaching the raft almost at the same instant, placed her fore-hoofs on the edge, though somewhat doubtfully, to follow. This gave additional impulse to the raft, and it was soon ten feet from the shore.

Even yet Will could have escaped by clinging to the overhanging willows. But he was too much terrified by the attack even to notice for some time that the raft was moving away. He was not so frightened, however, but that he made the shore ring with cries for his father. Mr. McRobert had been attracted from one flowering cactus to another till he had gone some distance up the river. Then he observed an enormous ammonite — a fossil sea-shell — projecting from a high bank still farther up. Laying down his cactus roots, he had broken off a pole, had climbed the hill, had inserted the end of the pole beside the petrified shell, and was just rolling it down the bank, when he heard the voice of his son again and again. Dropping everything, he ran down the bank and along the shore. But it was slow work at best —logs and boulders and tangled vines intercepted him. His hat was knocked off. Once or twice he fell in his haste. It seemed to him as if he would never reach the spot — blaming himself as he went for leaving it even for a moment. He neared it, at last, bare-headed, anxious, exhausted. With an eager bound he leaped over a rock that hid the place from view. One glance showed him that the raft was gone, and the next the infuriated cow rushed upon him.

CHAPTER VIII.

THE RAFT.

Swifter, and still more swiftly, floated the raft down the river. Several times it struck against projecting points of shore, where Will could have leaped ashore; but he was too much alarmed to move from the spot on which he lay, poor fellow! afraid to stand, and holding on to a cross-piece with all his might.

On and on he swept. Now he would cry for his father, and then he tried to steady himself on his knees and pray to God to help him. One thing encouraged him: he remembered that Hark was in the boat at the mouth of the San Hieronymo waiting to catch the raft. But he now began to observe, to his dismay, that as it floated down-stream it was drifting towards the other side — the eastern side — of the river. As the globe revolves on its axis, spinning so swiftly towards the east, all things on its surface have a tendency to be left behind by the motion, throwing themselves towards the west. This is the reason that the western banks of rivers are more worn by the water than the eastern, and why drift-wood is thrown rather to that side than the other. But it so happened, also, that there was a current strong enough to counteract this, which swept the other way. Now, Will was only a little boy. He was but as a grain of sand compared to the great globe he was on. Yet there was a Providence in regard to Will in this grand motion of the globe on its axis. We shall see how.

By this time the raft was nearing his uncle's ranch, which lay on the same side of the river, and between where he was and his father's property. Will knew that Francisco was somewhere there, and he began to shout for him as loud as he could. Francisco *was* there, mending his saddle. He heard the cries, and ran down to the bank as fast as he could. But just before he got there the raft had swept around a bend below, and was out of sight. Francisco remained for half an hour on the shore, gazing in every direction, and shouting, and he began, at last, to think it must have been something supernatural that he had heard; so he only crossed himself, and went back to the mending of his saddle. He could not have saved Will if he had seen him go by. Why, we will see after a while.

As soon as the boy had passed his uncle's landing, he began to shout for Hark. By this time he was driven by the current to almost the opposite side of the river. Hark was sitting in the boat, the oars in his hands, waiting for the raft. At his feet was a large tin bucket, in which was his dinner; but he was fast asleep. The boat was not tied, but the end of it was high enough up on the sandy bank to keep it from floating away. Negroes cannot sit still anywhere for half an hour of a summer's day without going fast asleep; and though Hark was as fine a black man as you would wish to see, as tall and strong as Rohamma, his wife, was short and fat, he was not superior to his nature.

Will was almost opposite him with his raft before Hark heard his cries. Then he started up and began to back the boat out in a desperate hurry; but before he could do this and get turned fairly around the raft was far down-stream on the other

side. There was a Providence in this, too. Negroes, however smart on land, are perfect fools on water, unless they have been very much used to it: when in the least danger, they lose all their presence of mind. Even one who can swim is ten times more apt to drown than a white man. I am sure he would have drowned both Will and himself if he had awakened before the raft had passed him; perhaps that was the reason he was permitted to be asleep.

Poor Will! he now sank on the frail structure that bore him, exhausted with terror. Although three years older than Josie, he was more feminine and easily frightened than he. There was no hope now. He began to have strange fancies that he was on the back of a great bird that was flying away with him. Then he thought the wild cow had got on the raft, and was trying to get at him. Once a garfish two feet long jumped through the raft beside where he lay, flapped about on him, and then slipped off again.

By this time he began to hear the roar of the rapids below him, but in his fainting condition he imagined it was Hark or Rohamma grinding hominy in the steel mill. Near the rapids the frail structure began to give way; it was not meant to endure such a strain. As the raft reached the middle of the boiling waters, it parted in two. One glance at the blue sky, one swift thought of little Bessie and his mother, and, with a half prayer on his lips, he sank beneath the turbulent waters.

Do you think it was without the ordering of some one that in all that dense forest there was one human being, and that he happened to be, not miles and miles away as usual, but upon the east bank of the stream? And he could not have told for his life why he was there, for he was sitting on a log doing nothing. For several minutes he saw the raft before it came to him, and the boy on it, too. In an instant he had waded out into the rapids. Just as the raft reached him, Will sank through it into the water, and the same instant the stranger dived, so as to let the raft pass over his head. When he emerged, dripping, the scattered rails were strewn over the whole surface of the river below, tossed and torn apart like straws by the rapids.

But that was a trifle. They had first borne the boy safely to him, and he now slowly struggled ashore, bearing him upon his bosom — for Will was very small and slight for his years, very much like his mother. The man was ragged and emaciated, his overgrown hair mingling with his unshorn beard, yet no mother could have laid the boy down more tenderly than he. For several minutes he rubbed and chafed the cold body with painful anxiety, and murmured prayers. At last, there were signs of returning life, and the large tears rolled down upon the wet mass of beard as he exclaimed to himself, "Thank God, thank God!" as if from his very soul. And when the boy opened his eyes and drew a deep breath, his companion sat on the grass beside him, weeping aloud,

overcome either by weakness or emotion, or both combined.

From this, however, he was speedily aroused by the sound of oars, and there came Hark, rowing down the river with all his might, his back to the rapids, intent only on pursuing the raft with its precious burden; for Hark would a great deal rather have lost his own black 'Markable any day than his young "Mass Will." It may be a shame to him as a father to say it, but it is a fact; in this, too, he ought to have risen superior to his nature, but he couldn't; at least, he didn't.

"Back water! back water!" shouted the stranger to him, loud and earnestly.

Hark instinctively obeyed. And it was well he did, for it was all he could do to stop his boat before it had got caught in the rapids, and then he pulled ashore. In a few moments the stranger had borne Will in his arms and laid him in the bottom of the boat, while Hark looked on with astonishment and delight, his hands trembling with excitement.

"Lor, massa," he exclaimed, "whar did you come from? how did you catch him? Whar de raft?"

"You never mind," said the stranger, interrupting the volley of questions, and placing Hark's coat tenderly beneath the head of the boy as he lay. "You mind what you are about; row back carefully, take him to his mother, and tell her to give him something hot to drink; quick too! What's in this?" he continued, as he saw Hark's bucket in the boat, which had been covered by his coat.

"That's my dinner, massa."

"I wish you would give me some of it," said the man, in a quick, nervous manner, with a lighting-up of his haggard face.

"Give you some of it!" said the negro, seizing upon the bucket and pressing it with both hands upon the stranger, "Lor bless you, massa, you's welcome to it, and the bucket too! You might eat me too, if you want to! You welcome! welcome! mighty welcome!"

Without a word the stranger seized upon the bucket, and was up the bank and out of sight in an instant.

"Oh, you *is* a fool!" said Hark, as he rowed up-stream. "Why didn't you ask him to ride up in de boat to dinner at de house? Guess Miss 'Manda glad to see him. Looked as if he hadn't had anything to eat for a year. But you shut up, nigger. Row! dat's what you do, row!"

And he did row with a vigor that soon brought the head of the *Dolores* to the landing-place at the mouth of the San Hieronymo; and, rowing up its blue and winding water, the negro soon reached the flat rock near the house.

To fasten the boat, to take the exhausted boy in his arms and bear him into the house, was the work of a few moments. Mrs. McRobert, Rohamma, and Bessie stood breathless while he told the tale—and told it over and over again. It was terror and joy combined that paled the cheek of the mother as she laid Will on the bed and began to remove his wet cloth-

ing, while Rohamma hurried out to prepare something hot for him.

"Colorado water, eh?" said she to Hark. "You so fond ob Colorado water; I hope you got enuff ob it now. Floatin' down the ribber on a raft! nebber heerd of such a ting as dat in Virginny; dat's *Texas!* Country nebber made to lib in; made for Mexicans, centumpedes, qurantulas, and frogs with horns—not for white folks. You, 'Markable, you'd better bring dose chips, or I'll *Texas* you!"

But let us return up the river, down which we have drifted so unexpectedly. We left Mr. McRobert just as the infuriated wild cow rushed upon him. So sudden was the attack that he had barely time to leap to one side to escape it. He knew the ferocious nature of the creature he had to deal with, he had no gun with which to defend himself, yet all was nothing to him in comparison to his desire to follow the departed raft and rescue his boy.

Before the animal could turn again upon him he had seized the readiest mode of escape from the spot by plunging into the river as he was. A few moments' swimming placed him far down-stream. Landing again, and without waiting to dry his clothes, heavy and clinging to him with water, he ran on along the rocky shore looking eagerly for the raft at every bend.

Meanwhile the victorious cow, having driven all her enemies from the field, quietly resumed her feast upon the broken ends of the salty ropes. But not long. Uncle Frank and Madison had succeeded in killing a deer at the spring in the brake. As rapidly as possible they had flayed and cut it up, and were about starting with as much of the flesh as they could carry, when Hoogenboom, the Dutch wood-cutter, happened upon them with his axe.

Be patient a moment while a word or two is said about him. We all know that Germany has sent an enormous emigration to America, a large part of which has settled in Texas. New Braunsfeld is a town in the valley of the Guadalupe wholly settled by a colony from Germany—a prosperous town it is too, as German in everything as any town in Germany. There are other like towns in Texas, besides thousands of German families scattered separately about. They have notions of their own in regard to the style of their houses, are exceedingly fond of lager-beer and meerschaums, have by no means as strict notions as to the observance of the Sabbath as is common in America; they are, however, a valuable kind of population—industrious, saving, sober, honest. There are two distinct classes of these emigrants. The most numerous are poor people who have come over to better themselves, in which they eminently succeed. The other class consists of highly educated men of all learned professions, who have left their own land in search of more liberty of thought and action than is allowed them there. Hoogenboom was one of this class. He had been a professor in some German college; was a learned and talented man. Becoming implicated in the political troubles in Germany, he had fled to America a poor man. What little he possessed he had been defrauded of after reaching America, and he had been glad to accept the offer of Mr. Frank McRobert to cut rails in exchange for land. Somewhat disgusted with the world, he had made himself content with his family in his mountain cabin cutting wood, killing deer, reading, smoking — especially smoking. Besides his children he had only one pet; this was his Mexican dog Schlick, to which he took a fancy on account of its extreme ugliness, there being not a hair upon his whole diminutive body—yellow too, as everything Mexican always is.

This was Hoogenboom whom the hunters persuaded to assist them in carrying their deer meat to the raft. Very short in stature, very thick in circumference, a huge wool hat on his head, a pipe as large as a coffee-cup held between his lips by its six-inch stem, Schlick at his heels, a load of meat in his hands, Hoogenboom parted the brush and entered the spot in advance of his companions, who were toiling behind him more heavily laden. In a flash he was rolling— an enormous ball — on the ground, knocked over by the cow, while at the same instant Schlick flew high in the air, landing in the top of a thick cedar, from the horns of the animal.

"Take to the brush quick, quick!" cried Uncle Frank, as it rushed upon them.

In an instant the hunters had dropped their meat and plunged into the thicket. Whirling upon her heels, the excited animal rushed back upon the prostrate Dutchman. It seemed impossible for him to escape being gored. Too much stunned and astonished, he still lay helpless on the ground, without even attempting to rise. Where he had fallen happened to be the top of the bank leading down by some twenty feet to the river's edge. The cow, dashing upon him, placed her long horns against his side; but, according to his singular habit, Hoogenboom had on no one can tell how many thicknesses of clothing. At the same instant, too, he seized upon the horns and pressed them down to the ground, so that when the animal threw up its head to toss him in the air, it only rolled him like a hogshead down the slope.

As he rolled, a bullet from the rifle of the excited Madison grazed the cow's side, and back she turned upon them—turned only to receive a bullet from the steady rifle of Uncle Frank right between the eyes, and to sink to her knees, and then at full length on the ground, dead.

"But where in the world are your father and Will?" said the Texan, as he came out of the thicket with his nephew. "And the raft is gone too!" he exclaimed, as he reached the top of the slope.

"Oh, uncle, what can have happened?" said Madison, white with anxiety. "Here are the ends of the ropes. They look as if they had been chewed in two. And here is Will's fishing-line lying on the ground. Oh, uncle, what can have happened? Where's pa and Will?"

His uncle glanced at the dead cow, and the truth dawned upon him.

"Don't be afraid," he said, concealing his own fear. "They have only drifted down the river to Hark. They are safe there by now. But let's hurry—never mind the venison now. Are you hurt, Hoogenboom?"

"Not mooch," said the Dutchman, who had by this time sat up. "Dunder and Blitzen! vere's my pipe? And Schlick tight up in de tree! Zince you have turned to von leetle bird," he added, looking up at his dog, which was howling from its airy position with fright, "you must sing von leetle song — is dat it? heh, Schlick? Himmel! Men, help get him down before you go!"

But when he had scrambled to his feet he was alone; with his dog above him, the cow beside him.

It is easy to imagine the joy of Mr. McRobert, Madison, and Uncle Frank, when they got home after a thorough search along the river, and a hot and anxious walk, to find Will safe, and to hear his story and that of Hark.

"But who was the wild man that rescued Will? That's what I want to know!" Uncle Frank exclaimed.

CHAPTER IX.

WINE-MAKING—PECAN-GATHERING—ANTELOPES.

When Hoogenboom was assisting the hunters to carry their venison, he had promised to come over to San Hieronymo in a few weeks, and show them how to make "von shplendid vine," as he called it. Wine? but where were the grapes to come from, do you ask? Nature had planted and trained and ripened them in magnificent abundance. Standing in the door of the house at San Hieronymo, you could see, now that fall had come, all the woods around fairly loaded with them. The vines weighed down the dog-wood thickets with great clusters of black grapes as large as a bullet each, and larger. The vines ran exulting to the very tops of the highest pecans and live-oaks, and enriched the whole tree with glorious clusters. You could have loaded a train of cars with them. The children had eaten of them until tired; and very refreshing they were on the long hot days, if you only avoided eating the thick skin and swallowed merely the pulp.

According to his promise, very early one sparkling September morning, Hoogenboom made his rotund appearance, not a bit worse than Will for his adventure with the wild cow.

"I can't tell why it is," said Uncle Frank, who was standing in the porch as the Dutchman rolled up towards them, pipe in mouth, and almost extinguished under his broad wool hat, "but Hoogenboom always reminds me of Molly McGruder."

"And who was Molly McGruder?" asked Mrs. McRobert, who was standing beside him.

"Not know Molly McGruder?" replied her brother-in-law. "Why, Amanda, who could have had charge of your early education? By-the-bye, how young and blooming you look! and you are getting so rosy and plump too; and you smile oftener and laugh a good deal more, I'll be bound, than you ever did in your old Virginia."

"Thank you! but what about Molly McGruder?"

"Oh, only this. The morning of the battle of San Jacinto, Sam Houston held a council of his officers under the tree where he slept. The case of Texas had reached its crisis. A few hours would decide whether this magnificent country was to be still a miserable province of twice miserable Mexico, or whether it was to be a free and independent republic; whether we were then and there to give the Mexicans a drubbing, or whether they were to beat and then butcher us, as they had done Fannin's command. It was a solemn time. Houston and all the officers around him were serious — consulting the plan of battle. Suddenly in rushed a huge Irish lady —the very double of Hoogenboom, only in petticoats; but she had boots and copperas-colored trousers on, too —I saw them. The sentinels tried to keep her away, but they could not. No, see Houston she would, and in she rushed.

"'Which is Mr. Houston here?' she asked. I have told you how particularly polite he is to ladies; always bowing and saying 'Yes, lady,' or 'No, lady,' when he converses with them: so he replied, with a bow, 'I am, madam.'

"'And these here are your people, ain't they?' she asked, with a motion of her hand towards the Texan soldiers all around.

"'This is the Texan army, madam,' he replied, with dignity.

"'It is? Well, they are your people, I'm told. Now, you are all trespassing on me land—Molly McGruder's me name. It's me league you are on. You are frightening me cows and trampling down me grass, and I want you to get off me land straight away. I'm a lone widdy woman—Molly McGruder's me name; but I won't have nothing of the sort. You've got no right to come here: it isn't your league. Go right off—clear out—take your people away! I won't have it— it's me own land—Molly McGruder's me name—'"

"Good-morning, Mr. Hoogenboom," interrupted Mrs. McRobert, for that gentleman had by this time reached them. But the Dutchman, pipe in mouth, had only time to lift his hat with a bow. Soon he had the whole available force of the family at work. Hark and Rohamma and Mr. Morton McRobert were too busy to assist; but all the rest were soon up to the lips in wine-making. Uncle Frank drove the wagon under the trees, while Will and 'Markable clambered up into them and threw down the clusters of grapes by the bushel. Meanwhile Hoogenboom, assisted by Madison, had got ready the wine-press, which they had spent days before in constructing. This was simply a very strong box, larger than a barrel, placed against the trunk of a pecan-tree, in a level place near the house. One end of a long pole was confined in a notch cut in the tree above the box, to be used as a lever in pressing down into the box a heavy block made just to fit in it. At the bottom of the box were holes for the juice to flow out, and spouts so arranged that buckets could be placed to catch the juice as it flowed.

In a little time the wagon was alongside of it, heaped with grapes. These were thrown into the box, pressed down, and chopped up therein with a clean spade. The block was then put on, the lever fitted, and when Hoogenboom caught hold of the end of the lever and drew up his feet, suspending all his enormous weight thereto, the juice gushed out in a red torrent as fast as they could catch it in buckets.

"He looks like an enormous bug, don't he?" Uncle Frank asked of Madison, "only bugs don't carry big pipes in their mouths. Yet that man reads Homer, Virgil, Horace, as well as English and German, and takes cart-loads of scientific magazines. He writes for them, too—is really a learned and distinguished scholar. You would not think so, would you? Reading and smoking and writing are all he cares for."

When the grapes in the box were thoroughly pressed, they were thrown out and a fresh supply placed in; so that before night there stood by the press quite a long range of barrels filled to the bung-hole with grape-juice.

But the work was by no means done yet. For days—in fact, at times for weeks—Hoogenboom put in play all the wine-learning he had brought with him from the Rhine—changing the juice from barrel to barrel, using sugar and a little alcohol to help the work—until, finally, there were several barrels of a claret superior by far to anything to be purchased in the cities, and which brought a high price when sent to New Orleans; for one barrel was as much as they cared to keep for home use.

But the gathering of the pecan crop was the most exciting time yet. It took place not very long after fall set in. All summer the trees had been almost breaking down under the nuts, and there is not a richer sight than to see a noble pecan-tree, as tall as the tallest hickory, full of the oval nuts from bottom to top, growing in dense clusters, a shade darker in color than the leaves.

When at last the hulls began to fall off, the whole family—negroes, wagon, and all—went into the work of gathering them as into a grand frolic. There was south of the house, along the river, a bottom of pecan-trees, extending for miles. Some of their neighbors—about whom we have not had time to speak as yet—cut down the trees to get at their rich crops. But a better plan was adopted in this case. Hark, armed with a long, light, tough pole, was sent up into the tree. Clambering up, he would in a short time thrash the whole tree soundly, even to its farthest twigs. The nuts rattled down from the green cloud of foliage like a hail-storm—shaken out by the thunder and lightning of the dark Jupiter above. Pans, baskets, buckets, aprons—everything was used by the eager hands; and it is astonishing how soon the wagon would be filled level with the sides, and heaping too, with nuts—not small ones either, but as large as a partridge egg, and just about the shape too, and that when the hull was off.

Thirty bushels that wagon held, and quite a beaten road was made from the bottom to the house, hauling pecans and returning for more. They were emptied in an enclosed space on the clean rock near the spring, and were easily beaten out of the hulls. For two weeks after the gathering was over, all the children—Bessie included—looked as if they had on black gloves, their hands were stained so with the juice of the hulls. It was with regret that they were compelled at last to cease from gathering, leaving the edge only of the pecan forest near the house touched—the vast forest of pecan-trees, loaded with millions of bushels, remaining to supply the wants of peccaries, bears, squirrels, birds, and other hungry tenants of the green woods. As to the family hogs, they increased beyond all count, fattening upon the abundant "mast," not only of the pecan, but also of the oak trees.

"Some day, when I can get time, I intend," Josie said, "to invent a machine for thrashing out the nuts."

"Humph! you will?" Madison said. "Next you'll say you can invent a machine to thrash the trees."

"I *have* invented one," Josie said, gravely.

"Doodle-bug! what a whopper! What will you bet?" Madison exclaimed.

"Ten thousand dollars! Where's a Bible? I'll bet you a million dollars on it!" Josie said. "Don't you see, I'd wait for the frost to do it. One white frost would rattle them out as quick as you please!" which was a fact.

When the wine was sent to Port La Vaca to be shipped to New Orleans, the pecans were sent too, sewed up in strong two-bushel bags. In return the merchant in New Orleans remitted a large amount in cash, besides sending enough family groceries to last for many a month.

But the pleasure of it was, that it was all the joyous labor of their own hands. With all its privations,.there is a free, untrammelled, independent exuberance of life in Texas—unbounded like its prairies, pure like its sky—which goes far to reconcile, and more than reconcile, the Texan to his home.

Anyhow, whether it is the Colorado water, or what, people who once leave the old states and the old enjoyments for the free pleasures of a wild life ever after look back upon the hours spent in Texas, if they go back to the older states, as among the sweetest of life—sweet, like life's earliest youth.

The first days of December found the farm advanced beyond anything they had hoped. It is astonishing how much can be accomplished by willing hands, prompted by warm hearts. As to the servants, they had done more work, and that more willingly, than during double the same length of time, even under the sharp watch of Watkins, the keen overseer.

Hark's name was really Hercules, first contracted into Harklis, then into Hark. He was of gigantic build, as black and as strong as one of the genii we read of in the Arabian tales, worth three common men—he was so active and powerful. He had taken a special pride in laying hands on the place from the start, when nothing had been attempted, and doing all that needed to be done. The family loved him and his family only less than they did each other. The affection between the dwellers in the house and those in the cabin was, as is often the case, strong and sincere beyond anything imagined by those who have never known the relation—a love, esteem, respect, and cordial attachment absolutely unknown, unconceived of, between the two races elsewhere.

And the white members of the family had done more real work since they entered Texas than during

all their life before put together.
Since May they had thought, planned,
consulted, toiled, enjoyed, more than
during a lifetime in Virginia: it had
been to them a long and happy picnic.
Buy a league out there, make a home
on it yourself from the start, and see
if it is not the fact. Never had the
family enjoyed such health and spirits. The blessing of God, so often invoked at table and family altar, had
descended upon them. The chief
lack was of an opportunity of having worship on the Sabbath.

The second week in December had
come: the weather had all along
been delightful, growing warmer instead of colder, until it might almost be called hot. One morning,
at breakfast, Uncle Frank, who had
just come over to ride out with
Madison in search of cattle, paused
as he carried his fourth cup of coffee
to his lips:

"Hear that? — a norther sure
enough at last!" he said. "You've
never seen a norther yet; if you
don't be gratified, and that right
soon, I'm mistaken."

"I cannot see that the wind has
risen," said his sister-in-law: "yonder is a tree, and the leaves are perfectly still."

"It was not the wind—it was the
wild-geese I heard flying overhead,"
replied her brother. "It's not a *sure*
sign, for they are sometimes mistak-
en; and nothing's certain in Texas
but uncertainty. But generally when
you hear them, look out for a norther."

"All ready, uncle!' cried Madison,
riding up to the door and leading his
uncle's horse.

As the Texan mounted, he looked
all round the horizon and shook his
head.

"Run and get two Mexican blankets, 'Markable," he said; and continued, as he received and strapped
them to his saddle behind, "I don't
much like to go out on the prairie.
However, we won't go far." The
blankets on so warm a day excited
the amusement of Madison; but,
putting spurs to their horses, they
were soon far out on the prairie
northeastward.

They had ridden two or three
hours, but had found no cattle of
their brand.

"Not an inch farther to-day, my
boy," said the Texan, reining up on
the top of an eminence, which, like an
island at sea, commanded an expanse
of twenty miles around. Unslinging
from his back the spy-glass which he
always carried when out on the prairie after cattle, the Texan swept the
whole horizon to detect what he
could among the long brown grass
which tufted the whole expanse.

"Ah, yonder is a herd, I believe!"
said he at length. "Pshaw, no!" he
continued, after gazing longer; "it's
only antelopes."

"Antelopes, uncle? Antelopes!
Where—where?" cried his nephew,
eagerly. For months he had suffered
under the singular enthusiasm in regard to this kind of game which
seizes upon those new to Texas—an
enthusiasm which pursuit of them
only serves to whet—a kind of in-
sanity.

"See that knot of timber about a
mile from here?" said his uncle, point-

ing northward. "Well, look to the right carefully—"

"Yes, yes, I see them," interrupted his nephew; and, shifting his rifle from the pommel of his saddle to his shoulder, and driving the spurs into his horse, he was off like a shot.

"Stop—halloo—hold on!" cried his uncle, endeavoring to rein in his own horse. But in the attempt, encumbered with his spy-glass and rifle, his half-broken animal was almost too much for him, and it required all his attention to keep from being thrown, as the mustang dashed forward, then reared under the powerful curb, then kicked up, whirled around to the right and left, backing and pitching worse than any boat in the roughest sea. The passenger on board needed all his attention to manage his wild mustang, and all his breath to whoa! at him; so that when he had at last got the upper hand, his nephew was far out of hearing, tearing across the prairie towards the knot of timber.

"Whoa!" cried the Texan. "I like to see spirit in a boy as much as anybody—hold up!—but to start off after antelopes—take that, you fool! Might as well try to run a hawk in the air. There goes my blanket! Real grit of a boy! Whoa!—hold up, I tell you! Only let me get that blanket strapped on and I'll show you!"

But it was rather his mustang that showed him. The Texan had dismounted, gathered his fallen blanket, and was about mounting when the animal caught sight of it, gave a sudden bolt, and was gone.

"Well, here *is* a pretty fix!" said the Texan, gazing after his flying steed. "Ever so many miles from home, past two o'clock, a norther coming up, me on foot, and that boy gone after antelopes! One good thing, that mustang has gone towards home; I may catch him, and when I do—!"

"Ah! woful *when*," sings the poet. Following on foot, the Texan soon caught sight of his mustang. It had stopped to graze. As he cautiously drew near, his master could see that the coil of rope had fallen off the horn of the saddle, and was trailing at length on the ground from the animal's neck. Creeping stealthily up, with many a honeyed term of endearment on his lips, which was only the sheerest hypocrisy, the hunter laid his hand upon the knotted end of the rope, but before he could grasp it firmly the suspicious animal was hundreds of yards away upon the trail leading home. Again he would stop to graze, and again escape, half for the joke's sake, just as his master made sure he had him. It was wise in the mustang, for he must have known the vengeance in the bosom of his master, burning more and more fiercely at each escape; but it was terribly inconvenient for that master, who was now panting and perspiring under the load of telescope, rifle, and heavy blankets—especially as the afternoon heat was very great.

"Exactly—just as I thought! a norther, sure enough!" said the Texan, as he observed a herd of cattle, before hidden from sight in a hollow of the prairie, now running in a long line for the nearest timber. Yet, besides this, there was no sign of a rising wind whatever. The day continued sultry, the sky cloudless.

"What did I take him out this morning for?" said the Texan, in tones of deepest anxiety, as he strode on more and more rapidly in the direction homeward. "What will Amanda say? What will Morton do if Madison—" Here the Texan, gathering his blanket in a roll upon his shoulder, began to run. It was dark, however, before he reached the timber, for he had been much farther out on the prairie than he had supposed.

As he entered the woods a murmur deepening into a roar began among its topmost boughs, while a sudden chill pervaded the air, and he reached the McRobert place at last almost worn out with his long walk. Hastening first to the cabin, he called out Hark, and sent him to the stable to saddle up the two best horses there, with an injunction to be as quick as possible. Hurrying then to the house, he met his brother, who was coming out to see if the absentees were yet returning. The elder read in the agitated manner of the younger the evil news, even before a syllable was spoken. In a few words he told him everything.

"Don't alarm Amanda," he said; "but put on your warmest clothing, get an extra blanket or two, a bottle of brandy, and come with me as soon as you possibly can. Hark's getting the horses saddled."

"The best plan is to tell Amanda everything just as it is," replied his brother. "You go on to the stable; I will follow you as soon as possible."

But, short as the time really was, it seemed hours to the Texan before his brother joined him at the stable.

"Isn't she screaming and crying?" he asked, as his brother rapidly strapped the blankets upon the saddle before mounting.

"No; she never does that. She is pale, but cool and calm; never fear for her," replied her husband.

As the brothers were riding rapidly out of the stable-yard the Texan observed that Hark was following them on a mule.

"No, Hark, no; stay at home," he said to him suddenly and sharply. "Cold that only hurts us kills the negroes dead; he would be of no use," he continued to his companion, as they rode rapidly along through the darkness and the increasing wind, which was excessively cold. When they got out of the timber and upon an eminence which commanded a view of the prairie, the Texan suddenly reined in with an oath.

"I beg your pardon, Morton; but see yonder," he said, pointing northward. "As I live, the prairie is on fire! and on such a night!"

But only for an instant could his companion gaze upon the red glare that shone upon the sky in the direction pointed out.

"Morton," said his brother, rapidly, in a loud and almost harsh manner, "let me command for this one night. You stay at home. It'll take all you and the rest can do to fight the fire off the field and the place. You remember I told you how to do it. I was careful to tell Hark too. Call him out right off, and get at it. It'll take your level best to succeed. You leave Madison to me. I'll attend to him, and be back as soon as I can. Hurry about it, Morton, if you want a rail or a shingle left!"

And before his brother could speak the Texan had taken from him the brandy and the blankets, and had spurred out into the gathering darkness, the roaring wind, and the bitter cold.

CHAPTER X.

OUT IN A NORTHER.

WITHOUT a thought in the world except antelopes, Madison had dashed across the prairie, greatly inconveniencing Slow by his excessive use of both his enormous spurs.

He rode keeping the clump of timber between the antelopes and himself. Arrived at its edge, he crept cautiously through it, leaving his horse behind, and peered out with levelled rifle upon the spot where he had seen them feeding. He might as well have expected to have found still resting on the brown grass the shadows of yesterday's clouds. As lightly, and far more fleetly, the drove had swept on almost at the instant the young Texan had first driven spurs into his horse's sides; for of all animals they are at once the most timid and the keenest of hearing and of scent.

A few hundred yards beyond where they had been feeding the prairie rolled up into a billow that concealed the view. In his eagerness, the boy ran half-way up its slope before he remembered that he had left his horse. Hastening back, he untied and mounted him with trembling haste, sprang upon him, and was soon near the crest of the hill. Alighting here, he threw his coil of lariat off from the horn of his saddle upon the ground. One end was already secured around Slow's neck; at the other end the lariat was knotted to an iron spike some ten inches long. Sticking the sharp end of this into the earth, he drove it in to its head by a few stamps of his heel, thus securely staking out his pony. Then, with his rifle ready in his hand, he crept carefully to the summit of the hill, burrowing as he went into the long, thick, dry grass.

Looking over, he saw that the ridge he was on was as the rim of a vast bowl, circling miles around, and in the very bottom of the bowl he could see the antelopes feeding, seeming more like a drove of goats than anything else. As he gazed he observed another and larger herd running towards them from the east; and he noticed that they did not bound along with occasional "lopes" like deer, but moved much more swiftly and evenly over the ground in a rapid trot, making the movement of the drove more, literally, like the flying of the shadow of a cloud across the grass than anything else.

The antelopes were very nearly the color of the brown grass. None but a Texan could have seen them at all. Madison had by this time practiced considerably at looking for cattle and game upon the prairies; and, like a sailor used to the sea, he could detect small objects very far away on the expanse. It is practice—practice! A music-master by perpetual practice trains his fingers to astonishing agility on the keys of a piano. So a rope-dancer can train his feet to the narrowness of an inch rope till he can walk such a thread-path for a long distance and with Niagara roaring beneath him. There is no telling to what degree practice in anything will carry a man. Only patient, persevering practice, and the end is certainly attained. What comes to very few indeed as the result of genius can be attained by any one who will only *practise* persistently towards it.

Thus Madison came to see twice as far and as distinctly as he could when his father's wagon-wheels first struck Texas soil. Untiring energy attains all the results of genius. But where the eyes are at all weak the prairies of Texas, by their vastness, are terribly trying. New-comers have often to travel with goggles on, making them look exactly like owls; and to come out of the narrow streets of cities and towns, or from the hollows and thick forests of other states into the unbounded magnificence of the prairie, *is* as the flight of an owl from its dark nook into the splendor of open day. They say that living amid such vast expanses makes a man large-hearted and open-handed. Sailors certainly are just that. If you have ever travelled in Texas, you know whether or not you found Texans to be such. Perhaps their tendency to exaggeration and enthusiasm may be traced to the same cause. At any rate, Madison had become twice as animated and expanded—a nobler, manlier youth in every respect —since coming out West.

In Virginia he certainly would never have dared to leave his uncle so impulsively, and he now turned his fascinated gaze from the antelopes, half remorsefully, in search of him. He knew him too well, however, to suppose that he could offend him seriously when game was the cause.

"I'm in for it, as I was that day uncle left me in deep water," he said to himself. "And my only way is to do now as I did then—strike out for the bank—go through with it! And your best plan, my young friend," he continued to himself, "is just to go back, get Slow, ride down out of sight around this biggest of bowls till you get entirely on the opposite side —they are nearest that side—then take a crack at them. Even if you miss, you will drive them towards uncle, and he never misses."

No sooner said than done, only it took him much longer to make the circuit on his pony than he had imagined.

There is nothing so deceiving as a prairie. You may journey all day towards a prairie knob that seems not ten miles off when you start for it in the morning, and yet camp at night far enough off from it. It is the singular transparency of the atmosphere which produces the delusion.

It was near sunset before Madison reached the other side. And then, when he had staked his pony, and crept carefully up to the summit of the ridge, as he lifted his head out of the brown grass to look, off went the drove of antelopes in a fleeting cloud, like a pinch of gunpowder from the ground when a spark is applied. On and on they went, with such incredible smoothness and speed that it was a pleasure, even to the disappointed hunter, to see them, till they disappeared over the very spot where he had knelt on the opposite side of the bowl.

"Never mind, my fine fellows!" said Madison, as he saw them vanish. "As sure as you live, I'll get you some of these days—see if I don't!"

The sun was fairly down as the boy mounted and turned towards home. He did not fear to lose his way, for right to the west of his father's house towered Mount Hoogenboom, as the boys had named the cedar brake in honor of the Dutch rail-cutter whose cabin was perched thereon. This lofty point could be seen far over the prairie, and served as an excellent landmark; it was destined to be seen farther over the prairie than ever before that night. As he struck a straight line across the bowl for the opposite side, he strained his ears, expecting every instant to hear the crack of his uncle's rifle at the antelopes.

But it grew rapidly darker and colder, and a chill struck into the heart of the young hunter as he reached the opposite crest, after a swift gallop, and could see nothing of his uncle, and could barely detect the dim outlines of Mount Hoogenboom through the gathering night. A sense of desolation and alarm filled him as he spurred on, such as he had never before known.

At this instant a singular sound behind him caused him to look around. Far down in the north hung a small black cloud, in which the lightning came and went incessantly. It was but the banner, black and fire-starred, of a tremendous foe, rushing with such artillery and forces upon the field as man can never either marshal or withstand. On it came, like a solid body, across the prairie, gathering fury and force as it came—a Niagara of wind. The instant before it reached the flying boy the air was as calm and cool as on a pleasant summer day; the next the norther was upon him, furious as a tornado, cold as midwinter. For the first time in his life, he was absolutely terrified. With all his urging, his tired pony seemed to creep rather than gallop over the ground. The darkness, too, had become appalling. He could only urge Slow along in the direction in which he had aimed when he last saw Mount Hoogenboom. What rendered it worse, the blankets were with Frank McRobert, and almost bitter thoughts rose in his mind that his uncle should have so deserted him.

He had heard often enough about the northers, and how people overtaken by them on the prairies had perished.

"If I could only get to that knot of timber where we first saw the antelopes," thought he, "I could shelter myself."

But he had gone too much to the right to hit it, for, as is well known, the beating of the heart upon the left side forces one unconsciously towards the right, if he has no object in sight to aim for; and thus, in time, a man will make a complete circle when he imagines that he is going forward. Even if he had entered the clump of timber, the trees were so small and the elevation so great that there would have been no sufficient shelter.

Still he rode on, till at last the cold became insupportable. At a sudden thought, he jumped off, and endeavored to screen himself behind his horse from the mad fury of the wind. There was no shelter in this. Then the shivering boy uncoiled his rope, threw it around the legs of his horse about the hoofs, and pulling the lariat to him, at the same instant pressing against the side of the animal, he succeeded in throwing Slow over on his side on the thick brown grass. The creature seemed to understand his master's object, and lay still, while Madison endeavored to nestle himself on the grass inside the legs of the animal. Some little protection from the fury of the wind was thus obtained by the body of the horse interposed.

The storm, however, seemed to grow in violence, as the boy, exhausted with fatigue and cold—having only light clothing on, it had been so warm—sank into a kind of doze. It seemed to him as if the very grass must be torn up by the roots; but it was only a moment or two that his doze lasted. Strange that he did not think of his saddle-blanket, but it never once occurred to him. Even if it had, its protection would have been insufficient. As it was, he was shivering, was perishing with cold, the sudden change causing the temperature to affect him even more than it would otherwise have done. And the cold continued to increase, and hail began to fall. Soon the horrors of a furious hail-storm were added to the darkness of the dreadful night.

"O God, have mercy on me!" said the poor boy, clasping his quivering hands together on his breast. And, notwithstanding the bitter cold, he thought of all his occasional disobedience of his parents, his unkindness to Will, Josie, and Bessie. He thought especially of an oath he had uttered—it was the first, and it had been the last, that had ever passed his lips. Associated for a time with some wicked boys, there had one day sprung up in his mind a singular craving to use profane language like theirs—a *craving* the direct and powerful temptation of Satan. He had yielded to it on the instant, and now he thought of it with horror. He dreaded to die —that oath, that oath! If God would but spare his life this once, this once, he would try to be a better boy. Not a sin of all his past life, not a prayer for him at family worship by his father, not a quiet talk with him by his mother, kneeling by his bedside at night in the dark and silent room, but rose to his remembrance. For the first time in his life did he pray fervently, sincerely, lying there on the grass in the black and bitter storm.

And miles away another was also praying for him—his mother kneeling, with Will beside her, by the bed at home, praying—oh, how fervently!—for her boy. And, seated far above the roaring storm, God was hearing them both—"A very present help, . . . therefore will not we fear though the earth be removed." The disjointed words kept ringing in the ears of the boy; he did not remember having ever heard them before.

As he held his hands clasped upon his breast, he had felt something hard there for some time. It now occurred to him that it was a box of matches his uncle had handed him that morning to carry—he had not thought of them since. Instantly he had them out. Making an arch of his body among the horse's legs, by resting his head and knees on the ground, he endeavored to strike a light under him near the ground against the stomach of the horse. Over and over again the flame caught, and was instantly extinguished by the wind. Pressing himself still closer against the animal, sheltering the flame still more carefully by his hollowed hand, at last there was a blaze. It is a wonder it had not exploded the powder-horn, which hung down by its strap from the young hunter's breast, actually into the blaze, with only a paper stopper. At the instant, however, that Slow felt the smart of the new element, and saw its sudden light, he struggled to his feet, and Madison with him, holding on to the lariat, and trembling lest the storm should extinguish the feeble flame.

But no, the grass was a yard long, very thick and matted, besides perfectly dry. The whole prairie was like an immense straw mattress, three feet thick, with the ticking off. It seemed to the boy that it was but an instant before the grass was on fire for twenty yards before him. Mounting his horse, he reined him back, and gazed with terror at the rapidity of the conflagration. The flame could not rise upward at all, but was driven by the wind in long tongues of fire, level with the earth, into the thick, dry grass ahead, travelling through the brown tinder-like hay with incredible speed and fury, the hail and rain not having penetrated deep enough to wet it.

Madison had supposed that the fire would only spread *from* him before the wind. In any case, it had been madness to strike the match; he must have been crazy not to think of the consequences; better, he thought, that he should have perished! He now saw that it ate its way with only less rapidity towards him, and against the wind. The truth is, he had kindled the fire only to warm himself, without any thought beyond that. And now he reined his terrified horse farther and farther back before a danger more appalling than the storm. With his little match he had *set that awful tempest on fire!* The thought filled him with horror and dread inconceivable. He would gladly have extinguished it if he could. He even attempted to do so. The fire, just before imprisoned in the little red drop on the end of a splinter safe in the box in his pocket, had escaped like a wild animal from its cage—like the awful giant of Arabian story from the fisherman's box. On the wings of the storm it rushed along, red and roaring, and as unchainable and past his control as the storm itself.

The cold was forgotten, as was the night, in the heat and glare of the conflagration: escape was the only thought. At one instant he turned to ride backward, but he could not endure the idea of going a step from home; besides, the fire seemed to travel almost as rapidly in that direction. Then he thought of putting spurs to his horse and dashing straight ahead through the fire; he even put the stopper of his powder-horn into his mouth, and moistened it thoroughly for this purpose, lest a spark should get at the powder.

Suddenly, he recalled the instinct of animals, and, dropping the rein upon the neck of the struggling horse, with a loud cry, and applying both spurs, he let the animal take his own course. Plunging once or twice, it turned and dashed off to the right, till it got beyond the flame, then it turned again to the left. This brought it again in the very track of the wind and the fire, but it was the straight line to its stable; and beyond this its instinct could not go. So thick and matted was the grass, however, that it could advance but slowly—at least, so it seemed to the rider.

Once or twice the horse fell with him in the unevenness of the way. Madison was thrown once completely over his head, but he alighted on the soft, thick grass, the coil of the lariat in his hand, and speedily regained his seat. All this time the fire was pursuing them like some fiendish foe, roaring with exultation in its red fury. Madison glanced behind at the blaze; but when he looked forward again, the darkness was doubly black before him, until at last he determined to look back no more, but to ride on, the hail rattling about his ears, as fast as possible.

In a short time, he felt, by the unevenness of his horse's gait, that they had reached a "hog-wallow prairie." This is a prairie pitted all over with hollows, as with a gigantic small-pox, all alike, of about eight feet diameter and one to three feet depression, formed, as is conjectured, by the cracking of the ground during long droughts, the earth afterwards filling in. Why the depressions should be so regular is not accounted for.

Hardly had they advanced a hundred yards into this, when Slow suddenly stumbled forward over something in his way with more violence than before, throwing his rider far over his head. The grass had now become much more thin and bare, and the boy struck with considerable violence on the earth. Before he could regain his feet, Slow had disappeared like a dream. In vain his master attempted to whistle or call—his voice was drowned at his lips by the roaring of the storm and the beating of the hail. Exhausted with terror, cold, and fatigue, he crouched upon the ground, powerless for the moment. As he did so, he felt beneath him the object over which Slow had stumbled.

6

It was the wreck of an ox, which had bogged and perished in one of the hog-wallow pits years before. The bones had been cleaned and scattered around by the ravenous wolves; only the hide remained whole—shrivelled up on the ground like the shell of a turtle—and it was over this that the pony had stumbled.

But the sound of the approaching fire awoke Madison from his stupor. He turned around, and saw that the sea of fire would sweep its red surges over the spot on which he then was in a few minutes. As to escaping on foot, that would have been impossible in any case; and he was far too much bruised and overcome by weariness and cold. Almost instinctively he tore his powder-horn from his neck, and cast it from him as far as he could hurl it. Then, murmuring incoherent prayers for help, and holding to his darling rifle, even in death, he crept under the hide, coiling himself up beneath it as well as he could, with his face against the earth, and submitted to his fate.

CHAPTER XI.

THE NIGHT OF THE FIRE.

ALMOST before Uncle Frank had disappeared in the darkness, Hark, 'Markable, Rohamma, and Will, led on by Mr. McRobert, were hard at work "fighting the fire."

Before fencing in his field, Mr. McRobert had, under his brother's advice, ploughed up the earth for thirty feet beyond and outside the line of fencing. Thus a comparatively bare space lay between the cedar rails which enclosed the field and the thick grass of the prairie. The field extended between the prairie and the timber, in which the house was built; so that if they could only keep the flames off the rails, all would be safe. Even if the fire had seized upon the rails only, it would have been a terrible loss. Almost a single spark, under such a wind, would have burned the long line of fence, containing thousands upon thousands of rails, into merely a black line upon the ground, like that left by a train of powder when fired. Each rail cost on the ground nearly five cents; besides, it would be impossible to enclose it again in time, so that the next year's crop was involved. In a word, before morning Mr. McRobert was to be several thousand dollars poorer, unless the fire could be kept off; and if you had stood there that night where Will stood, and had seen the oncoming ocean of fire, you would have thought, with him, that it was hopeless. So his father feared; yet he was determined to do what he could; and, aided by every busy hand there, he fought the fire. With water, of course, you say? No, sir. It would have taken the Colorado for that. With fire.

There is a practice in medicine called homœopathy—that is, the conquering a disease in any one by employing the same agent of disease, only in a very much smaller quantity. "*Similia similibus*" is the motto—the use of poison to drive out poison. Whether homœopathy is right or not, this was the practice adopted by Dr. McRobert that night for the saving of his imperilled property. Under his direction, all hands being employed, the prairie was set on fire some sixty feet from the fence. With the help of the storm, the grass was thus speedily consumed up to the very rails, but without setting them on fire, as they were closely watched, and the conflagration had not headway enough to be unmanageable. Thus, all along the fence there was, in half an hour, a broad, bare, blackened belt sixty feet wide, upon which there was not left a straw unconsumed as fuel for the approaching conflagration. The same process was repeated farther out, and soon the belt had been widened eighty feet broader.

But now it behooved them to bestir themselves, indeed. The storm of fire was, by this time, full in sight. Busy as he was, Mr. McRobert could not but pause a moment to gaze upon it, keeping Will close to his side. Right across the prairie, more vivid for the blackness of the night, more terrible for the roaring of the tempest of wind and hail, was a horizon of red fire, curling high in the air, darting hither and thither upward, crackling and roaring even above the storm. But the most appalling of all was the swiftness of its advance. But just now it was a mile or two off, and now it was almost upon them. To gaze upon the inrolling of the crimson ocean, it seemed the folly of a child to attempt to check it from sweeping all the world before it. Small time was there to admire its sublime splendor. Already the wind came hot and full of sparks and smoke upon them from the approaching furnace. Another belt must be burned, at least, or all would be in vain. Rohamma and Hark ran a hundred feet beyond the blackened line, each with a blazing torch. Hurrying Will in to his mother with 'Markable, Mr. McRobert went to work still harder.

But Hark was the hero of the fight. Notwithstanding the storm, he had cast off his coat, and, with his old hat drawn down over his eyes, he ran, with almost superhuman energy, along the line of grass he was firing, stooping every step as he ran to thrust his torch an instant into the grass; and, fat as she was, Rohamma did good service. It was close work, for the heat from the approaching fire was almost intolerable. By the time Hark had run out at one end of the line, Mr. McRobert and Rohamma had run out at the other, and all the grass was in a fierce blaze. It was a close race between the two fires. But the larger fire assisted the smaller by casting in its rain of sparks and cinders. Having done all man could do, Mr. McRobert, seated on the fence, watched with breathless interest the result, as well as the stifling smoke would permit. Never before had he been so thoroughly aroused. Whatever the result of the fire, he could never again be the same listless, somewhat sluggish, Virginia planter he had been before. From a sudden development of this sort no man ever can wholly recede.

"Dey tell me, Mass Morton," said Hark, standing beside him, steaming with perspiration and smoke, "dat a Dutchman—Squeezeborn I belebe his name is, de farmer down de ribber—allus hauled his rails home after he gathered his crap, carried dem out again next spring when he done plantin' his seed. Folks here laugh at him. I nebber laugh at him any more after dis night."

"Nebber hab such doin's in Ole Virginny," groaned the panting partner of his bosom. "Nebber see such crazy wind as dis dare; nebber see such world on blaze as dis dare; nebber lebe bed fightin' fire all night in Virginny. Texas! Oh, how I hate de country! All dis worser dan ole Watkins eben. And where Mass Madison all dis time?"

Where, indeed! The excitement and intense struggle against the fire had not kept that thought an instant out of his father's mind. But what could he do? And the storm of fire, whose billows were now breaking in upon his very feet; had it, indeed, passed over his boy—his brave, noble boy? He did not know before how he loved his son—how he was beginning to look to and lean upon his manly growth. As he sank his head upon his bosom, a hand was laid upon him from behind. He turned with surprise to see his wife standing quietly behind him, on the inner side of the fence on which he was seated.

"Never fear about me," she said, in reply to his exclamation. "I am so strong and well the storm will not hurt me. Besides, I am warmly clad. I left 'Markable in the house with Will and Bessie all safe. Josie is here with me. I came out for a moment to see if I could help;" and she shielded her face against the blast.

"Work's done, Miss 'Manda," said Hark, eagerly. "See, our fire done burned out; and prairie fire just reached its far edge—good two hundred and fifty feet from here."

Sure enough, the conflagration — rushing magnificently on, reaching the edge of the burned belt, had suddenly subsided for lack of fuel— was rapidly sinking. Still the air was almost unendurable; not so much from heat as from the smoke and sparks.

"Get two buckets of water each, as quick as you can, you and Rohamma," said Mr. McRobert to Hark; "one go one way, the other the other way, along the fence, lest some of the sparks should lodge in the cedar bark of the rails. When all is safe, come to the house, Hark, with Rohamma. There'll be supper there for you."

As soon as they returned from the river, which flowed along one side of the field, with the water, Mr. McRobert—after helping them wet the rails, and seeing that the shower of sparks had ceased—assisting his wife through the darkness across the ploughed ground, hastened to the house.

"I am not so much alarmed about Madison," she said, cheerfully, as they sat down by the fire. "It's my belief that it was he who started the fire to warm himself, not knowing. Then, he has only had to keep up with it on Slow to keep warm in spite of the norther. What do you think? But can that be the wind roaring so?" she added.

"Just what I always think, my dear," said her husband, turning upon her, with half the anxiety gone from his brow, "that all things are for our best interest, in some way, if we only do our duty. It always has been so, it always will be so with us. As to Madison—"

But the remark seemed to meet with a flat contradiction on the spot.

"Cedar's on fire, Mass Morton," interrupted 'Markable, putting his head in at the door.

Mr. McRobert sprang to his feet. "Are Hark and your mammy there still?" he asked, as he grasped his hat and rushed out.

"Lor', no, massa, dey's at de fence. It's de cedar *brake* dat's on fire!" and a ruddy glow upon the midnight sky to the west explained it all. Hastening down to the spring a hundred yards below the house, and turning—so as to see over the top of the rocky hill, which sheltered them upon the north—Mr. McRobert beheld the sublimest scene he had ever witnessed. As has been said, on both sides of the San Hieronymo from the house the rocks ran up into a mountain, crowned miles away, and to the summit, with cedartrees. This had been the vast storehouse from which the brothers had cut and hauled their logs and rails for building and fencing, for years in the case of the younger brother. A great deal, too, had been sold to neighbors around, until the best of the cedar nearest the house was cut off. There was still an immense quantity, but some of it was farther off west, and most of it lay upon the mountain on the other side of the river. The fire had scaled the mountain from the prairie, and was now storming upward like an army. The direction of the norther drove the conflagration off to one side from the house; thus there was no danger so far as it was concerned. Mrs. McRobert had, by this time, joined her husband, and stood beside him, watching the magnificent spectacle. As the flame reached higher and higher, feeding eagerly upon the lopped-off branches and heaps of brush left from the axe of the rail-cutters, the whole mountain was literally on fire. Vesuvius could not be more awful, for here the flame ascended not from a central crater, but from the sides as well as the summit—a solid pyramid of light, a mountain of fire. The wild contortions of the spires of flame, broad at the base and narrowing to a long, flexile tongue each, till the lofty points were lost in the dull orange of the smoke overhead; the awful roar, rising high above the storm—the prairie on fire was tame in comparison. The house, the spring, the river, all were lighted up by the glare, the shadows of the garden posts fell clear and distinct on the earth. Notwithstanding the cold and wind and sleet, the husband and wife stood fascinated, unable to move their eyes.

"Well," said Mrs. McRobert, at length, "if Madison *did* start the fire from a match—not that I blame him in the least, dear fellow!—he will certainly have an illustration to last him all his life of one passage of Scripture, at least."

"Yes, I know," said her husband, and added, "Behold how great a matter a little fire kindleth!"

But she only said it to cheer up herself and her husband—both of them silently but exceedingly anxious in regard to Madison.

"But what about Hoogenboom, and Francisco too?" his wife said, suddenly.

"I don't know. I have not forgotten them; but what can we do?"

"And there is a fire in the east, too!" exclaimed Mrs. McRobert, as they turned towards the house, pointing to a ruddy glow through the smoke rising from the prairie.

"Yes," replied her husband; "but that is a fire of God's own kindling—it is day that is breaking." So saying, he hurried on with her to the house.

"Now for Madison," he said, eagerly, as he passed on towards the stable. There he found that Hark had already saddled his master's horse, in anticipation.

"By-the-bye, when did you see Duke last?" he asked, as he mounted.

"Mass Madison tied him up before he left yesterday," replied the black; "but he howled so 'bout dark dat I let him go. Habn't seen him since. Massa," continued the negro, drawing nearer as he spoke, and sinking his trembling voice into a whisper, "Slow is in de stable. I found him whickerin' at de bars dis mornin', an' let him in; but whar Mass Madison?" he continued, with deep anxiety, laying his hand on his master's knee.

Mr. McRobert sprang from his horse, hastened to the stable; there stood Slow eating at his manger, as if there was nothing unusual.

"I lef de saddle and bridle on him, just as he come; his rope was trailin', de spike broken off," said Hark. Mr. McRobert walked once or twice around the animal with eager eyes, but nothing could be elicited.

"Hark!" he exclaimed, suddenly, and in a voice so altered that the negro did not recognize it, "tell the rest to say nothing to Mrs. McRobert of this. Get a mule as quick as you can, and follow." And he spurred out of the yard. Before him, when he got beyond the field, lay the expanse of the prairie, black and bare as far as the eye could reach. The sleet had now ceased, but the wind still blew with unabated violence, driving before it the smoke and ashes. Reaching the first eminence, Mr. McRobert halted till Hark could join him, sweeping the desolate landscape with his eye, eager, yet dreading to detect any unusual object. Nothing was to be seen save here and there the blaze from a fallen mesquit-tree.

"I hear Mass Frank say dey gwine

by de five-mile mot," said Hark, closing with Mr. McRobert.

"Very well, we'll aim for that first," replied his master; "it's all we can do." And they galloped on in the teeth of the wind.

"Dere's no wolves on de prairie, massa, anyhow," said the black after half an hour's swift ride. "De fire done drove 'em out into de ribber bottom. I saw whole pack runnin' 'fore de blaze last night. Mass Madison's body—I mean Mass Madison safe from dem for to-day."

Mr. McRobert could not reply. It was the darkest hour of his life. Though he could scarce keep his seat for the fury of the wind, his glance ran incessantly on every side as he rode, without a thought of anything but his son. It might have been the balmiest of summer mornings to him instead, for what he observed of it.

"Why didn't we think of it?" he exclaimed, suddenly drawing up. "We might have tracked the way Slow came in."

"No, massa, no," said his companion, shaking his head. "I tried dat dis mornin' hard. De wind cover de tracks wid ashes 'tirely."

Again they drove on at full speed. On the summit of every rise they would pull up; and, though the wind seemed as if it would tear them from their saddles, they scanned the expanse closely—fearfully, yet closely. Not a living thing was to be seen, all was black, bare; the heretofore hidden rocks and ravines showing plainly in the increasing light, as the sun struggled, as if itself against the wind, above the murky horizon. In another hour they had come in sight of the five-mile mot. Yesterday it was a green clump of live-oaks; now it stood a dwarfed and shrivelled group of leafless trunks.

"Oh, massa!" exclaimed Hark, suddenly, "I see a man on a horse ridin' towards de mot. But Lor', Mass Madison hab no horse."

A few minutes' gallop, and they could see that it was Uncle Frank, and alone. There was no gladness in his haggard face as they joined him at the mot.

"Not a thing of him, not a thing of him!" he exclaimed. "I've been riding around the edge of the fire—into it, for that matter," he continued, pointing to the singed fetlocks of his horse, "and I can see nothing of him. I've been here a dozen times since day broke, sweeping the prairie with my spy-glass. Nothing can I see. I'll try again." He did so, slowly and thoroughly, then shook his head, and handed the glass to his brother. In vain his brother attempted the same; the trembling of his hand and the dimness of his eyes made it useless.

"Let me try, Mass Morton," said Hark, and, taking the glass and rapidly adapting it to his focus—for he had often used it for cattle—he carefully scanned the whole expanse—once, twice, thrice. "Hah!" he exclaimed, suddenly; but then, in an altered voice, "Psho, it's only hide of ox burned so black. Yes," he continued, "and yonder's a wolf—no, you fool nigger, it's Duke circlin' round and round! Hi on, dog! good dog! Hi on! Hunt him, boy!" he exclaimed, at the top of his voice; and slamming the tubes of the glass together, he thrust it in his bosom, and was off in a moment, followed by his companions. It was with difficulty they could detect the form of the dog, for it was Duke, now on a crest, next lost in a hollow, as he ran with his nose to the ground.

"He got 'larmed 'bout Mass Madison las' night," said the excited negro; "but de ground too hot for his foot—too hot now, but he huntin' up his massa. Hi on, boy! hunt him, fellow! 'good dog!" he exclaimed, almost beside himself with eagerness, though the dog was still far beyond sound of his voice. It was but a few moments, however, before they were up with him, ascending an elevation as they did so. The dog was running before them towards a burned and blackened heap, lying in a hog-wallow, motionless.

"Hold up, Morton, for God's sake!" exclaimed the Texan, seizing upon his brother's bridle, and reining both horses back, while the tears gushed from his eyes and rolled in torrents down his cheek and beard. "This is no sight for you to see. Be a man, brother! be a man! Here, Hark," he continued, sharply, "stop! you stay with your master!"

Mr. McRobert had caught sight of the object yet distant, and, yielding to his feelings, sank, as his brother spoke, upon the pommel of his saddle in unutterable grief. He had dreaded it—it was what he knew must be; but the reality was too painful. The strong arms of the negro were around his master in a moment, and both seemed convulsed equally with grief, the negro weeping aloud, as the Tex-

an rode ahead alone. Suddenly he dismounted—it was to pick up a powder-horn lying on the ground, exploded and black. A moment more, and he he was beside the dread object. Suddenly the negro and his master started with surprise.

"Oh, you everlasting scamp!" was the exclamation they heard. "If I only had a mesquit branch handy, if I didn't let you have a taste of its thorns I wasn't at San Jacinto, that's all! I have seen folks play 'possum before," he continued, as his companions ran up, "but this beats all!"

He had seized upon the shrivelled hide of the long-ago-dead ox, and there, beneath it, coiled up in the smallest space, lay Madison, looking stupidly around, and wondering where he was, just waked out of a sound sleep, his rifle beside him.

It were vain to describe the revulsion of feeling as they assisted the young hero to his feet. Even Duke himself ran round and round with delirious barking, knocking his young master over once or twice in his exuberant joy.

"The wind blows too hard and cold to stop to hear about it now," interrupted Mr. McRobert, at length. "Up behind me, Madison, and home to your mother as fast as we can go."

The norther was now upon their backs, and even seemed to help them on with its force as they rode. Never summer breeze filled happier homeward sails. It seemed but a few moments before they were near the edge of the timber, Mount Hoogenboom still smoking with fitful flames upon their right. In his eagerness, the father had ridden with his son quite ahead.

"Mass Frank," said Hark, earnestly, drawing back the Texan as they approached the house, "I want to show you somethin'. I clean forgot all 'bout it till dis moment, lookin' for Mass Madison. He's in my cabin. Dis is de way it was—"

"Who's in your cabin?" asked the Texan.

"Lor', massa, dis is de way it was: I see him once, twice, 'fore las' night—day he saved Mass Will from ribber, and odder times. Las' night I see him fightin' de fire like mad. He keep at my end'ob de fence, in dark, so Mass Morton couldn't see. He holp me mightily, I tell you. Did more'n I. 'Don't tell your massa, boy,' he said, ebry time we come togedder in de smoke and wind. After de fence saved, Mass Morton go to de house, and I hurry down to odder end ob fence, and dare he lay, where I seen him fall—in corner ob fence. Rohamma and me we take him up—he limber as if dead—and carry him in our cabin, put him in bed. 'Don't tell any one, don't tell any one!' he groan. But, Lor', I mus' tell. I keeps nuffin from my massa. I thought I tell you fust."

By this time they had dismounted and reached the cabin of the negro. Throwing open the door and entering, there, on the bed, bearded, emaciated, covered to the chin in blankets, his sunken eyes sealed as in death, lay the wild man who had so long haunted the house and the woods around.

CHAPTER XII.

MR. CRITTENDEN.

"Mass Frank say he and Hark gone over to de ranch; back arter while," was the announcement of 'Markable to the family as they sat down to the breakfast-table. Now that Madison's adventure was all over, it seemed more like a dreadful dream than sober reality.

"But it wasn't so wonderful at last, my escape," said Madison at length, when he had somewhat brought up the arrears of his long fast. "Only," he continued, "it does seem fortunate that Slow should have thrown me just in the hog-wallow. If I had kept on him only a little longer, he would have been in the thickest sort of prairie grass; and Slow was getting to be so slow that I do believe he could not have kept ahead of the fire to save our lives. We would have been burned up, certain."

"But I can't imagine how being in the hog-wallow prairie saved you," said his mother.

"Why, ma," exclaimed Madison, "didn't you ever notice how thin and green and short the grass always is in those damp hog-wallows? But it's well the hide was there, too. I declare it does seem as if the very things that seem worst for us at first turn out afterwards to be the very best things that could possibly happen. I didn't want to go into the brake that morning at all; yet I killed my first buck by going. I didn't want to be sent back that other morning by Uncle Frank; and it led at last to my killing that big bear. If I had shot one of those antelopes—I'll kill one yet one of these days—I do believe I would have perished out in the cold. The very hide that pitched me off of Slow was my salvation from the fire. You see, I crawled under, and pretty near gave up, I was so worn out. I was hardly under, when there came tearing along a herd of something—wolves I believe—running from the fire. One of whatever it was actually stood on the hide above me to look back on the flame. It was only a moment, and he was off like a shot. I could hear the fire roaring and crackling nearer and nearer. The smoke got dreadful bad. If it hadn't been that the wind was so strong, I would have been smothered, sure. I drew in my feet, put my mouth with my hands beside it close to the damp ground, and breathed as slow as I could. The hail made the grass harder to burn, too. Somehow it was on me and past me in a flash, like; and after that I fell asleep, although terribly cold, I was *so* worn down. But I thought my feet were frozen when Uncle Frank stirred me up."

"Next time, my dear boy," said his mother, "don't be so impulsive—it is growing on you."

"But you wouldn't have me hang round like cousin Gus, would you, ma? He isn't older than I am, and he chews and smokes and idles about all day so fat and lazy."

"No fear of your being a lazy man," replied his mother, with a mother's pride as she glanced at her son—black-eyed, black-haired, straight as an Indian, and almost as brown, lithe, and active in every member, his face sparkling with animation.

"No," said his father; "but there is no use going to either extreme. When I was in college at old Hampden Sidney, there were two youths in the Freshman class with me—Bob Winslow was one. He was rich and short and heavy, extravagantly fond of good eating. He went to bed at eight, and was never up at chapel hardly, scarcely out to breakfast even, except when it was the season for buckwheat cakes. He never learned a lesson well in his life. We called him 'Log,' because he drifted along like a log on a current. The very opposite of him was King, or Rex, as we used to call him. He was thin, poor, sharp, active, eager. Up earliest of all; to bed last of all. Hard at it all the time. He went into mathematics like a skater on ice, into shinny on the Campus in the same way. He would never take less than a half-dozen books out of the society library on Saturdays at one time. He was the fastest walker I ever tried to keep up with. And what was the result? He was the swiftest and shallowest man I ever knew. He was everlastingly stumbling, he went so fast. It was no pleasure to converse with him, he was perpetually interrupting you; before you could finish half a sentence he would have the other half finished for you. You couldn't keep his eye in yours a minute. He was a fussy man — a headlong, haphazard harum-scarum. Don't be either, Madison; be just between the two, neither too slow nor too impulsive. The noblest style of men are those who combine in themselves opposite excellences without the extremes of either."

"Half of Texas and half of Virginia, father, I suppose," said Josie, who often made queer remarks.

"Without the extremes of either," added his mother; and she continued, "It must be the climate of Texas, or the strong winds, or the broad prairies, or all these combined; but I never heard so much exaggeration in my life. In all this neighborhood, if anybody is sick, they are always reported as *very* sick. And if really and seriously sick, it is immediately said that they cannot possibly live. It is always terribly hot or awfully cold, pitch-dark or splendidly bright. Everything is either the very biggest or smallest, the *very* best or the *very* worst ever known. Both of you boys are catching this Texas brogue fast enough."

"Oh, it's the country, ma," said Josie. "Nobody ever saw such a grand fire as we had last night in good, dull, easy old Virginia; and I am certain I never heard such a norther as this there in my life. And such splendid *long*-eared rabbits, and such heaps of grapes and pecans, and such great big flowers on the Spanish dagger-tree. And brother Will might

have got to be an old man and never had such a ride on a raft there," he added.

"Thank you, I could have done without," said Will, who was by no means as sturdy as Josie.

"That's right, Dodles; stand up for Texas always," said Uncle Frank, who had entered; for the family had lingered long around the table. "All safe over at the ranch," he added, drawing up to the hearth. "Hoogenboom was driven down to it with his family from the fire in the brake," he continued; "he will stay there till it is done burning. He thinks his cabin has escaped, as there was a clearing all around it."

"There must have been immense mischief done," said Mrs. McRobert.

"Oh, I am so sorry!" said Madison. "I declare I would almost rather have frozen to death. The fact is, I never once thought about it."

"You never mind," replied his uncle, who invariably stood up for his nephew. "If the prairie's burned over, it will only help the young grass when it rises in a month or two now. As to the brake, it was mostly trash that was burned from where we cut our rails. A great deal of good cedar is burned too, but there's plenty left. Mustn't be so headlong next time, Madison. A rifle too quick on the trigger is almost as bad as one of those old Yagers that keep snap, snap, snapping all day at a deer without going off. Besides, you'll never kill antelope that way all your life. You must be cool, patient, persevering, that's the way."

"How long will this norther continue, I wonder?" said Mrs. McRobert, lifting the curtain and gazing out upon the stormy scene.

"Just three days exactly," replied the Texan, "and then a lull of half a day, and back all the wind comes again from the south, dampened by the Gulf, till matters are balanced once more. I hate the return wind worst of the two, it's so chilly."

"I'm afraid our cattle will suffer," said his brother.

"They would if we lived farther from the mountains," answered the Texan, "but they can find something to eat there all winter. It's astonishing how thick and rich the mesquit grass grows up to the very tops of the mountains, out of holes drilled by the rain in the rocks; and it's the richest grass for stock in the world."

"But I have often seen skulls of cattle on the prairies," said Will.

"Well, very often they do die from one cause or other, though Texas is the best stock-raising country in North America, at least; you never have to feed; prairies always open, and fat with grass. And it's the most profitable business, too," continued the Texan. "You know that white calf I gave you, Will, last spring. Five years hence, without any care on your part except to drive up once a year and brand the calves, that one calf will have increased to no less than thirty head of fine cattle. By the time you want to get married and 'set up' a ranch for yourself, say ten years after that, you will have from that one white calf a herd of one hundred and fifty head to begin the world with, at the lowest calculation. As to the skulls you speak about, most of them are buffalo skulls, as you can tell by the shortness of the horns. Bessie said the oddest thing the other day when I took her out for a ride before me on my horse. She saw one of those skulls, and she cried out, 'Oh, Uncle Frank, look! thomebody hath hurt that cow.'"

"But it is such a dry country," said his brother; "that is the grand objection to it."

"Well, it is dry for two or three years at a time," replied the Texan. "But you ought to have seen Hoogenboom this morning. Down he had come in a hurry from the fire, hardly time to bring anything but his wife and children; yet he had managed to lug along also a block of wood, cut from a post oak, about six inches long and eight or ten across. I thought it was a stool to sit on; but he showed it to me. It was the section of a tree, and he had planed and polished and varnished one end so as to show the rings—the yearly growths of the tree. He had told me about it before. There were eighty or a hundred rings, showing the growth of the tree for that number of years past. You could tell the wetness or dryness of all the seasons for that time back by the comparative thickness or thinness of the rings. He had made out a table, showing that the seasons went wet or dry in separate groups of six or eight years each; but a large number of the seasons had been very wet, and a majority of all favorable in the highest degree. He says experiments all over Texas have proved the same, and that he has tested his tree-almanac by what is well known in regard to seasons for the last twenty years. Its rings for that time and the facts agree. He is a learned man, Hoogenboom; it's his broken English makes him seem ignorant. I think a great deal of him."

"As you would of anybody, Frank, who says a good word for Texas," said his sister-in-law.

"But we are so out of the world here," said his brother, "you can hardly reason that objection away."

"Only till railroads are built," replied the Texan, warmly; "and their tracks are already graded for them over the country in every direction by nature itself. The cedar brakes are full of cross ties, ready. Coal for the locomotives plenty — the mountains crammed with it."

"Coal?" asked his sister.

"Yes, iron too, in abundance, copper, and lead. As to gypsum, Texas has the largest known bed of it in the world. Only wait a little and the world will know what Texas is, I tell you!"

But there was one thing which the Texan did not tell them. As the result of a rapid conversation with the man whom he had found in Hark's cabin, he had bundled him up, and, aided by Hark, had hurried him through the tempest over to his own ranch, and there put him securely and comfortably to bed under the care of Francisco. And from that moment there sprang up a singular interest in his warm heart towards the stranger. As he slowly recovered during days after, under the care of the Texan, many and long-continued were the conversations between them, no hint being ever given to the family at the San Hieronymo of his being at the ranch. So carefully — for whatever reason — had the matter been kept secret that six or eight weeks had passed before it was known to the San Hieronymo family that there was such a person. One day, however, Madison came suddenly into his uncle's ranch in search of a powder-horn to supply the place of the one lost in the fire. He was startled as he entered the log cabin to observe a grave-looking gentleman seated by the fire absorbed in reading. The stranger sprang to his feet at first, greatly alarmed and embarrassed, and the boy noticed that he had turned ashen pale — sprang up, in fact, as if on the point of flying from the spot; then stopped with a hesitating, palpitating manner like a snared bird. Madison, confused by the confusion of the other, was retreating when the gentleman, as by a sudden and strong effort, calmed himself, and begged him, in courteous tones, to be seated. As he complied with his request, Madison observed, in a glance, that he was a closely shaven, pale-faced, sad-eyed, student-like man. "Looked like a minister," said the boy afterwards. The quick glance of the young Texan showed him, too, that he was plainly but neatly dressed in black, and had the appearance of great mental suffering and long-continued ill-health. It was some time before either party could be perfectly at ease. At last, after some hesitating conversation, Madison spied the horn he was in search of hanging against the wall, and, taking it, he was about leaving.

"Are you going directly home?" said the stranger, suddenly, as Madison bade him good-bye.

"Yes, sir," said the boy.

"Be so good as to wait a few moments," said the stranger, "and I will accompany you;" and he withdrew into the next room.

Madison waited some time for him to reappear. At last he rose and sauntered to the book-case, which was a set of rough shelves nailed up against the logs which partitioned off the two rooms. As he stood there with a book in his hand his eye fell through a crack in the wall upon the stranger in the adjoining room. He had knelt on the floor beside his bed, and, with face buried in his hands upon the coverlet, was as silent and as still as a statue. With a glow of shame on his cheek for having thus unwittingly intruded upon the privacy of another, the boy stealthily resumed his seat. In a few moments the other reappeared, hat in hand, with an aspect of perfect composure; and they proceeded on their walk.

There was a certain gentleness and refinement in the face, bearing, and tones of his companion that impressed Madison with a sense of respect, and almost awe, towards him. Both education, society, and suffering had united to give to him, apparently, an indescribable air of purity and refinement unmistakable, yet so difficult to analyze. The boy knew that he walked with one superior to the mass, though why he thought so he could not have told. As it was, he felt strongly drawn towards him. On reaching his father's house, he showed him into the parlor, while he informed his mother—his father being absent—of the arrival.

"Permit me to introduce myself, madam," the visitor said, rising and bowing as Mrs. McRobert entered the room. "My name is Crittenden. I am a minister of the Gospel. I have been on a visit to your brother at his place, and have taken the liberty to accompany your son home this morning to have the pleasure of becoming acquainted with yourself and husband."

There was something in the tones of his voice which caused Mrs. McRobert to hesitate a moment, coloring and embarrassed in spite of herself, and without knowing why. Soon recovering herself, however, she engaged in conversation, and learned that it was his intention to remain in the neighborhood for some time, in accordance with the request of Mr. Frank McRobert, making that house his home. Mrs. McRobert learned, too, in the course of the conversation, that Mr. Crittenden was a minister of the same communion as her husband and herself, and that it was his intention to preach and visit as a minister of the Gospel as he had opportunity. This was glad news to her, as both herself and family had yearned for the worship of the Sabbath; it was the greatest of their privations so far; and upon this the conversation became more animated and interesting until Mr. McRobert came in. In accordance with their cordial and repeated request, Mr. Crittenden remained to dinner. Long before he left, a great change had come over him, his eye kindling, his wan cheek flushing with a new life.

The conversation of the family, the artless prattle of Bessie, seemed to give him exquisite pleasure, as if long ignorant of such things. It was late in the afternoon that he rose to leave, his face mantled with smiles and pleasurable excitement — a pleasure reciprocated by the rest, who were charmed as in the society of one of the most fascinating men they had ever met, even in their old home. At this moment Uncle Frank suddenly entered the room. At sight of Mr. Crittenden he uttered a sudden exclamation of astonishment, which he endeavored to cloak, first by a cough and then by pleading that he had not known that Mr. Crittenden had come over. He soon, however, recovered himself in the quiet self-possession of the minister's manner.

"You see I could not wait for you to introduce me, Mr. McRobert," he said, "so I came over myself."

"I trust that we may often have the pleasure of seeing you," said Mr. Morton McRobert, accompanying him to the door.

"Thank you, sincerely," said Mr. Crittenden, as he stopped in the doorway, his hat in his hand. "I should have told you," he continued, "that my daughter Agnes will soon be with me. She is an orphan, has no mother now, and I hope — I think — you will like her. I fear she will be very lonely during my absences."

"Where can I have seen him before?" thought Mrs. McRobert often during the rest of the evening, pausing in her sewing to think. "In Virginia? Where can it be?"

It was but a short time, however, before all felt as if Mr. Crittenden had been known to them for years. On the Sabbath after his visit worship was held, at Uncle Frank's request, in the largest room of his ranch. He and Hark had constructed some rude benches in addition to the seats already there—that is, unplaned planks supported upon chairs. At the appointed hour, not only the family from the San Hieronymo, but several other families, had gathered in. A small cedar table had been placed on one side of the room as a pulpit. When the hymn had been read, to the astonishment of all, Uncle Frank, who had whispered to Mrs. McRobert beforehand to help him out, raised an old, familiar tune, in a bold, clear, and sweet voice—one he had learned from often hearing it in his father's family. Hoogenboom sat beside him growling a deep bass, almost equal to an organ; while all the rest, male and female, joined in cordially and harmoniously. Rough as was the room and small the audience, it was none the less the solemn worship of God. Every heart was stilled, and warmed with devotional feelings long unknown to most there. A fervent prayer, the very breathing of childlike feeling, by the minister, in which he solemnly and touchingly dedicated the room they were in as a sanctuary to God; another familiar hymn, and then, in a simple and natural manner, the minister expounded to his hearers a passage of Scripture. His manner was unstudied, easy, colloquial, familiar, yet solemn, and full of rich and instructive thought. The hearers could not but listen. It was a conversation held as with each of them, personally, upon the momentous questions of the soul and eternity. There was no lack of animation in the speaker, nor any strong gesticulation or uplifting of voice unsuited to the small room in which they were assembled. The attention of all was held unslackened to the close. Then another prayer, gushing from the heart of the speaker, and sweeping all other hearts there upward with it to heaven; another hymn, closing with an old-fashioned doxology, and the benediction was laid upon the bowed heads of the audience like a reality of good, and the worship was over.

Notice had been given, before the conclusion, of future services by the same minister there and at other points around. No language can express the gratification of the family as they walked slowly back to the San Hieronymo. It was the sudden, unexpected supply of just what they most desired.

"And could we possibly have had a better preacher?" said Mrs. Mc-Robert. "Surely he comes among us sent of Heaven. Where did I meet him before?"

CHAPTER XIII.

AT THE RANCH.

"ONE entire year in Texas has rolled round," Madison wrote to his cousin Charley in Virginia, "and oh, how swiftly! More has been thought and felt and accomplished and enjoyed in this one year, reaching from May to May, than during any ten years before. We have had a bit of danger now and then, it is true; but that was only as the rocking winds to the oak — it but roots us that much the more firmly to Texas soil. Emigration is pouring into the state from Europe and from all the old states; railways are being constructed; the whole area of the state is being explored and settled; an empire is rising rapidly around us. Virginia was well enough in its way, but it belongs to fifty years ago. Texas to-day, and hurrah for Texas forever!"

"'It is all the same old story,'" Madison read aloud from the reply when it came, of his cousin Charles. "'Everything drifts along on the plantation in the same way this year as last year. You write to me about your rich soil, and we have to butter ours with guano an inch thick to make it yield. You tell me about your game, and a squirrel is the largest I ever have a shot at here. I am so tired of nothing to do and so much to eat. Gus was at the university, but he did something or other, and was expelled. He is at home now, the idlest of us all. I go to school, but it is school, school, all the time. Not divided up by work and hunting as with you. I wish my father would let me visit you in Texas. But people don't respect Texas here at all. It seems to them only a sort of refuge-place at the ends of the earth for scoundrels and poor folks. But I would rather be hard at work there, by a long shot, than lying on a sofa in the parlor all the time here. I feel tied up, nothing to do. The girls are always fixing themselves up, and seeing about their dresses, and visiting and being visited —busy enough; but we boys, what under the sun is there for *us* to do here? Watkins, your father's old overseer, is cutting and slashing the negroes like everything, we hear. He wants to squeeze double crops out of the ground and double work out of the hands. He seems almost mad after money. I met him on the road once, thumping his horse along by keeping up a beating on his sides with both heels at once, his head leaned forward between his horse's ears, his face as sharp as a hatchet, white and cold like steel. He's too keen for us Virginians, cuts every way, and as smooth, too, as an oiled razor. It is astonishing how the people hate him. Tell a hand you'll sell him to old Watkins if he don't walk straight, and it does more good than a rawhide any day. But what am I talking about Watkins for? I was only saying how tired I am of this slow, dull, do-nothing life, and how glad I would be to visit Texas. I don't

blame Uncle Frank for running away from here so long ago, at all. I've half a notion to do the same myself, only I know your father would send me right back. I tell you—'"

"Never mind about the rest, Madison," said Josie, who was waxing very impatient, and had stood now some time with his hat on. "They are all over at the ranch ready to rope calves this morning. Let's go. Hurrah! Make haste."

Sure enough, it was Saturday morning, and work enough there was to do before night. As speedily as Josie himself could desire, they were on their way to their uncle, Will joining them as they went.

"I can't imagine what's come over Francisco," said the younger brother as they walked along.

"Oh, I've noticed it," said Madison. "It's ever since Mr. Crittenden came to live at the ranch. I suppose it's because he is a Catholic, and don't like a Protestant preacher to live in the same house. And Miss Agnes, too, he seems to be afraid of her," for Mr. Crittenden's daughter had arrived shortly before. "I don't see why, I'm sure; there is not a nicer girl in all Virginia. She's so gentle and quiet and smiling. I'm always glad when Mr. Crittenden is off to preach, and she comes over to stay with us till he comes back. I heard ma say that she loved her dearly."

"Beautiful people always love each other," replied the younger philosopher of the two. "But I must tell you about Francisco," he continued. "We were in uncle's boat fishing together last week. I hadn't caught anything—got tired of trying. I was lying down in the front of the boat, and I got to thinking about the queer name uncle gave it. 'Dolores, Dolores, Dolores,' I said, half aloud to myself. You ought to have seen how Francisco jumped. I thought he would have pitched overboard. Then his brown face turned almost white. He took his big knife out, and told me to hold his line at the other end of the boat a while. Then he went to the bow of the boat, leaned over, and began to scrape the name out. He wouldn't stop for all I could say, but worked at it till he had scratched it out on both sides. Then he took his line again, and fished just as before. For a long time he wouldn't talk to me at all. At last I said, 'Don't be so cross, Francisco. What does Dolores mean?' 'It means sorrows, troubles,' he said, at last. Queer, wasn't it?"

By this time they had reached the corral, or pen, belonging to the ranch. This was made by inserting in the earth the ends of ten-foot rails placed upright, and as close together as possible. For whole weeks all hands had been riding over the country for many miles around, driving up all the stock bearing the McRobert brand. Almost every cow had a sleek little calf trotting beside it. These calves, several hundred in number, enclosed in this pen, were now bleating uproariously; rushing hither and thither, pressing their noses through the cracks in the rails, doing their best to get out—just like

fish in a huge net after a successful haul. Inside of the pen were Uncle Frank, Hark, and Francisco, hard at work.

"No better fun in the world!" said Madison; and he soon had off his coat and was with them as busy as any. They went at it in this manner: First Francisco would catch a calf. It was astonishing how skilfully he did this. Without stirring from his place, he would throw his coiled lariat at a calf, catch it in the noose around its neck or any leg he pleased. As soon as he drew the rope tight, Hark would throw the struggling and protesting victim on its side and sit down upon it, taking care not to hurt it, however. Then Josie would hurry up with a small furnace full of coals glowing hot—the branding-iron among the coals, having a long handle with a corn-cob on it, to protect the hand from being burned in using it. This brand was simply the letters "McR," about three inches long. Taking this in his hand by its cob handle, Uncle Frank would hold it half a minute upon the hide of the calf. There would be a puff of smoke and a ba-a-a! from the victim, and then the noose would be slipped off, and Francisco would have another down in a moment. If a calf belonged to him, Uncle Frank branded it on the right fore-shoulder; if to Madison, on the left fore-shoulder; if to Will, on the right hind-quarter; if to Mr. Morton McRobert, on the left hind-quarter—so that any one could tell ever after, whenever he saw the calf, after it had grown and as long as it lived, whose it was at a glance. It was exciting but hard work.

"Look here, Dodles," Uncle Frank said, when they seemed to be through and the corral was empty of cattle, "I want to show you something;" and, taking a new branding-iron from the furnace, he applied it to a nicely planed bit of board a foot square, leaving this brand :

"That is your brand, Dodles," he added.

"Mine !" exclaimed the boy, opening his eyes with astonishment.

"Yes; yours and Bessie's in *cahoot* — that is, partnership, you know. Take care !" and the wondering Dodles had to run to one side, for at that moment a whole herd of mares were being driven into the corral, each with her colt beside her. For a week before, Uncle Frank and his nephews had been gathering them up from over the prairies for twenty-five miles around. At Uncle Frank's request Dodles sat on top of the high fence, and picked out the two colts he liked best—one for him, one for Bessie—and in a twinkling they were roped, thrown, marked as the property of the new firm, and let go again.

"You see," the uncle explained, "such a brand was never heard of before. Will showed me a drawing you had made for your stock, you told him, when you got old enough to own any, and that is it. You said that whenever and wherever it was seen, for a hundred miles around, the neighbors would say that they had 'seen the elephant,' and you never could lose your stock, or fail to learn where it was. It was a smart idea, and you have got the best colts in the corral;' and, without waiting to hear the thanks of the overjoyed boy, his uncle plunged into the herd, running round and round about him, and went to work, putting his own mark upon the rest, giving one colt to Will and Madison also, but not with Josie's brand.

For an hour or two Mr. Crittenden leaned against the gate of the enclosure, looking in upon the active scene. His daughter Agnes stood beside him. For many weeks now she had been with her father, and her presence had lighted up the whole place. She was still quite young—barely entering on womanhood; but it was evident that, as with her father, sorrow had cast its shadow upon her path. Not that she looked gloomy — far from it; a more fresh and cheerful smile never beamed from the eyes or rippled the cheek of a maiden into dimples. She was very beautiful — only very quiet and still, with a low, sweet voice, and a laugh clear and silvery, but never ringing out loud and long. There was an inexpressible home-like sweetness about her, very different from the flashing beauty of the ballroom belle. Not a flower in all the prairie, dewy with morning, more like a thing of nature than she! Firm and decided enough she could be, too, when necessary—as the boys could testify any day. Uncle Frank had given up one of the rooms of his house, with a shed-room adjoining it, to Mr. Crittenden and his daughter, and every day Madison and Will came over to school to Mr. Crittenden — reciting, in his absences at preaching - stations around, to his daughter. No queen could command more respect than she, and Victoria herself had not more loving and loyal subjects. It is astonishing how rapidly the boys learned, and especially when it was to her that they had to recite their lessons. In fact, the whole neighborhood regarded Mr. Crittenden and his daughter as among their most valuable new arrivals for many years. During her father's absences she made her home with Mrs. McRobert, going back to Uncle Frank's when he returned; and Uncle Frank hardly knew his own home or his own table for the happy reformation effected therein—everything was now so neat and clean and orderly. As to himself, up to the arrival of his brother and family he had paid no attention whatever to his appearance, taking things as they came. Ever since, he had been much more particular in his dress and manner, but ten times more so since Mr. Crittenden took up his abode with him. As Will said, however, it was only too plain that Francisco regarded Mr. Crittenden's arrival as the unhappiest possible event. He would never even speak to him or his daughter, under pretence of not understanding English. He understood, well enough, all that Uncle Frank had to say, however, and his swarthy face would bright-

en up with life and joy whenever he was near. And it is astonishing how close he would keep to him. No dog could follow up his master's steps more closely, watching his every word and movement with quick and constant affection. The happiest time of all the day to the Mexican boy was after dinner in summer. Then the Texan would sit swinging in a hammock slung under the trees near the house, smoking cigarritos almost as fast as Francisco, sitting on the ground near by, could make them— and no cigar-maker could be more expert. With a pile of shucks beside him, a paper of tobacco, and his sharp hunting-knife, his expert fingers would have the shuck cut into right lengths, the tobacco put in, and the cigarritos twisted into shape in a twinkling. Young as the Mexican was, never, except when eating, was a cigarrito out of his mouth. As to the Texan, he treated Francisco almost exactly as one would an affectionate Newfoundland dog. Since Mr. Crittenden came, however, he had become apparently ashamed of the Mexican, spoke to him less frequently, even avoided him, and had almost given up the smoking altogether. It seemed cruel towards a creature that seemed to live only for its master; and after every such neglect the pitiful look of the swarthy boy was touching to see. It was a distress to Mr. Crittenden, and especially to his daughter, that Francisco remained so shy towards them. Miss Agnes especially did everything in her power to gain his affection—offered him articles of clothing, books with pictures, endeavored to get him to permit her to arrange his room more neatly—but all in vain. Once or twice the boy seemed moved by her gentleness and beauty and singular sweetness of manner, but it was only to sink back into a deeper reserve.

It was late in the afternoon when the last colt was branded. Mr. Crittenden and his daughter were standing again at the gate of the corral. Leaning against the fence beside them, their host was gayly laughing and talking with them; and never before had Agnes seemed so beautiful and happy. The Texan was endeavoring to induce her to mount his favorite horse, that was staked near by, and take a lesson in riding. At last, she consented, provided the horse was led. There happened to be no side-saddle at the ranch, and his master told the Mexican to go over to the San Hieronymo and borrow one from Mrs. McRobert. In a few moments, Francisco had his own mustang—a spirited, vicious little black animal—saddled, was off, and back again with the saddle before they could have supposed him half-way there. Had they noticed more closely, they would have observed that the boy seemed under the influence of a fever—almost delirious. He dismounted, and stood looking on, while the Texan carefully placed the side-saddle upon his horse, buckled the surcingle very carefully, then led the horse to a stump near by, and helped Agnes to mount. Strange to say, but it so happened, that she had never been on a horse before in her life. She was determined, however, to learn, and sat as composedly as she could, while the Texan showed her how to hold the reins, leading the animal slowly and carefully along. If they had not been so much occupied, they could not but have noticed the conduct of the Mexican. He had never before seen a side-saddle, nor a female so unused to riding. As he glanced from under the broad brim of his hat, he murmured his contempt in strong Spanish to himself. Once, when the horse started a little, and its rider gave a half shriek of alarm, the Mexican actually laughed out so rudely that the Texan glanced angrily around upon him. Eight or ten times did her host lead the horse slowly along, up and down the open space before the house, and then led the animal again to the stump for its fair burden to dismount.

"Ah, you'll never be a real Texan, Miss Agnes," said he, as he assisted her to dismount, "until you've learned to ride."

"I'm sure I will be glad to learn," she replied. "I can think of nothing more delightful than a gallop over the prairie in the morning, before the sun gets high, only I'm afraid I will never dare to do it. I will do my best to learn."

"I'll take care of that, if you'll permit me," said the Texan, his handsome face in a glow. "Only ride a short distance every day, as you have done now, and, in a few weeks, you will ride with the best of us."

"Wouldn't it be grand to see Miss Agnes on a mustang, after a long-eared rabbit as hard as she could tear!" said Will.

"Just wait till I learn, Will, and see if I cannot leave you far behind in such a chase," answered she, laughing.

By this time, they had reached the front porch.

"Only look at Francisco!" exclaimed Dodles, who took a new interest in horses, altogether, since he had become a stock-owner.

And it was worth looking at. The boy had again mounted his mustang. His lariat hung at the pommel of his saddle, and a huge spur armed each heel. With his hat down over his eyes, his long black hair streaming behind, his cheeks glowing with excitement, he rode his horse at a swift gallop as far as the space before the house permitted, then whirled him around at the end, and was back again in a moment, as much at home and at ease on his horse as if he were seated in a chair. Turning his mustang, he rode back again at full speed, gathering his lariat in his hand as he rode, and as he passed amid a group of cows, scattering them to every side, he, in a turn of his hand, had the noose of his lariat around the horns of one of the wildest of them. As the rope tightened about the animal's head, he turned the head of his mustang towards it, and backed it away from the struggling victim, thereby holding its head to the ground, bellowing and frantic. Suddenly the cow made a bolt at him, but, in an instant, he was off on the other side; the rope tightened upon it in that direction;

and so he continued, till, with one sudden jerk of the lariat to one side, he threw the struggling animal on her back, its hoofs in the air. Springing off his mustang, he jumped upon the animal, had the noose from around its horns, and was off again, with his lariat held coiled in his grasp. Galloping swiftly back, the noose flew from his hand right and left, like the fang of some fabulous monster—like something itself endowed with life. Now it held a struggling calf by the hoof; then it was loosened with a shake, and around the neck of Duke, looking on with astonishment. Hark held out his hand towards him as he passed, with a "You see dar!" to 'Markable, and the next moment Hark was running to keep up with the wild Mexican, the noose fastened like a manacle around his wrist. In vain did the geese attempt to escape by rushing into the brush. One throw of the lariat, and the leader of the hissing flock was being dragged through the air after the flying rider, like the white tag to the tail of a kite. The boy seemed possessed with a fury. Before Madison had done wondering to see the branding-furnace dragged along the ground after the hoofs of the mustang, encircled in the noose, he felt his own hat taken from his head in the same manner, and, a moment after, replaced evenly on his head again by the rider, as he whirled and rode back past him. Turning his foaming mustang, and dashing along up the corral, he seized 'Markable, as he passed, by the waistband, and held him, dumb with astonishment, over his head, and, riding at full gallop, dropped him into a chaparral-bush at the end of the course.

"I thought he crazy 'fore," said Hark, at this juncture, "but now I *knows* he is. Time to send for doctor, *I* think!"

Leaving 'Markable squalling among the thorns, the Mexican dashed back again, clearing a wagon at a leap as he came. Arrived opposite the portico, he threw from his pocket a handful of dimes on the ground, and continued on. Returning at full speed, he kicked the stirrups from his feet as he came near, and, winding his legs around the horse, he dropped towards the ground as he passed, picking up a dime as he did so, without drawing rein, and so back and forth, till all the pieces of silver were again in his purse. Suddenly the Mexican rode full towards the portico, his black eye glittering as with fever, and the Texan sprang forward between Agnes Crittenden and the rider just in time to receive on his breast the noose thrown into the group. Shouting at him loud and fiercely in Spanish, the Texan held the noose an instant and cut it in two with the knife from his belt. The Mexican only laughed, and dropped the remainder of the lariat. By this time it was quite dark, and the group on the portico entered the house, while the Mexican rode on and out into the prairie.

The Texan seemed gloomy and absent-minded during the conversation that followed around the supper table.

"The Mexicans are singular people," he said, at last; "the laziest beings in the world. Eating, sleeping, smoking, riding, and herding cattle is about all they are good for. But let them get excited, and they become crazy. It's very rare for them to become so about anything singly—they go in masses like sheep."

"I am sorry Francisco has taken such a dislike to me," said Agnes. "He is so handsome and spirited, with his black eyes and raven hair and bronzed cheeks; he looks like what we read of young Spanish cavaliers. He will have nothing to say to me whatever. What can be the reason, Mr. McRobert?"

The Texan hesitated to reply, coloring violently up to the very hair of his head under the calm inquiry of her clear blue eyes.

"Be guided by me, Miss Agnes," he said, at length, "and have nothing whatever to say or do to him. He is a singular creature; let him have his own way. He will not be with us long. I intend sending him away soon."

"Where to, Mr. McRobert?" asked Agnes, quietly.

"Oh, to San Antonio—to the Port—to Chihuahua. The arrangement is not all made yet."

"Shall I show you those drawings of mine you asked about this morning?" said she, as they arose from the table.

"Thank you, thank you, but not to-night. There is something I must attend to," and, as he said it, he left the room.

CHAPTER XIV.

OFF FOR THE LAMPASAS.

MAY and June flew by on swiftest wings. Every lovely morning the delicious jargoning of mocking-birds, swarming like bees in the trees around the house, made sleep nonsense and an absurdity. Then family worship, which even restless little Bessie had learned to love, with its few Scripture verses so read by the father as to interest every child; its sweet, familiar hymn in which all joined, even the bird-like discord of Bessie assisting therein; the short prayer acknowledging the mercy of a Father during the night, and an entreaty for his guidance and blessing during the new day. Next a cheerful and hearty breakfast: eggs in abundance, from the hen-house of Dodle's own building; tender chickens from the same prolific structure; radishes, raised exclusively by Will in his own particular garden; honey, too, from the forest or from the long stand of garden hives; venison, supplied by Uncle Frank or Madison from his last Saturday's hunt; sometimes birds, brown and delicate, or even squirrels, the result each of near twenty shots by Will in his hunting—for Will was by this time aspiring to a buck.

Very often Mrs. McRobert herself, tempted out and down the banks of the spring by the Eden loveliness of the early dawn, would make her contribution to breakfast in the shape of a gasper-goo — a delicious trout, not half an hour before very much alive indeed in the cool and transparent water, but now lying brown and juicy on the dish, its mouth open in unutterable astonishment at the swift change in its situation in life. As to the light rolls, clustered in one, like bubbles on the plate, and the coffee, and the cooking —these were from the hand of the dark Ceres of the kitchen; the snowy hominy being from the steel mill, driven at daylight every morning by Hark-power, its noise loudly objected to by the protesting mocking-birds. And Bessie—breakfast would not have been breakfast without the many wise remarks made by her in the intervals of her busy spoon—remarks which always produced redoubled wisdom from the lips of Dodles, the two being singularly mated to each other somehow.

There was real meaning now in the blessing invoked by the father upon his happy table. It may be Texas *is* a dreadful country to live in. People with their noses in the air, and their feet barely touching its soil with disdain, have said so, with the intimation that, to them at least, the descent from some previous condition in the old states to Texas was very, very far down hill. "What did you slide down to us for, and why don't you hasten to return?" is the question which dwells upon the tongue of Texans towards such persons, sometimes even breaks through the lips in trying cases. It may be that the McRobert family did not attach that value to mere paved streets, and fine houses, and all the rest of it, that they should have done. The fact is, somehow or other, all the members of this household had learned to look for, and be entirely satisfied with, so much of happiness as was to be found within their own circle. They might have made themselves profoundly miserable, forced to live by misfortune there, out of all the world, on the San Hieronymo. As it was, they were, in spite of their exile, as happy as people ever get to be in this world—a calm, deep, every-day happiness. None had ever said so, yet they all felt that their coming to just that spot, and all that caused it, was, upon the whole, the happiest event in their lives. And they had no peculiar disposition to cheerfulness under trouble. Their religion was to them the deep central fount of all their happiness. It was that which diffused perpetual summer upon their roof—as it is the same that makes heaven itself sunny forever. Acknowledging the perpetual presence of God as a guest in their family, they were trying, at least, to avoid those ten thousand wrong-doings of hand and tongue, great and little, which produce unhappiness, as certainly as thistle-seed produces thistles.

"Crop laid by, Mass Morton," said Hark, one June evening, as he reached with his hoe the end of the last row of corn, and his master too at the same moment.

"And a splendid crop it will be, Hark," said Mr. McRobert, as he climbed the fence and stood upon the top rail, holding by one of the stakes. I am afraid to say how many acres of green corn he could see, head-high nearly, green and glorious. "Hard work we all have had at it, Hark," he continued.

"Yes, massa," replied the negro, leaning on his hoe with a sigh of satisfaction. "Ef since we come fust on dis San Hieronymo, anybody's been idle, I don't know who 'tis. 'Tain't you, Mass Morton, certain; hain't been Mass Madison, sure. I nebber see white boy hoe corn like Mass Will. Mass Dodles done his sheer. Little Missy drop seed in dozen rows. Rohamma, she growl and grumble at Texas, an' work her hands off. I done little—what I could; 'casionally, at least. 'Markable, I give him a treshin' once or twice ebry day, and he work. An' if dar's been any time —quarter hour—idle, I don't know when dat time o' day from dat hour, las' May year ago, we fust saw dis place till dis moment."

"You never saw such soil as this in Virginia, either," said his master.

"Guano foot thick not equal to it," said the negro. "You can jest see de corn growin'. An' look at dem punkin vines. In my patch we worked by light ob de moon. Watermillion vines hide all de ground; plenty of millions long 'fore Fourth ob July. An' what takes me, massa," continued the man, wiping his streaming brow, "is de case ob de work. It may be de air, or de soil, or de startin' a new place, or de habin' ebrythin' to do from de start, but de work come like a corn-shuckin'. It all a frolic. Rohamma say she pine for Ole Virginny. Virginny 'spectable place for ole folks; but Texas for me eny day. High time I begin to make de rails into cribs for de corn."

"There's the supper bell, Hark. I'll see you about the cribs early in the morning," replied his master.

At an early hour next morning, Hark was at work at the cribs with the zeal of a Sir Christopher Wren. Not earlier, however, than Uncle Frank, Madison, and Francisco had started on a trip to the sulphur springs, with the zest of so many Mungo Parks. Ever since the arrival of the family in Texas they had heard of the sulphur springs of the Lampasas, not a hundred miles to the east of them. Since the opening of summer there had been perpetual discussion of a family trip there. A great deal was to be said for and against. It was not so easy a thing, the queen-bee argued, to leave one's home, even for a week or two: the hawks would get among the chickens, the hogs into the garden; the turkeys were about hatching; a hive might swarm; nobody was sick and in need of sulphur water; Indians might be about the springs; Josie was forever at work with his hatchet, and might chop his hand off; Bessie might get bitten by snakes or something there; watermelons were getting ripe at home; there was so much sewing to do; what were they doing but picnicking already where they were? Sulphur springs! Could any spring by any possibility be superior, or even equal to, the San Hieronymo, which gurgled full of coolness and fish there before the very door? Every voice had been heard fully on the subject. Mr. Crittenden and Agnes had been several times over to supper for the express purpose of assisting in the discussion. At last one final tea was drunk over the matter.

"It would be well enough for Madison to go," said Mr. Crittenden. "The boys have both studied hard for months; now they deserve such a trip—"

"Oh, ma!" interrupted Bessie, who always thought aloud, "Rohamma says she see enough of Texas where she is, right here; don't want to see any more."

"As to myself," continued Mr. Crittenden, "I cannot go, as I have appointments around to preach. Never in my life did I have so much pleasure in my work. People crowd the cabins wherever I go. Latterly we have had to worship out of doors under the trees for the crowd. I never saw people so attentive, so hungry for preaching, in my life. Some of the wildest and roughest characters I ever met have made a profession of religion, and others"—and here his eye lingered seriously and pleasantly upon Uncle Frank sitting opposite at table—"are, I have every reason to trust, thinking of soon taking the same step. I never enjoyed myself so much in my work. I never wanted to live so much before, that I may carry it on;" and his pale cheek glowed with earnestness. He had only hinted thus at the hard, incessant work in which he had been engaged since his first sermon at the ranch. Not only at every neighborhood near by where he could get an opportunity to preach, but not a cabin in reach that he had not visited with the personal and pressing message of the Gospel. In all the region no man was so looked up to and revered and loved. Suffering seemed to have separated him from all else to his work. He loved Agnes, his daughter (none could help loving *her*); yet even she was second in his thoughts to this. There was a fervency of devotion in the man which none had ever witnessed before in any one.

"I only meant," he now added, "to say why I cannot go; but don't let that prevent others."

"As to myself," said his daughter, when called on for her vote, "I will be glad to go, but not without Mrs. McRobert; since she remains, I prefer to do so too."

"Oh, I don't care so much about going myself," said Uncle Frank, who happened, by the merest accident in the world, to be seated next to Agnes, and whose turn was therefore next to speak. "Upon the whole," he added, "I believe I won't go either."

Now up to a moment before the Texan had been loud in his resolves to go. At his frank and set af change of vote the cheeks of his nearest neighbor at the table became even rosier than before, while a gathering of the dimples upon the cheeks of Mrs. McRobert, and a merry light in her eyes, proved the remarkable powers of female intuition possessed by her also; while the younger people laughed out loud and heartily, to his great discomfiture.

"My decision," said Mr. Morton McRobert, suddenly, and with a shake of his head, checking the children, "is this: compromise. Let Frank and Madison and Francisco, say, go up on an advance trip to the springs; then come back and report. We can then decide."

And this was the way that these three started that clear June morning for the springs. Madison had slept at the ranch to get an early start with his uncle. They had left, after a hasty breakfast, with Francisco; but they missed him before they had gone far. He had ridden back with a sudden turn. Arrived at the house, and seeing that his companions were out of sight, he had walked his restive mustang once, twice, thrice, slowly around the whole place—looking lingeringly, devouringly-like, at everything. Then drawing his broad-brimmed hat further down on his eyes, the struggling mustang had soon rejoined the other party on the prairie.

"I declare I don't like what Hoogenboom came down to tell us last night about the Indians," the Texan was saying.

"But how could they attack so

see a a crowd as will be at the springs?" asked Madison.

"They come down to take off the horses staked out near by. The Rangers are out, that's one good thing."

"How many Indians are there in Texas, uncle?"

"Nobody can even guess. There are the Apaches, Lipans, and Comanches, continually coming and going like the wind, down through New Mexico into Texas, and back again, perhaps ten thousand warriors in each tribe. When game gets scarce on the northern prairies, they come down for stock—take anything they can lay their hands on. They are afraid to go near a house on account of the rifle-balls from between the logs. If they catch anybody out alone on the prairies, they always spear and scalp him."

"Why don't the government make treaties with them?"

"It has made a thousand; but they pay no attention to them. Sometimes government tries to settle and civilize them. That may do with some tribes like Cherokees and Chickasaws, but not Comanches and the like; it only makes them more cunning. Instead of being in the fields at work, they are at the old game— out murdering and stealing cattle. Government sometimes pays them annuities to keep quiet; that has failed, too — only makes them insolent. From all I know of Indians in Texas, the only way is to exterminate them at once. It seems cruel; but it is only what will have to be done at last, and that after

they have killed any quantity more of whites."

"Hoogenboom told me last night," said Madison, "that he was once with a ranging party. They surprised and killed a party of Indians that were running off cattle. One of the bodies happened to fall into an eddy of the river near the camp, and in a few hours they noticed that the water had washed some sort of dye off its skin; and, sure enough, it was a white man fixed up to look like an Indian."

"Yes, there are gangs of horse-thieves and murderers who make a regular trade of that in Texas. Scoundrels! they deserve being killed over and over again fifty times. Their inroads are not a hundredth part, however, of what is done, and by real Indians. But worse than Indians — worse even than the renegades among them — are the Indian agents of the government. They sell whiskey and arms to them, and habitually cheat government and Indians. Rascals!"

"It seems hard, though, uncle, our driving off the native owners of the soil before us."

"Yes. I remember seeing how that is done, and seeing how they liked it too. I was out with a surveying party. As we drew near one of their villages on the frontier with our theodolites and chains and flags and stakes, they swarmed out to see what we were up to. As soon as they understood that we were actually dividing out and marking off their prairies, you ought to have seen them. They would have speared and scalped us to a man if they could. We were too strong for them, armed each of us to the teeth with rifles, bowie-knives, and revolvers. So they could only scowl upon us in sad and sullen hate. Their children at first came running about us for beads and buttons and crackers — little naked, brown monkeys; but as soon as their parents found what we were doing, they beat them terribly to make them keep away. We ran our lines through their village. In fact, I had to carry a chain right through one of their very tents, going in on one side, coming out on the other. Did I ever tell you about it?"

"No, sir. How did they like it?"

"Needn't ride so fast, Francisco. Hold in your mustang, Madison. Plenty of time before us. Well," continued the Texan, "when I got in the tent, there lay on a buffalo robe on the ground an old, old Indian. He was a chief, his hair white as snow. He must have been a magnificent warrior — broad chest, splendid eyes; looked, as he lay, like a king, say King Lear. I stopped a moment, hated to do it; but I had either to run my chain over his body as he lay, or to move him aside. So I took the edge of his robe, and pulled it with him on it to one side of the tent, out of the way, you know. I need not have been so particular—did it half for devilment, for I was a hard case once, my boy. How he looked! It was greater *anguish* than I ever saw even in a white face before. I was half sorry, couldn't help it, and drove ahead.

That was morning. Late that afternoon we all came from the prairie into camp. It was pitched near the village. At sunset we saw quite a crowd of Indians gathered on a sort of mound on the river bank, and some of us strolled up to see. There, in the centre of them, on the highest part of the mound, was the old chief seated on his robe—not lying down—sitting as erect as a king on his throne, dressed out in his full war-dress. He was making a sort of set speech, all the rest listening with solemn, bowed faces. I knew enough of their language to make out what he was saying. Pointing to the river sweeping by, he seemed to make it an emblem of the passing-away of his people from before the whites. Then he chanted a long account of all he had done in glorious days ago, keeping his eyes fastened proudly on the setting sun. All around listened as if for their lives. With his left hand he pointed to the sinking sun, and, just as it disappeared below the prairie, with his right, which all this time held a long knife under the blanket, he plunged the sharp blade into his bosom, right through his heart, and fell forward dead, grim and kingly to the last. Not a man of us but had a tear in his eye, but a revolver, too, in his hand. We expected them all upon us certain, and I declare they would have been right."

"I did not know that Indians ever committed suicide," said Madison.

"Oh yes! Not long before that we had captured an Indian with his squaw and children—five, six, I don't remember how many. He was a tiger of a fellow, and we put him and his family in a tent, with sentinels all around. There was plenty of food and water left in reach for them, but they were all chained. It was near dark when we put them in. There was not the least noise inside all night. Next morning when the sentinels went in with their breakfast they hadn't touched their supper, but there they all lay together dead. The father had got loose, and had killed them all with his knife, himself last. I think it must have been the chaining that broke his heart."

"I can't think such Indians can be cannibals, as some people say they are," said his nephew.

"Why, yes, but not from love of such fare. The Tonkoways always cut off the right hand of an enemy slain in fight, and make their women roast and eat it, that they may have brave children. The same tribe, I believe it is, always cut open the bosom of a slain foe, tear out the heart, cut the tip-end of it off, and eat that raw—to give them braver hearts, they say."

And thus they beguiled their road over the rolling prairie. At noon there was a short halt to graze their horses and to take a snack and a nap. At night they stopped on the bank of a crystal creek—the San Gabriel—rather a river than a creek; staked out their horses; boiled a cup or two of the invariable coffee; ate a very hearty supper broiled on the coals; then, with their heads on their saddles and their broad-brimmed hats over their faces, slept without stirring, sweetly, profoundly, till break of day. To breakfast, saddle up, and be away again took but a few minutes.

It was but little past noon on the day after leaving home that, entering a belt of timber, they halted to water their thirsty animals at the Lampasas—a broad, beautiful stream. The three animals thrust their noses eagerly into the tempting water, and together drew them out again, snorting and coughing with indignation and disgust, the water streaming from their mouths. No wonder. Long before their riders had reached the water, they had perceived the strong smell of sulphur in the air. The entire bed of the stream shone coated with a silvery sediment of brimstone. A few shanties stood around for the use of visitors to the embryo Saratoga.

Staking their horses to graze as well as their thirst would permit upon the rich grass under the magnificent live-oaks near by, the travellers proceeded to examine the springs. The first they came to gushed up out of the soil near the bank, more like milk, creamy, almost thick with sulphur. Gourd after gourd did the Texan drink, smacking his lips with relish after each, proving then and during the rest of his stay the assertions as to the enormous quantities which can be swallowed, the thirst for the water increasing with its use. Francisco drank too, because his master did—sullen, silent, dejected in doing so, as he had been, and to an increasing degree, for months past.

As to Madison, though thirsty, the smell of the water was more than enough. Doubtless nature causes those to thirst for such waters who need and are benefited by them. Sauntering farther along, they came next upon a chalybeate spring, which all agreed in rejecting. Crossing the stream upon a narrow and tottering bridge, they hastened in search of the famous gravel spring. And there it was, sure enough; a pool of water ten feet across, in the centre of which rose a natural fountain boiling and foaming furiously with gravel and water. The day was hot, the spot secluded, and in a few moments both of the travellers had laid aside their dusty garb and were luxuriating in the stormy bath. Plunging into the centre of the crater, the boy was thrown out again like a cork by the turbulent surges of pebbles and water. It was like bathing in the surf. The struggling water, the grating gravel, the foam and fury of the water rushing up from unfathomable depths, made it the most exhilarating bath ever taken. It was almost dark before they could tear themselves away. When they returned to where they had made their camp, they found that Francisco had the coffee-pot bubbling and slices of venison and bacon hissing upon the coals under the live-oaks. Another visit to the horses to see that they were strongly staked, and, with their heads upon their saddles, they were soon asleep—sound enough.

CHAPTER XV.

ALONG THE SAN GABRIEL.

"I say, men, any o' you know a man name o' Crittenden?" The speaker was seated, one morning after our friends had arrived, smoking his pipe, upon a log near the main sulphur spring. Low in stature, red in hair and beard, full and sensual in lips and cheek, narrow and retreating in forehead, dirty beyond description in garb—out of all the motley crowd there you could have picked him out in three minutes as a desperado and a bully. Whoever his companions might be, there was no doubt of who and what he was.

"There's a ugly-mouth *Chit*tenden lives on Goose Creek down Trinity," replied an old farmer, nursing the lame leg which had drawn him to the springs for its cure.

"Been long thar?" asked the first speaker.

"No; some twenty years or so."

"Not the man I'm after."

"There's a Jim *Bit*tenden cheats at peddling; drives around in a green wagon," ventured an old lady in green spectacles and fly-away cap. "He sold me some wonderful ointment for my eyes—made them smart like fire, almost ruined them. You see, gentlemen, my eyes has been ailing now nearly fifteen years. Cold, one doctor said; gnats, another doctor said. Rheumatics, I believe. You can't tell what trouble I've had with them. Somebody said these here springs—"

"Did your chap have black hair, black eyes, solemn-like face, marm?" interrupted the first inquirer.

"No; sandy hair, whitish-like eyes; solemn enough, though, he was at a bargain. I bought a pattern of calico of him once, paid forty cents a yard; came to unroll it—"

"I know a man answers to your description," said another of the crowd, coughing in the last stages of consumption. "He's my brother—my name's Litten—but he died of consumption ten years ago. In fact, I'm the only one of the family that escaped the disease." And he coughed again as if he would die.

"I tell you what it is, gentlemen," said the first speaker, rising to his feet, and putting his pipe in his pocket; "*my* legs ain't hurt, *my* eyes are sound as a bell; you don't ketch *me* coughing. I didn't come here to drink this here water for *my* health. I'm after a man. People come here from all parts of Texas, and I know that this is the very spot to hear about him. I'm from South Alabamy. Dyson's my name—Buck Dyson. People know me about home. Now, there's somebody in this crowd must know my man. I'll tell you what I'll do—as they do when they pass around a hat at meetin'. I'll go around to every man in this here crowd, and ask him separate; and I'll do the same thing to every stranger that comes while I stay here. If that don't bring what I want, I'm mistaken. I can try it, anyhow."

There was one person in the fifty or sixty grouped about on the benches and logs and grass around the spring who heard with painful interest these words. It was Madison. For four days now, his uncle, Francisco, and himself had been at the springs. They had fished, had shot deer, turkeys, and even a bear in the wild region around, until they were tired. They had become restless for home—Uncle Frank himself, even, and for the first time in his life. He had all the time seemed despondent, uneasy, unlike himself. In fact, for months now—why, Madison could not guess—a sort of gloom had rested with increasing darkness upon the otherwise open and sunny face of his uncle. He had been the first to propose leaving for home, and this they had determined to do early next morning. It was now near sunset. While his uncle and Francisco had gone to look after the horses, Madison had strolled down to the spring for a last look. Clustered about it were people of all sorts of ailments, and it reminded him of the Pool of Bethesda. The boy knew, almost from the instant the stranger spoke, that it was *his* Mr. Crittenden for whom the inquiry was made. A few months before he would have spoken out impulsively, but he had learned a lesson as to the evil of impulse that night under the hide, with the billows of the prairie fire surging over him. He was older and manlier, too. Besides, he had so strong an aversion to the bully, partially intoxicated as he was, and to the profanity of his language—which seemed more shocking to him than he had ever heard from human lips — that, restraining himself, he resolved to have nothing whatever to do with him. Besides, and above all, there was that in the manner of the man that urged him to conceal from him the home of Mr. Crittenden — he scarce knew why. But when the man announced his intention of putting the question in turn to every one on the spot, he felt his heart throb, not with fear, but anxiety. If he had hesitated before whether or not to tell, he now slowly and fully decided the matter. But could he deny any knowledge of Mr. Crittenden? A lie? no—never! Suddenly it occurred to him that his easiest plan was to withdraw quietly from the spot. Accordingly, he arose slowly, and began strolling away, hoping to escape the notice of the man, who was still at the other end of the crowd. Now, had he been a large man and a determined-looking one, the desperado might have made it convenient not to observe his leaving; but being merely a slightly built youth, the case was different. The man had, in fact, laid his command upon all there to sit still until questioned; to leave was contempt of his authority.

"Hallo! you there — stop!" rang in loud and insolent tones upon his ears.

What should he do? Run for it? For an instant he thought of doing so. But no; he felt his heart sicken even painfully in him, and knew that his cheek was ashy, but all the George Washington he had so often read and dreamed of rose to his lips. Slowly and quietly he turned to face his foe, for he felt him to be such in every nerve.

"Look here! I say, sir, you stop in your tracks!" said the man, hastening towards him with a volley of oaths interspersed. "Didn't you *hear* what I said? What are you leaving for? This is meetin'; 'fore you go you've got your catechism to say!"

By this time he had reached and stood face to face with Madison on the bank of the Lampasas.

"Look here, buddy," he continued, "do you know of a man named Crittenden down your way?" The man already saw, in his pale, set face, that the boy did know such a man, and the very man he was after.

"I refuse to answer," he replied, with lips so dry he could hardly articulate.

"You re-fuse to answer!" shouted the bully, his brandy-reddened face growing redder than before, his red whiskers and hair bristling with rage. "You re-fuse to answer! Game, *you* are, ain't you? Now, I'll just tell you what, my chicken — you've *got* to answer. See this," he continued, unbuttoning his vest and displaying a revolver in the belt next to his greasy flannel; "and do you see this?" he added, drawing a long, broad bowie-knife from his collar back of his head. "Now," he continued, "if you don't tell me all you know about the man I'm after in less than no time, I'll kill you — certain, sure.

8

Buck Dyson is my name. You won't be the first I've killed."

Madison glanced at the breathless crowd. It is astonishing how apathetic even the bravest men are when spectators of such a scene. "It's dreadful; somebody ought to stop it; but it's none of *my* business," is the brief and satisfactory reasoning of each under such circumstances. With drier lips than before, but as mechanical as steel, the boy replied as before, his cheek pale as death, his eye resting steadily in the inflamed orbits not ten inches from his—"I refuse to answer."

With a savage curse, the desperado drew his knife back.

There was a shudder in the crowd—a shriek from the old lady in the green spectacles. "Dear me, why don't *somebody* stop it?" was the thought of each. They were sure the knife would be driven into the bosom of the brave boy. He thought so himself, and shut his eyes for an instant with a swift, silent prayer; then opened them calmly in the glaring eyes of the man again.

"You came in an ace of it then," said the man, with hideous oaths. "I only didn't kill you because then I couldn't get out of you what I want. Now," he continued, with fearful meaning in his eyes and tones, "next time I will *kill* you as sure as you live. I *love* killing! Once more, where's my man?"

Madison knew that his hour had come. But there was no flinching. He was a thousand times more determined than ever not to tell, even had it been the most harmless ques-

tion in the world. He seemed to have turned to cold steel.

Again he replied—as his enemy drew back his knife with his right, while he grasped the boy, to make a sure stab, by the shoulder, and turned him a little to expose his bosom more to the sweep of his blow—in a low, slow tone—"I refuse to answer."

At that instant there was a rush of feet behind the desperado, the descending knife was wrested from his grasp, and its owner hurled, head-foremost, down the bluff into the Lampasas. Madison could only see that it was his uncle who had done it, and sank, weak as a babe, upon the ground, the high-strung excitement suddenly ceasing.

At the very beginning of the strife between the two, some had hurried off, and found and told the Texan all that was occurring. His most intimate friends would have hardly recognized him, so deadly pale, so dangerous he looked, standing on the bank, his rifle in full aim on the floundering bully.

"Hold on!" he said, in a strange, savage voice, as the man swam towards the shore. "If you swim another stroke, I'll shoot you." And Madison was appalled at the awful oaths and curses which streamed from the lips of his uncle, from whom he had never before heard an oath. He did not dream he could swear. "You let your feet strike ground; tread water if you can't," his uncle was saying to the man, "but come an inch nearer shore, and I'll kill you."

To the astonishment of Madison,

the man obeyed, being a coward, as all bullies are. He would certainly have been shot if he had not, and he knew it. As it was, the water reached to his chin as he stood in the creek, to the inexpressible gratification of the crowd that lined the bank, the bead of the Texan's rifle drawn full on the centre of the bully's forehead.

"To get his revolvers too wet to use. I see it. Ah, yes, very right," said a gentleman in a raccoon cap, shaking his head approvingly, and fixing himself more comfortably to see, while he cut up some tobacco in the palm of his hand for his pipe held between his teeth. And now that each one felt relieved of all personal duty in the matter, it is astonishing how unanimous they were in their sentiments—derision for the bully, admiration for the boy. The backwoodsman contemplated Madison, as he sat by his uncle, through the smoke of his cob pipe with solemn approval, his skin cap back on his head for a more unobstructed view, and he continued:

"Whenever *he* runs for Congress, he's got my vote, sure. Game, pluck, spunk, clear grit! Curious, too, the game ones *always* turn white, bullies red, when in a tight place. Singular." And he resumed his pipe in meditation upon this circumstance. As to the old lady in green spectacles, she actually threw her arms around Madison's neck and kissed him, saying, "Bless you, honey! you come of good stock, I reckon."

"I wonder, wonder, whether I'd not better kill him at once and have done with it; it'll save a world of sorrow and trouble hereafter," said the Texan to himself, half aloud.

"Oh no, uncle; no, no!" exclaimed Madison. "'Thou shalt not kill.' Don't you remember the command? Don't, don't—please don't." And he laid his hand on the rifle, and pressed its muzzle down to the ground.

"You may come out, man," said the Texan, shouldering his rifle, to the desperado. The man obeyed, and, passing dripping through the facetious crowd, disappeared without a word behind the shanties. Tearing themselves from the flattering attentions of those around, the Texan and his nephew proceeded to the live-oak under which they camped. It was now dark, and Francisco was waiting supper for them. Wearied out with excitement, Madison was asleep on his blanket in a few moments after. It seemed to him about midnight when he felt a hand upon his bosom, and he sprang to his feet from his dreams with a cry.

It was only his uncle, and Francisco stood by in the darkness with the three horses all saddled, their blankets and cooking utensils strapped on them ready for a start.

"All right, Madison; mount as quietly as you can. Heap more wood on the fire, Francisco. So now *vamos!* Quietly, quietly," said the Texan.

Madison rode after his uncle mechanically, and as in a dream, a mile or more through the darkness. Becoming at last wide-awake, he asked, in a low voice,

"Were you afraid he would shoot us as we slept, uncle?"

"Pshaw! no. Dyson's spirit's broken as far as *we* are concerned. He don't even *care* to hurt us. I was afraid he would follow us to find where Mr. Crittenden lived, if we waited till day. Don't ask any questions now, and don't say anything at all about this at home. I gave you as much sleep as I could before we started. Ride faster."

The night was very dark; it seemed to Madison as if day would never dawn. At last, the risen sun found them beside a bayou, nothing but a wide prairie all around.

"We've come far off to the north of our road home, to throw Dyson off our trail, you know," said the Texan. "We'll rest awhile, and breakfast. Stake out your horses—you needn't unsaddle. That's it. Catch a grasshopper, Francisco. Madison, you make a fire down the bank there; no leaves; not a puff of smoke, if you can possibly help it. Indians are only too plentiful about here." While he was speaking the Texan had tied the end of a line to his ramrod, baited the hook with the grasshopper, lowered it to the water, and almost immediately drew up a catfish, then another, and another.

"One apiece," he said; "that'll do. Clean them as fast as you can, Francisco. Here's a paper of salt."

In a short time each sat over the fire cooking his own fish by a ramrod thrust through it lengthways.

"No bread; but never mind," said the Texan, as he finished the last morsel. "Now unstake and off."

A ride of a few hundred yards brought them to a rise in the prairie. There, in the valley beyond, nearer to him than he had ever seen them before, was a herd of antelopes. To the pleading of Madison that he might try to get a shot at them his uncle gave a decided refusal.

"But, uncle, we have nothing to eat," his nephew argued. "I couldn't eat any supper hardly last night, and as to that cat this morning, I couldn't eat it at all. I'm so hungry."

"Well, that's a fact, Madison," replied the Texan. "They are not so shy out here. Crawl up on them through that clump of timber yonder. Tie this red handkerchief around your head, your hat on top of that, and keep as flat upon the ground as you can. Don't be flurried; shoot slow and sure."

Without a word, the boy slipped off his horse, and, leaving it with them, darted down to one side and disappeared in the hollow. Half an hour elapsed, and Francisco and his master, peeping over the top of the grass, could see that the antelopes were still grazing quietly. Another half-hour, and the antelopes had raised their heads, and were gazing at a red something several hundred yards from them in the grass. They would run towards it, then run back, and seemed much excited.

This continued for nearly an hour, the timid creatures drawing nearer and nearer to the object all the time, but very slowly.

"That boy's getting to be a cool hand," said his uncle to himself; "he couldn't do it better if he had been hunting antelope all his life. If he ain't genuine Virginian stock, I'm a Greaser!—Now's your chance, Madison!" he exclaimed aloud as the drove rushed nearer than before; and at the instant he spoke a puff of white smoke rose from the red spot, and, soon after, the faint crack of the rifle came on the wind to their ears. They saw Madison running towards the drove while it fled from him and disappeared like the wind. Riding on towards him, they saw him standing with his face to them upon something—probably a dead antelope—waving his red handkerchief and shouting at the top of his voice.

In the same instant, however, the crest of the prairie behind the young hunter seemed suddenly alive with men and horses, dashing down upon the boy.

The very soul of the Texan sickened within him. Indians! Indians! There was but one thing to do. Running his hand over the butts of the revolvers around his waist, glancing to see that the cap was on his rifle, he rode down to meet the foe.

"Unloaded, and with his back to them!" groaned the uncle. "On foot too. God help us! we are in for it, *sure!*"

Long before he could get in rifle-range, the Indians had swarmed around the boy like angry bees. He could merely catch sight of Madison clubbing his rifle and raising it to strike, when he seemed trampled down and swallowed up in the *mêlée.*

"Cool, cool, Dolores!" he said, in Spanish, to the Mexican. "You take red blanket; I'll take white; and as

he spoke, at the simultaneous crack of their rifles, two Indians fell headlong from their horses while rushing upon them.

"Draw your knife and hold it in your teeth, Dolores. Cool, cool! Revolvers is the word now. Drop your rifle!"

By this time the Indians, staggered for a moment by the fall of the slain, were almost in arm's-length of them. They were appalling foes to fight with. Almost black, naked to the waist, the long hair hanging down their neck behind full of coins of gold and silver, their cheeks barred with various colors, armed with bows and arrows, riding as if they grew upon their shaggy ponies—a herd of ferocious wolves would have been less dreadful to meet. The instant before closing with them, a thought flashed upon the Texan. Lifting his hat from his head, and half turning in his saddle, he waved it with a shout towards the ridge from which he had just descended. "Hurrah, boys!" he cried, as if exultingly. "Here they are! here they are!" Then, dashing his hat with reckless confidence in the faces of the enemy, notwithstanding the arrows whizzed upon him like hail, he discharged his revolver right and left, but with deliberate aim, hitting at every shot. Even in the heat of the fight he could see that his stratagem had its effect.

The Indians were at that instant flying with Rangers on their trail. The cry of the Texan, and his riding upon them instead of attempting to fly, and in the direction from which they were expecting the Rangers, together with his dashing confidence, impressed them with the belief that their dreaded foes were at hand. And they were right. As if in response to the cry of the Texan, there rang a wild hurrah from behind him, and helter-skelter, down the slope, rode the Rangers, their captain at their head. They were not in line of battle at all; but all were racing as hard as spurs would drive—their teeth set, their faces glowing, their rifles ready. But it was a fatal instant when the Texan looked around to see. The hindmost of the flying Indians had drawn his arrow to its head upon his bow, aiming at the bosom of the Texan. But, although his gaze was averted, other eyes saw the aim; and the Mexican, rushing between, received the arrow in his side, and fell from his horse as the Indian disappeared over the hill after his comrades.

For a moment the Rangers—bearded, sunburnt, wool-hatted, most of them in their shirt-sleeves, their coats strapped behind them—drew rein round the Texan supporting the Mexican in his arms upon the ground. In a few rapid words they learned everything—examining with contemptuous curiosity the bodies of the Indians lying on the ground.

"Not much hurt, I hope," said a Ranger in a red shirt, drawing near, with sympathy in his face and voice, "Oh pshaw! tut!" he added, with a sudden change in tone and manner—indifference, not to say disgust, taking the place of sympathy. "Why, it's only a *Mexican!* and I thought it was somebody! I say, old fellow," he continued, to the Texan, sharpening his knife upon his hard palm as he spoke, and, in wheedling tones, "come, now, let *me* scalp these redskins—come, do. They killed my father last month—some of them;" and, without waiting for a reply, the Ranger whipped off the scalps and had them tied to his saddle by the buckskin strings in a few moments.

"Come, you hush up!" he said to one whose low groan gave evidence of life; and, pausing as he mounted his horse, he shot him through the head with his revolver, exactly as he would have done had it been a rattlesnake instead. "Clever of you!" he said, nodding to the Texan as he rode off. "I'll do the same for you some day. My name is Bud Jenkins, and I live at the forks of the San Gabriel. Drop in and have some coffee when you happen to pass that way. I can't be with you always. Take care of yourself. Good-bye!"

"Iron-Jacket, was it?" said the captain, as he parted with the Texan. "All right. I thought so. They've got your nevy, have they? Our mustangs are badly used up, but we'll fix them before night. Come on as soon as you can. Hurrah, boys!" And in a minute after the Texan was alone upon the field of battle, the Indians lying grim in death beside him. But he seemed to have forgotten even his nephew in his anxiety for his servant. A look of the deepest anguish sat upon his brow as he supported the drooping head upon his bosom.

"Water! water!" groaned the other in Spanish. The Texan glanced around: it was his only way; and, bearing the wounded Mexican in his arms, as if it were a child instead, he hastened up the slope towards the bayou beyond, where they had breakfasted. Often would he have to stop and rest, changing, as he did so, the position of his bleeding burden. It was much farther than he had supposed, but it was his only chance; and the afternoon was far advanced when he laid his servant gently upon the grass on the edge of the bayou beneath a mesquit. Hastening to the water, he filled his hat and returned; and, having satisfied the burning thirst of the Mexican, he proceeded to bathe the pale face with water, smoothing out the long raven hair across his knees from the head supported in his lap. Their broken conversation was now altogether in Spanish, and no longer the language of master and servant.

In fact, that servant was really a Mexican girl. The Texan had married her during a trip into Mexico, upon a sudden whim. Long ago had he repented it. His affection had never been anything that merited the name of love; he had hardly even professed that it was. But her affection for him was all that is usual in her warm-hearted race. It had been for a short, a very short time that he had even tried to reciprocate the love she lavished upon him. She was a *Mexican*, was too far his inferior, and he had required her now for years to be rather Francisco than Dolores to him. The coming of first his brother's family, and then of Mr. Crittenden and his daughter, had made her even less to him than she had ever been. He *could* not love her; she was to him a grief, a burden, a perpetual repentance. But she had given her life for him; and, with the softest and sweetest of the endearing words of the melting Spanish, he now endeavored to assuage her dying hours.

And she seemed perfectly happy. Her dark eyes fastened with eager fondness upon his face, she murmured softly, in reply to his soothing words. "I crept to her bed one night to stab her, but she looked like the Virgin Mary as she slept: I couldn't!" And as the shades of evening fell around, the Texan sat with the dying girl in his arms, the tears flowing down his cheeks. He did not know when she died. One moment the moon shone on her face, and she was alive, and gazing fondly up into his eyes. A cloud swept over the moon; when the light rested again upon her face, it was cold in death—all light gone from the glassy eyes, still fixed upon his.

For hours the Texan sat in the darkness, almost motionless, all his life passing in review before him in the solemn stillness, the awful burden resting upon his lap, as the sweeping clouds hid or revealed the ghastly face. His own early training, the influence of his brother and of Mr. Crittenden, his own experience, observation, and conscience — all these had long been working a revolution in his bosom, and this night completed it. Who could detail the whole process?

With the earliest gray of morning, he wrapped the body—it was all he could do—in his blanket, weighting it heavily with rocks. He stooped to kiss the pale brow, once, only once; he had cut a long tress of the raven hair, but he took it again from his bosom and placed it back beside the face of the dead. Bearing his burden to the brink of a dark, secluded pool in the bayou, so deep that he could not see its bottom, he let the shrouded form glide from his embrace, down and down, into the quiet depths. Then, kneeling beside the brink, he made confession of a lifetime wild and reckless; made humble acknowledgment of present weakness and folly; made fervent supplication for help in the new life before him; and rose from his knees another man—humble, but determined. Then he walked rapidly to the battlefield. There he found his horse where he had got a Ranger to stake it for him, the wolves flying from around the dead bodies, and the buzzards rising reluctantly on his approach. With his eyes fastened on the trail of the Rangers, and putting spurs to his horse, he rode rapidly on—hunger, watching, fatigue, Dolores, all forgotten for the time; Madison, Madison the one ruling thought!

CHAPTER XVI.

AMONG THE INDIANS.

MADISON was not killed on the spot by the Indians, for two reasons. They prefer taking boys and girls prisoners to killing them, with view to selling them to Indian agents for spirits and ammunition. Besides, they had with them many spare horses which they had stampeded and stolen, and they needed the assistance of the boy to drive these. Between being taken a prisoner and being killed outright, the latter, as a general rule, is preferable. As it was, the boy was badly wounded in his knee and through one arm. Almost at the instant his foes came upon him, before he had time to think, he had been lifted upon a mustang and was galloped off between two of the tribe; for, having the Rangers on their trail, they had no time to stop. Before he had gone very far, he heard the crack of rifles behind him, and knew that Francisco and his uncle were in the fight. It flashed upon him as a sudden hope that they might be taken prisoners also, so that he might have them with him; but he well knew that all the probabilities were that they would both be killed and scalped. Even in that moment of terror he noticed, and with a sort of pride, too, that one Indian had thought his antelope worth bringing, and now rode with it slung behind him on his horse.

After dashing on for a long time at full speed over the prairie, the Indians slackened their pace a little at a gruff word from one of them. Madison had read, and had been told also by his uncle, that the only way to propitiate Indians when in their power was to be as fearless of them as possible; so he raised his drooping head and assumed as bold a port as he could, and for the first time looked full at the Indians between whom he rode in front, while the rest of the band came after, some fifty in all. He recalled what he had read in Cooper's stories about the noble red man, but he saw at once that if such Indians ever existed, they were no more like his captors than Grecian statues are like Hottentots, or lions like wolves. Cooper's Indians were, in fact, purely ideal; these were the *real* savages. The Indian who rode upon his left was almost as black as a negro. His hair was cut square off over his eyes, and hung down behind almost to the stirrup as he rode—plaited and mingled in with all sorts of coins, gold and silver; it was a wonder to the boy how his head could sustain the strain of such a load. Buckskin and blankets made up the rest of his dress; but his face — it was that which puzzled Madison. He had imagined that Indians always had a ferocious aspect, but this Indian had a fat, grave, even benignant face — not at all like the savage he had read of in books. It reminded Madison strongly of the pictures he had seen of Franklin. A more serious, composed, sanctimonious face even, could not be seen anywhere. Apart from his hue and his costume, he looked like some respectable deacon riding on his way to church — one who had scarce harmed even a fly in his life. And yet that Indian had murdered, cruelly tortured, and butchered many a human being; and would have put Madison to the most terrible suffering, and then killed him without moving a muscle of his benevolent countenance.

Madison, who did not know this, was greatly encouraged, and now glanced at the Indian on his right. This was a tall, lean, haughty-looking warrior, who reminded him as much of pictures he had seen of Don Quixote as the other did of Franklin. But the most striking thing about him was his armor. This consisted of a coat of mail covering him down to the thighs, and formed of innumerable small steel rings woven curiously into each other with consummate skill. The Indians were supplied with leathern shields painted over with various emblems, and with bows and arrows in cowskin quivers. As he looked at the arrows projecting from the quiver hanging under the arm of the right-hand Indian, he knew that it was Comanches in whose hands he was. His uncle had told him that every tribe grooves its arrows, so that when they have penetrated the body of a deer the blood may trickle out and drop upon the ground, leaving a trail by which the game can be followed. The arrows of other tribes are grooved spirally, or otherwise irregularly, while those of the Comanches have, his uncle had told him, a straight groove from the barbed end to the other. And Madison knew, too, that it was Iron-Jacket who rode by him, a renowned chief named after the mail he wore, of whom he had often heard.—Iron-Jacket! He was well known over all the West, among the Indians especially, as the owner and constant wearer of a coat which rendered him, as was supposed, invulnerable to arrow or bullet. In some way it had come down from Cortez—or some follower of Cortez—into the hands of this chief, who was a chief in consequence of owning it, and who would not have exchanged it for all the cattle on the prairies.

And now Madison began to wonder how he was going to escape; and then imagined how interesting it would be, when at home again, to tell Bessie, Doodle-bug, Will, and all of them about it. His wounds began to smart severely; yet by a strange reaction, from sudden terror his spirits began to rise also wonderfully. Next he breathed a fervent prayer to God to help him, and hope, and even joy, filled his bosom as he rode. Then he wondered whether they had captured Francisco and his uncle yet, and would soon bring them along. And then it came again to him that the same Father whom he worshipped at the family altar at home was as near to him, and as powerful and willing to help him, now as then; and this was a consolation to him inexpressible. Then another thought rose in his mind. His hands were not tied, and he quietly slipped them in his pockets as they trotted rapidly along. Gathering up the contents of each pocket in his hand, with his forefinger he managed to punch a hole through the seam in it, and cautiously pushed his knife through. It gradually worked its way down his leg and fell upon the ground. He dreaded lest the Indians clattering behind should see it; but they were too busy looking around and talking to do so.

By this time it was becoming dark; still they rode on without a halt. Scarce a word had been uttered by any one since the last Indian had galloped up after sending from his bow the arrow which bore death to the Mexican. As it became darker, Madison dropped through the hole in one pocket everything there—two half-dollars, three Mexican dollars, his pocket-comb. Then, out of the other pocket, a fishing-line rolled up on its cork, a brass buckle, a bunch of buckskin tied up, a box of caps, a charger made out of a boar's tooth. All these not at once, but scattered along a mile or so apart. His object was to help any persons who might endeavor to trail him; and it answered the purpose admirably afterwards. He would have had all these things taken from him; but the Indians had not yet had time, dreading to stop lest the Rangers should catch up with them.

All night they rode, the boy almost falling from his horse, at last, with hunger and loss of sleep; a sense of utter wretchedness and despair, too, began to creep upon him. When the next morning dawned upon him, the benignant Franklin was still riding on one side, and Iron-Jacket on the other, as composedly as if just started on a little pleasure excursion. The horses, however, could hardly walk; and at full sunrise Iron-Jacket called a halt upon a little stream. The animals were allowed to graze to recover strength; for an Indian cares for his horse only for the present use it is to him, having no idea of affection for it. Madison fell heavily on the grass, and lay there sound asleep, the Indians paying no attention to him whatever. When he awoke the sun was high, and the savages preparing to start. A fragment of jerked beef was thrown to him by Iron-Jacket, like a bone to a dog; but so ravenously hungry was the boy that he ate it greedily. And so on and on, over the prairie the whole of that long day, the boy being forced to assist in driving the loose horses, among which he recognized his brother's pony Slow, which Francisco had ridden. It was even a consolation to have this old acquaintance along. Once when a young Indian drove his spear into Slow to make him go faster, Madison shouted at him fiercely, and the whole band broke into a loud laugh. In fact, the boy began to feel at home with his captors, weighed down though he was by heavy thoughts as to the fate of Francisco and his uncle, and in regard to his own destiny. And so night came—then a fragment of beef, a sound sleep on the grass, and up again by day, and off on the wearisome march. Thus passed a whole week; though it seemed to the boy like a year. He was now naked except half a blanket tied by him around his waist, everything having been appropriated some time ago by the In-

dians. His hat, too, had long decked the head of the young Indian that had speared Slow. From head to foot Madison was dirty and blistered by the sun, his naked feet bleeding from the rocks, his wounds exceedingly painful. He almost began to doubt his identity; he felt as if he were rapidly becoming an Indian himself, almost imagined that he had always been what he now was.

Morning and evening he ceased not to pray to God, often remembering his deliverance, when escape seemed impossible, from the prairie fire. As he rode during the day, or lay awake at night, all the verses of Scripture and hymns he had ever learned passed through his mind; he loved to repeat all he knew, and was astonished how many he remembered. Home, too—that dearest spot on earth, under the live-oaks by the San Hieronymo — it was before his eyes all the time, clad in a kind of glory to him. He wondered he had never prized it more. Oh, if he were there again, how he would love the very rocks and earth! And his father, mother, Will, Josie, Bessie, Hark, Rohamma, Duke, Snap — how keenly he appreciated and loved them now! It seemed as if it would be to him like Paradise with its angels if he ever got back. Plans of escape, too, had often crossed his mind — such a whirl, a current, a cataract of things had rushed through his mind since he had been taken!

It was the tenth day after he had been captured. The Indians had now reached their camp on the

Colorado—a helter-skelter collection of rude skin tents with swarms of squaws and children. All his romantic notions of such things vanished before the reality. The filth was unutterable; not a spark of kindliness or gentleness had he yet witnessed. It was a den of wild animals with their cubs—nothing more. He was continually employed in bringing wood or water, a miserable slave, as squalid in appearance as any of them, almost. His long black hair all tangled about his eyes, his naked body blistered by the sun, grimed with dirt, a great sore on his knee, another on his arm; he could scarce have been told from the Indians. He had thought best not to wash himself when at the river for water, but to seem as much at home with the savages as possible. But under all his miserable outward appearance he was his uncle's own Madison still, as the young Indian who had wounded Slow found to his cost. In passing Madison once, he spat at him. It was on the top of a high bank of the river, and the next instant the Indian had been knocked down the bank into the river with a splash. All the Indians near ran to see, and laughed heartily. Madison waited for the discomfited savage to rush up the bank and kill him. And he did come up the slope, but with his brown face all in a good-humored grin, and to shake hands with the captive. Ever after Madison had in him a stanch friend. It illustrated the fact that treaties and tribute only encourage the Indians to insolence. Fear is the only means to keep them in order.

The tenth, eleventh, and twelfth days of his captivity were spent by Madison in the camp. The savages occupied themselves in dressing hides, broiling beef on the coals, and in eating, smoking, quarrelling, sleeping, going out hunting or returning with game, their squaws making baskets, moccasons, and bows. The filth and stench—to say nothing of the vermin with which all were alive—were abominable; it seemed to the boy that he was among a species of monkeys rather than human beings. They had scouts out in every direction, and were keeping a sharper lookout in reference to the Rangers than he knew.

The fat, grave Indian whom he thought of as Franklin sat all day on a log, smoking solemnly, absorbed in unutterable meditation. Iron-Jacket stalked haughtily about, never removing the armor in which he trusted. It was to him his confidence, his glory, the one thing that separated him from and elevated him above all the world besides. No monarch could be prouder of his crown and kingdom; and the rest of the tribe rendered him the homage due as owner of an invulnerable coat, creating him justly and rightfully their superior. It was kept clean and bright, covering his entire person to the waist. Glittering in the sun, he moved about the Achilles of the camp. As to the captive, he kept up as stout a heart as possible. Occasionally he would steal down to the river to weep, for he could not help it. He thought how its waters flowed by his father's door so many miles below, and he would even kiss the surface, sending his love thus to that spot which now seemed to him to hold in itself all repose and joy in the world, and yet as far away as if in another planet, from which he had fallen ages ago. Whenever he dared, he would loiter to where Slow was staked on the prairie, and hug and kiss him and whisper his hopes. "What do you think of things, old fellow?" he would say. The horse would shake his head despondingly and pause from grazing a while to consider matters, but, making the best of circumstances, would then resume his grass as steadily as if at home. As Madison would turn from Slow to the miserable camp again, it was like coming down from human companionship to that of brutes. If there had been anything womanly in the squaws, it would not have been so bad; but they were all of them hideously ugly, dirtier than the men, and always squabbling with each other or with their little rats of children—rats small, but with keen, quick eyes, malicious and wicked. It was after this that the governor of a western territory made an official proposition to the War Department that he be allowed to invite all the Indians to a grand feast, and kill them to the last man by poisoned food; a little more experience of them, and Madison would have favored, it is to be feared, even that.

"What makes the vast difference between these creatures and white people?" he often asked himself. "If they lived on a different globe, they could not be more unlike us."

As his father might have told him, that which made the chief difference between savages and civilized people was, in a word, the possession and use, and for generations, of the Bible.

The morning of the thirteenth day since he was taken had arrived. The Indians were eating their breakfast, their mustangs grazing around as usual. Suddenly a single naked savage was seen riding towards the camp from the prairie, yelling and brandishing his arms. In an instant the whole camp was in a whirlwind of confusion. Each squaw dropped everything else and pounced upon her own children like a hawk, carrying the youngest in her arms, the elder running closely at her heels, and making for the bottom timber as fast as they could. The men, in a minute's flash, were on their mustangs armed for the foe; Benjamin Franklin, on his animal, as serious and benevolent in his aspect as ever. But Iron-Jacket was the hero of the hour: seated on the most spirited horse there, fully armed, resplendent in his coat of mail, he rallied his warriors around him with a yell and a wave of his hand. However it fared with the rest, he was certain that no bullet could harm him, and was composed and confident accordingly. The savages had little time to spare—so little that they seemed, for the instant, to have forgotten Madison. Close at the heels of the Indian that gave the alarm the company of Rangers came tearing on for the camp, outyelling the Indians. And a motley crew they were, as has been already said: some with broad wool hats; some with handkerchiefs tied around their heads; some with coats; some in their shirt-sleeves; old, white-headed frontiersmen with a long score of outrages to settle up; bronzed middle-aged men; youths not twenty. Not a man there but had lost a father, brother, mother, sister, whose scalps they knew were at that moment drying in possession of the Indians; or, at least, had lost cattle and horses by them. As before, there was no line of battle at all—helter-skelter on they came as hard as their mustangs could bear them under incessant spurring—Colonel Ford ("Old Rip," as he was most generally called) at their head. The in-running warrior fell with a dozen balls in him, and lay dead far behind in a short time; and then came the fight in good earnest. Soon after the first surprise, an Indian had snatched Madison up from the ground, lifted him on a horse—it happened to be Slow, to which Madison always kept as close as possible—leaped on another, and was off with him in a twinkling, the contest raging louder and louder behind them as they fled. They had gone a mile or more before Madison recovered his presence of mind. He was almost stunned with anguish—so near rescue, and to be thus carried off, as from the very grasp of his friends, into captivity, hopeless captivity! He would rather be killed on the spot! He was becoming desperate.

Suddenly a thought struck him. Right ahead were several openings in the ground like deserted wells. In carrying out the horses to graze, with the Indians, he had often noticed them, and wondered what they were—had even sounded one or two of them with a stone. As he approached them he laid his hands upon the neck of his horse; as he passed them he suddenly sprang off and ran for his life. An arrow from the Indian whizzed through the very place in which he had been the moment before, but he had disappeared down the well in one desperate jump, crashing through the brush that almost covered its mouth, and followed in his descent by a shower of dirt and pebbles from the banks. Almost as soon as he had escaped the Indian had ridden his shying horse as near the mouth as possible; but the sound of battle waxed louder and louder behind, mixed with the rush of coming hoofs. How to get the boy out puzzled the savage. There was only one remedy; and, standing over the mouth of the opening, he sent arrow after arrow from his bow down into the darkness. Then, as the contest rolled upon him, he sprang on his horse again and with a yell mingled in it.

The fight had been from the first a retreat on the part of the Indians; the bravest of the warriors plying their arrows upon the Rangers, but giving way before them all the time, as slowly as possible, to give chance for the rest to make good their escape. First among the Rangers was a Texan in his shirt-sleeves, pale and calm, while all the rest seemed frenzied with excitement; silent, while all the rest were cursing and swearing as if their oaths could kill like bullets. An arrow was sticking in his clothes, but he rode steadily on; another passed between his arm and his side, but his object seemed to be to get among the Indians, while his quick glance ran like lightning rapidly around in search of the prisoner. Benjamin Franklin spurred upon him only to receive a ball in his benevolent face. Sliding, as the fight rolled by him, slowly and decorously from his horse, he lay at length upon the earth dead, with countenance as sanctimonious and dignified in death as in life.

But Iron-Jacket was the most active and desperate foe, and the most conspicuous mark for every Ranger. Their assaults, however, he treated with contempt, confident in his invulnerable armor. Suddenly, however, in the thickest of the fight, and in the height of his confidence, a loud "Waugh!" burst from his lips. He had been hit! Instantly his courage gave place to consternation. Who can tell the agony of the man at the sudden destruction of the faith and reliance of his life? And as he turned, another ball struck him full in the breast. With mortal anguish, and disappointment even more agonizing, he fell headlong from his mustang and soon expired under the hoofs of the Rangers. At the sight the rest of the Indians ceased to make even a show of battle, and fled for their lives, the Rangers spurring after them and picking the scattered and flying foes off their horses with rifle and revolver as they got the chance, keeping up all the time unceasing yells. There was not a plume, not an epaulet, not an inch of gold facing, not a brass button, not a sword, among them, nor any other show whatever of martial splendor. There was not even a fife, a drum, or a bugle—nor anything resembling discipline or drill. Yet they out-Indianed the Indians. Each man "fought on his own hook," a Ranger with the least white feather about him being a bird never yet heard of in Texas.

Spurring at full speed through and through the abandoned camp in every direction, around and around it, again and again, rode Uncle Frank, shooting the Indians only when they got in his way. Madison! Madison! where was he? Not a trace of him! Suddenly he dashed ahead of the rest of the Rangers after the flying Indians. Outstripping them all, he rode hard upon a young Indian wearing a wool hat which he recognized as his nephew's. One shot from his revolver brought down the Indian's horse, and, before the savage could rise, the Texan was on him, had plucked the hat from his head, crushed it up in his hands, and stuck it in his belt.

"Where is he?" he shouted to the Indian, in Spanish, choking him so at the same instant as to render reply impossible. The Indian pointed ahead, and indicated as much by gestures as words that the prisoner had just been carried on. Hurling him to one side out of his way, the Texan sprang on his horse again and spurred on.

"Throw away an Indian!" exclaimed a voice behind him. "What a wicked waste! Here, you, mister, take that with my compliments!" and as the Indian fell at the shot, the red-shirted Ranger added his scalp to his collection, already very large. "Never saw a man as careless about collecting his scalps in all my days as that fellow; it's sinful," he said, as he tied the last knot in the buckskin strings of his saddle to the bloody hair and remounted his horse in search of more.

By this time the Texan was far ahead among the leading Rangers. Still no sign of the boy. Turning rapidly aside to the top of a prairie knob, he could see the flying Indians, all of them racing for life. Swiftly arranging his spy-glass, he scanned eagerly their disordered ranks—again—yet again. No white-skin among them. Overwhelmed with distress, he rode on, not knowing what to do. Suddenly his eye caught sight of a familiar pony—Slow—standing off to one side and whinnying. But he could not stop for him now, and dashed on almost hopelessly after the Rangers.

Seven long hours afterwards the Texans came trooping back from pursuit, eagerly discussing the events of the day, as they walked their worn-out horses along. One only among them rode silent, and oh, how sad! Where?—how?—what possible chance was there now of trailing the prisoner? As he passed along he noticed Slow grazing about the same spot. Jumping off his horse, he walked up to him with the half-purpose of questioning him for his master. "For God's sake, Slow, speak out!" he said, half beside himself, to the horse. Slow recognized him, evidently; and, trotting off before him, stood at the opening of a sort of well, whinnying and pawing. The Texan glanced at the mouth of the well; the bushes were disarranged; there were breaks in the gravelly sides as if of soil lately knocked away.

"By—!" an oath rose to his lips and almost escaped, but was kept down by a sudden emotion, a new resolve.

"Here—I say, Mac—one of you boys—a lariat—quick as you can!" And all the Rangers pressed eagerly around the opening. Swift as thought, Uncle Frank had tied the end of a lariat around his revolver, and riding "straddle" of this he pushed himself off down the opening, while a dozen willing hands held the end.

"I'll bet my life, it's only an Indian down there," said a Ranger. "Anyhow, let him go down. It's a pity to lose the scalp. My scalp, if you please, old hoss!" he shouted down into the darkness.

"Hold!" cried the Texan from below. "Send down another lariat—another still. Now pull!" he again shouted, after a few moments, during which a hundred questions were poured down upon him without a reply. A hard pull it was, but it brought up the Texan bearing a body, evidently a dead body, in his arms. When near enough the surface, a dozen hands lifted Madison out of his uncle's arms, and laid him gently on the grass, almost dropping the Texan back again into the hole in their forgetfulness of him. There was not a dry eye among those rude but gallant men as they gathered around the body—naked, grimed doubly with dirt and blood, a wound in his side, in which an arrow was still sticking. The Texan sat down on the grass, and wept silently, the men standing around in hushed silence, most of them having taken their hats from their heads. At last, one of them knelt down, laid his ear to the naked bosom of the boy, then placed his finger upon his pulse.

"Gen-tle-men," said he, looking up with an air of grave importance, "calomel is pisen. Any man that'll give minerals to a feller-creeter is a murderer any day. I'm what you call a steam doctor. Thompsonian-Botanic is my sort of doctoring. But this here boy ain't dead. Stan-ned he is — see that bruise on his head? — fainted, too, from loss of blood. A han'kerchief, any of you? Some whiskey, too, if you hain't drunk it all up."

CHAPTER XVII.

THE RETURN.

"It's twice, now, you've made a goose of me, my boy. I want you to stop it. You play 'possum a little too well."

It was the uncle who spoke, and to his nephew lying pale and exhausted upon a buffalo-robe beneath a mesquit. Borne in the arms of his uncle into the camp so recently occupied by the Indians, attended by the Rangers with an eager sympathy, every means had been used for his restoration by the steam doctor, who had thus soared suddenly above all his fellow-Rangers into an importance absolutely sublime.

Sure enough, the boy had only fainted from loss of blood. The close air, too, of the pit had aided to prolong his stupefaction. Very soon the well would have been his grave also, had he not been rescued in time. As it was, there he lay naked, except the blanket around his waist; very dirty, too, except where water had been dashed over his face to restore him. Browned by the sun, and his black hair hopelessly tangled together, he looked much more like an Indian than a white man. He had already told, as well as he could, his uncle and the Rangers crowd-ing about him the story of his captivity. It was now past mid-night. Around their camp-fires, the Rangers had sauced their suppers—made up in large part from the lard-ers of the defeated Indians — with narrations by each man of his share in the fight of the day. After this, several uproarious songs had been sung, not a voice failing in the chorus. Next, a dozen or so of them had further refreshed them-selves after the fatigues of the day by joining in a double-shuffle dance for an hour or so, with the hearty approval of the rest. A guard had been stationed around the camp, outside of the grazing horses; and by two o'clock in the morning the moon shone, at last, only less brightly than the sun, upon the Rangers lying about, soundly asleep upon the grass, in every direction and attitude, some with their heads on their saddles, others upon buffalo-robes, some on saddle-blankets, a few flat on the ground.

The steam doctor was the last asleep, no one remaining awake to the story of his manifold cures, which he had continued to tell without pause from the moment Madison had been extricated from the pit—all through his restoration, through supper, through the song and dance—and had ceased only when the snore of his last companion left him without a listener. Not far from him lay the scalp-collector. Never had miser counted over his gold more eagerly, carefully, than he had his scalps before sleeping; and now, wrapped together in his coat, they made a pillow upon which he rested his head and slept as sweetly as an infant. Little undressing was needed for the repose of the Rangers. One war-whoop would have drawn every man of them to his feet, wide awake, armed to the teeth, and more than willing for a fight. Now, however, they slept deeply—scattered about over the prairie—leaving the uncle and nephew to their own secrets.

"There's one thing more I wanted to tell you, uncle," said Madison, at length, "before we go to sleep, and while we are all quiet here by ourselves. I can't take care of it.

There it is." And he drew out a corner—which had been tucked in securely—of the blanket around him, and, unrolling it, he produced a bar of dirty metal—square, some four inches long by one thick.

"Why, this is silver," said his uncle, after scraping it with his knife, holding it up in the moonlight, turning it round and round, and examining it closely. "Where on earth did you pick it up?"

"Nowhere on the earth—under the earth, uncle. When I first fell, or rather jumped, into the hole, I was so stunned and bruised I did not know anything—even that I was wounded by the arrow. After a while I came to myself a little. I could hardly move, and it was so dark I could not see. I began to feel around a little on the ground with my hands, expecting to touch a snake or a centipede every instant, when I felt that bar among the trash, with a number of others lying beside it. I didn't know what it was—iron, I supposed—till I held it up in the light. Then I thought I might dig out steps with it in the sides of the well to climb out by, so I rolled it up in a flap of my blanket, and tucked it in carefully, not to lose it, for I felt I was getting sick, as if I were going fast asleep. I never thought of it again till this moment. That's all."

"And a plenty," added his uncle, eagerly, who had listened with deepest interest to the narration. "Don't say a syllable about it to any one, Madison. I'll keep the bar safely for you. We'll talk about it more after a while. You go to sleep now as fast as you can."

In fact, his nephew was almost asleep before he had finished. Not so with the elder of the two. Lying down beside the boy, with his hands so that no one could see, the Texan rubbed the bar well with his sleeve, first moistening it with his lips, and then examined it carefully for an hour. It was a bar of silver, nothing more, nothing less, no stamp or mark upon it whatever. The Texan understood it none the less. He had often heard from Americans, and more especially from Mexicans, wonderful stories of the old silver-mines throughout the northwestern part of Texas, extending through Chihuahua and Sonora and Arizona, and so on up into California. On several occasions when among Indians, he had made careful and cunningly worded inquiry of them in regard to these mines, from curiosity more than anything else. They had uniformly denied any knowledge of such mines, but always in such a manner as confirmed him in his belief. The more loud and positive their denials, the more satisfied he had become that they knew of them, and carefully concealed the location. In fact, for days before the fight, in trailing the Indians with the Rangers, the Texan had observed that upon almost every eminence in the prairie were heaps of rocks evidently piled by hand. On one or two occasions, having ascended to these piles, he had noticed a something he would not have observed but for a hint he had once got from an old white-headed Mexican woman. This was that on the top of every such heap there was always one long rock pointing in a certain direction. Noticing this once or twice, he had taken the course in which the index-rock pointed with his pocket compass. Afterwards, during every day's ride, he had made a point of ascending the elevations on either side of the trail, as if to scan the country for Indians, and in every case there was the same pile of rocks, with the same sort of finger-rock pointing the same way. Laboring under a feverish anxiety in regard to his nephew, as well as full of thought only less painful in regard to Dolores, he had found a kind of relief in doing this while he urged on the pursuit, which continued in the direction of the rocks. He had forgotten all about the matter during the fight and since, and now it all came back to him in the bar of silver. Sure enough! sure enough! And so Madison had pitched down head-foremost into one of the old silver-mines!

"Pointed right, that's a fact," said the Texan to himself—"pointed exactly to the spot where I was to find the silver—and the *gold!*" he added, glancing at his slumbering nephew. "If chance is God of this world," he continued to himself, "then chance is singularly wise and astonishingly good. Things go crashing and smashing and ruining along right hand and left, just when they are working out—like a mill sluice on an overshot wheel—the best results. My opinion is, we've most to fear when everything seems going right. Providence! Providence! as Brother Morton says. And it shall be *my* religion, too, from this day out."

Concealing the bar of silver carefully in his bosom, the Texan breathed a fervent prayer to that Being whom he had now taken as his chief friend forever, and with a supplication for future guidance he composed himself to sleep.

It was three days before Madison was strong enough to go any distance, the Rangers remaining in camp to rest their horses a little. It was not till the morning of the fourth day that he ventured down to the river, and there took a thorough washing for the first time in weeks. He went in a savage, and came out a white man — except that he was badly sun-burnt. In one of the tents had been found a suit of buckskin, which Madison remembered to have seen a squaw at work on for the Indian whom he had knocked into the river, and who had robbed him of his hat. It was new, but far from complete. However, his uncle managed to eke it out from other spoils found in the camp, so that by the end of the week after his rescue Madison was clothed from head to foot—enough of an Indian in appearance to have frightened Bessie out of her wits had she seen him. The coat of mail and a complete equipment of bow, arrows, and quiver was gladly allowed him by the Rangers—who regarded him as rather the owner of the camp, the residuary legatee of his dear departed friends the Indians. He kept these spoils of war by him to carry home, as well as a skin paint-bag and a few other

mementos of his short but eventful experience of Indian life.

During the week of his recovery the Rangers were far from idle. They had hunted all the squaws and papooses they could find out of the bottom, and had guarded them in a tent for a time, but became so tired of the troublesome charge at last that they gave them provisions and let them go. Not a day but scouting parties were going out and coming in, with little success, however. Indians do not invade the frontier in an army, but in squads of from three or four to fifty. To fight them is like keeping off mosquitoes; while you are chasing them in one direction they are coming in upon you in another. When it is remembered that the frontier of Texas is many hundred miles long, the difficulty of the task can be somewhat appreciated. As it is, Rangers — *i. e.*, men perpetually *ranging* along the frontier—are the only ones to defend it; the pomp and cumbrous machinery of the Regular service is totally out of place under such circumstances.

To while away the hours around the camp-fires by night every expedient was put in play. Gambling was forbidden, horse-racing too. Drinking was also prohibited, as well as impossible from lack of whiskey. As it was, every man told his story of frontier adventure with Indians and all sorts of game. The steam doctor was always a great deal more than ready with *his* experiences; the scalp-hunter had a tale an hour long for each of his scalps. Not a man, too, but could sing. "When I can read my title clear" was the favorite, sung in the longest possible metre, although in singular juxtaposition with many other melodies exceedingly unlike it. One would suddenly lead off, when everybody was thinking of something else, and the song would close with every voice on the ground joined in. Dancing, too—such dances as would have appalled a French dancing-master by their peculiar figures and the breadth of prairie essential to their performance—was very popular. A wild, jovial, whole-souled, reckless set they were, kind as women to the sick or suffering among them, more desperate than Indians in an affray. The discipline of their officers was that of good-fellowship and personal popularity rather than of drill and routine and arrest. It was far, very far from being the place for a youth to learn life in; and it would have been worse for Madison than it was, had it not been for the unusual respect felt by all for his uncle. As to Madison himself, what was yielded to him first from pity was more than confirmed as he moved among the men, as he rapidly got well, in his moccasons and buckskin apparel, pale and weak, yet with a ready smile on his brown, frank, intelligent face; he became, in fact, the hero of the camp. Young as he was, he already possessed, unconsciously to himself, the magical influence of a youthful Napoleon, in virtue of his fearless, sincere, pure-minded intelligence, the result of his training, as well as of the "good stock" from which he sprang.

It was ten days after his capture before the march homeward was begun—and greatly to the joy of both uncle and nephew. Both knew the sickening anxiety under which the family at home must be suffering in regard to them; but they had found no way of communicating with these since they had left. The morning after his rescue Madison had heard from his uncle of the death of the Mexican—heard it with deep sorrow. Though to Madison—and to all except the Texan himself—that Mexican continued ever after to be only the boy Francisco. The girl Dolores slept in the depths of the prairie bayou, and in the deep, serene memory of the Texan, too, more as a dream than a reality. For all, it was well it should have happened as it did.

It was six days' steady travel before Madison and his uncle parted with their companions at the base of Mount Hoogenboom, the Rangers going on to Austin, the capital, to be mustered out of service, the boy and his uncle hastening towards their dearly loved home on the San Hieronymo.

"We will say nothing to any one except your father and mother about the bar of silver, just yet," said the elder, as they rode along. "Nobody knows certainly who the old silver-hunters were. They may have been Spaniards a hundred years ago; they may have been Mexicans hunting for silver only some fifty years since; they may have been the old original, mysterious aborigines of the country many centuries past. Nobody knows, and nobody ever will know, I suppose. I took many a look at the wells near the camp. They are all alike — old silver-mines long abandoned. It might be because no silver could be found, if it were not for the bar you picked up."

"I've been thinking, uncle," said Madison, "that it was in this way: perhaps the miners, whoever they were, had works there long, long ago for refining and rolling-out the silver, and perhaps suddenly fierce savages of some sort came upon them, killed them all—"

"And burned up their works," interrupted his uncle. "Just what I thought possible; and in groping about there one day—I had to be careful lest the Rangers should suspect something — I came upon two things, each of which told its own separate secret. One was a stick of charred wood, almost overgrown by grass and brush—*that* whispered of a fire. The other was a skull with a hole—a hole on its *left* side, mark, made in a *fight* therefore."

"How? Why, uncle? I don't see that."

"Suppose an Indian was face to face with you, fighting. He raises his hatchet in his right hand and strikes your head."

"Oh, yes, it would be on the left side, sure enough."

"Well," continued the Texan, "we've guessed the history so far right. Careful search would be sure to reveal more. Why, if we only found, say, a spoon, or a button, or a coin, or—"

"Even a buckle or a bridle-bit or a stirrup, uncle," interrupted his nephew.

"Yes, almost any relic would tell the whole tale."

"Some of these days we must go there for a good search, uncle."

"Yes, *sir!*" replied the Texan, with emphasis. "We might get silver enough, Madison, to buy you three or four thousand head of cattle to begin to raise stock with. A man isn't really set up in such a country as Texas until he has a brand of a hundred thousand or so. Besides the curiosity of the thing, there's no telling what we might come across there. And then, too—"

"Oh, yonder is father and Will in the field!" exclaimed his nephew, interrupting him; and, putting spurs to Slow, Madison dashed to the fence, bounded off his pony, cleared the rails at a leap like a deer, he hardly knew how. Now, when a wandering son returns home in rags a father always knows exactly what to do. But in this case, at a shriek from Will, Mr. McRobert had looked up in time to see an Indian jump the fence and make full at him. It was too far to see the brown face distinctly; but buckskin, moccasons, bow, quiver, everything—it was an Indian! Mr. McRobert took for granted that the rest of the tribe would come streaming after the first over the field in an instant; for the country had been full of them, he knew. Will had picked up a clod of earth and jumped behind his father, already slaughtered, scalped, and eaten up in imagination. Josie came running up, instead, brandishing his inseparable hatchet in his hand. As to his father, he had been plugging watermelons in the field, and had the butcher-knife in his hand. This he grasped firmly; then dropped it and almost sank on the ground as the ferocious Indian came bounding along among the green corn, exclaiming, "Oh, father, father!"

Who can describe the father's joy, Josie's and Will's, too, as their brother seized each in turn in his arms and lifted him from his feet, held him high in the air, dropped him on the ground and ran on down the row between the standing corn towards the house. But the voice of his father arrested him—

"Stop, Madison! you will frighten your mother—wait!"

By this time Uncle Frank had come up, and received an ardent welcome. On account of his dress it was agreed that Madison should wait, while the rest went on to tell of their safe arrival. As soon as they were gone — it will never be known whether it were thoughtlessness or sheer mischief—Madison turned aside towards the negro cabin. He ought not to have done it, but he pushed open the door and stepped in upon Rohamma, Indian as he was, without a word of warning. Stooping over the fire, she was toasting coffee for supper. She gave one half-glance, and, dropping her spoon, rolled over helplessly among the pots and pans beside her, an easy victim for the tomahawk and scalping-knife. There was only one word on her pallid lips, and that was one which held ample meaning with her—"Tomas!"

But now the air rang with cries of "Madison! my boy!" There was the sound of light but swift-coming footsteps along the ground without, and the boy stepped out to receive his mother — his dear, dear mother—in his arms, upon his bosom, in a gush of silent tears, and kisses more silent still. And Bessie—for a week after she complained how hard her brother had hugged her. "He squeezed me tho!" she said. There was Hark, too, and 'Markable, as glad as the rest. No tongue can tell the joy with which the boy, only just now a captive among the Indians, walked along towards the house as well as he could for loved ones clinging about him, clasping and kissing him at every step. And Duke and Snap, too. Oh, home! home! It seemed heaven itself to Madison; he could have hugged the very gate-posts as he passed them. He felt as if he had been gone for months—even years. It was not until he had laid aside his Indian attire for one of his own suits that he could sit still if but for a moment in the joyful confusion.

"Ah! it's mighty plain nobody cares a cent for me," said Uncle Frank, at length. He was seated on a step of the long porch in front of the house, his back against one of the pillars, Bessie in his arms.

"Oh, Uncle Frank!" exclaimed Bessie, with a hug and a kiss, "how can you thay tho? Didn't we all hug you tho? and didn't ma and me kith you tho?" Another embrace and a kiss upon his bearded lip by the little witch, who was fatter and rosier than ever, and overflowing with affection.

"Yes; but nobody cared for me

while I was gone," said her uncle, taking her little hands in his.

"Oh yeth we did!" re, .d Bessie, eagerly. "Pa prayed for you tho ev'ry day at prayers, and brother Will and I prayed for you by the bed every morning and night; and Dodles nailed up our el'fant plank to a tree for uth to thee ev'ry day; and Mr. Crit'den prayed tho for you! And, oh yeth, yeth, Mith Agneth—!"

"Hush, Bessie!" interrupted her mother.

"Oh yeth, ma—yeth, uncle," persisted Bessie—"I didn't thee Mith Agneth cry any, or pray any; but oh! the looked tho thorry, thorry for you; and it wathn't for brother Madithon, I know, becauth—"

Here Miss Agnes herself, who had drawn near unperceived, stepped upon the porch, her sweet face all of a glow — from walking, probably; but not more so than that of Uncle Frank as he rose to greet her, his face glowing—probably from sitting still.

"Oh, Mith Agneth!" burst out Bessie, "poor Franthitheo dead, killed — poor Franthitheo! ain't you thorry?"

CHAPTER XVIII.

THE COMMUNION SABBATH.

Two weeks, happy weeks, have passed—happy to all the family on the San Hieronymo because the affection of each towards every other is now flowing with a deeper stream as from fountains enlarged; only the San Hieronymo itself is illustration sufficient of that. It is the Sabbath morning, and the month of July lies like a charm upon prairie and forest and the silent-flowing Colorado. The labors of Mr. Crittenden have been greatly successful in that secluded region, away from the distractions of business and fashion. Yesterday a church was organized by the minister so wonderfully sent them. Besides many of the neighbors living around, and of whom one would have liked greatly to have said something, only one is so afraid of making this story too long, there was Hoogenboom and his wife, Christians in the Old Country, glad to be members again of a visible Church. Yes, Hoogenboom had united in the organization with a profusion of red pocket-handkerchief, parting for a while even with his meerschaum for the purpose, and his wife in an extraordinary bonnet, not worn before since she left Germany. Then there were Miss Agnes, and Mr. and Mrs. Morton McRobert, who had also been members of the Church before. Rohamma and Hark, too, had both been consistent Christians for years before leaving Virginia, and their names too were enrolled. But there were two who united with the Church now for the first time, Uncle Frank and Madison. Alike they had received an early training; alike had they been the special objects of prayer and effort on the part of their friends for a year now; in the last few months they had alike passed through scenes which had awakened deep reflection and new resolves. The joy of the angels above in the event found an echo, if possible, deeper and sweeter still in the bosoms of those who looked on below. Uncle Frank was so bearded and bronzed and nobly rough in his way, yet so grave and calm, resolved and happy, even Bessie could not but notice the new beauty in the face of her darling uncle; it would have been a blind man who could not have observed it. And beside him now, as in sport and danger, was his nephew. The loving eyes of father and mother fairly devoured him as he sat that day in Uncle Frank's ranch, where the organization was accomplished. Just turning, as on a sudden, from the boy into the man, modest and yet manly, humble and yet resolved, happy and yet calm, no wonder he had become the pride and joy of his father and mother. Dodles, as well as Will, felt as if his brother had, in the last few weeks, risen higher, somehow above him, and felt for him a new reverence as well as a more relying affection. Words cannot utter the joy with which Mr. and Mrs. McRobert grasped the glowing hand of their brother, feeling that he was now doubly their brother, and held Madison to their hearts as trebly their son. As to Hark and Rohamma, none the less sincere was the hard hand with which each grasped

that, first of "Mass Frank" and then of "Mass Madison," and welcomed them into new relationship with them in that body in which all are one, whether bond or free.

"May de good Lord bless you, massa, an' bring you to glory at las'!" they said. Nobody could doubt the sincerity of *their* tearful eyes and white teeth glittering through the hearty smile. The organization of a group of Christians thrown together in the wild West into a church is to the individuals themselves, minister and all, one of those rare luxuries which are reserved among manifold privations for settlers upon the frontier; and never did Christians enjoy feelings deeper or sweeter than on that Saturday in the log ranch.

But it was now the Sabbath morning—the day following the organization. The whole neighborhood had assembled at the ranch. Already steps have been taken to build a neat church on a spot near by; but until then the ranch is used, as it long has been, for public worship. Let us stand just inside the door and look on. It is the largest room in the ranch, of logs, about twenty feet square. There are six or eight rows of seats, made of plank laid on hide-bottomed chairs, and covered with bedquilts, and every inch of space is occupied by—apparently, at least—a devout worshipper. There, on the front seat, sitting, like the rest, with their backs to the door, are Hoogenboom and his wife, with several white-headed children clustered about their knees or sitting on the floor at their feet. On the same seat are Mr. and Mrs. Morton McRobert, with Dodles, Will, and Bessie. Madison next his mother, and Uncle Frank next him, fill out that plank. Not three feet before them is the little pine table, covered with a gorgeous Mexican blanket, which is the pulpit; and behind it, against the wall, is Mr. Crittenden. On chairs to his right and left are seated Hark, Rohamma, and a few other negroes of the neighborhood. The service is just completed. The singing has been of old familiar hymns; the prayers and the sermon have been delightfully adapted to the occasion; the bread and the wine of the sacrament have been distributed; and the plates and glasses are again on the little table, with the Bible and the hymn-book, before Mr. Crittenden. He has just engaged in prayer, thanking God, with the hearts of all there on his tongue, for the feast they have enjoyed, and for employing him as a minister, "so unworthy, unworthy," in the blessed work. He has now extended his hands, and all rise to receive the benediction, which seems to flow from his outstretched palms upon the bowed heads before him.

As those of the congregation standing outside the door for want of room within bow their heads with the rest, they are conscious that some one has ridden on his horse near behind. Almost at the same instant they hear, in a low, coarse voice, a deep curse, followed by the sharp crack of a rifle not a foot, apparently, from their ears. Instantly they turn, in time to see the back of a man as he rides off at full speed. On the instant there is confusion, cries, shrieks, a whirlwind of uproar, from within the crowded cabin, out of which comes Frank McRobert, his rifle in his hand, which he has snatched — it was his first thought — from its wooden pins on the wall. All who see him are appalled by the whiteness of his face as he speeds, or rather leaps, along after the horseman. He surely cannot expect to catch the man! He runs like a deer; but by the time he has reached the edge of the timber in which the ranch is built the horseman is sixty yards from him on the prairie, and will soon be over the ridge and out of sight. The Texan falls on one knee as he catches sight of the fugitive, and, as in the same instant, the horse falls, struck by a ball from his rifle, which has broken its hind-leg just above the hoof. Before the fallen rider, blaspheming like a fiend, can disentangle himself from under his steed, he is in the grasp of his pursuer, his red hair and crimson face in strong contrast with the rigid pallor of the man who holds him. And the Texan seems to be in a sort of dream; he is not looking at the captive, is paying no attention to his struggles and curses. He is talking aloud to himself.

"Oh no, no, don't! don't! for your life — for your soul, don't do it! Don't! don't!" he continues, earnestly, incessantly. It is with himself that he is struggling and entreating. For a minute longer he has to hold down the ruffian without him and the devil within himself; and then—and before, stunned by his fall, the captive can grasp his weapons—twenty men are around him, and as many hard hands have hold of him as can find space to grasp.

"Thank God! thank God!" says the Texan, silently to himself as he steps back, "*my* hands are free from your blood; it was a narrow, a narrow escape."

It seems not ten minutes since profound peace reigned in and around the ranch, and now all is confusion and terror. The ruffian has been brought into the yard, and has been woven into a net-work of all the lariats to be had on the place. The man seems to be more astonished than anything else; with volumes of oaths he exclaims,

"Why, surely, I couldn't have killed the wrong man. Why, men—you fools—gentlemen—it was only the *preacher* I shot—the *preacher*, I say. I've got nothin' agin none of you. You ain't such fools as to care for him, *I* know. He killed my brother two years ago and a little over in Alabam. I was bound to get him. Come, you let me go. I've done nothin' to none of you, hev I?"

"Killed your brother?" say several, in a breath.

"Yes, gen-tle-men, my own dear brother—the smartest chap you ever seed; a man as never had a card up his sleeve in his life, never killed anybody 'cept in fair fight; we have ate all our lives out of the same trough. My own brother, gen-tle-men. I was bound to kill him, certain, and I done it."

"Gentlemen," exclaims Uncle Frank, in a loud, clear voice, high above all, "I happen to know the whole story. Mr. Crittenden *did* kill his brother. But it was because his brother grossly insulted his wife. Mr. Crittenden was often from home preaching. Once or twice this man's brother, Bob Dyson, a notorious scoundrel, had insulted Mr. Crittenden publicly, because of his hate for religion and anything like a preacher. Crittenden bore with it for months patient as a lamb, never gave the man the least cause. Bob Dyson only got madder at him, determined to drive him away, bring on a fight, kill him. One day Crittenden came home from preaching somewhere off. He found Dyson in his house—actually *in* his house, men—insulting his wife, men—a poor, sickly woman, men—*insulting* her, men! In a moment Crittenden had picked up the tongs—it was in winter—and had knocked the man down—killed him at one blow. I know all about it from his own lips, and from twenty people—I wrote back—living around! Hold on! hear the rest. Mrs. Crittenden died in consequence of it all. We can't understand it—remember he's a *preacher*—but somehow his conscience troubled him. He was acquitted on trial right away; but that he, a minister, had killed a man, he couldn't bear to think of it—he couldn't bear to look anybody in the face, and he fled out here. He was around here for months, starving, before we found him out. Hush, men! one word more. Natchez under the Hill never saw two worse men than Bob and Buck Dyson. It's Bob Dyson Mr. Crittenden killed, men; that man there is Buck Dyson you've all read about. Killed his own father, you remember. *Buck Dyson!*"

"Yes, and I'll tell you what it is, men," said the ruffian, with oaths, "this here Buck Dyson will settle accounts with some of *you*, sure! You let me loose, it's only a preacher I've killed. I wish I could shoot down the whole raft of them! I'll mark every one of you; and as soon as I'm loose I'll not leave a man of you that ain't richer by an ounce of cold lead. Texas? Eh! Texas! you can manage yellow Mexicans—you can't manage Alabamy boys. Come, now, I want to get loose!"

There was not a syllable of reply. Hoogenboom was slowly winding round and round the ruffian an ox-chain which he had taken off the oxen that had dragged his family to meeting, regardless of the curses of his victim. The rest stood around in silence — not a whisper even among them. As the Texan walked away towards the house, one of the neighbors followed him quietly and laid his hand upon him; he turned almost fiercely upon him.

"No!" he exclaimed, "I won't—won't! Don't you say one word to me, Lem Johnson. You mind your own business. I tell you what it is. I won't stir a finger, and I won't hear one word;" and he disappeared in the house and suddenly came out again.

"Hoogenboom," he said, "you and Hark put that man in the ox-wagon and pack him up to your cabin. Take more lariats if he needs it. I'll be along to-morrow;" and he again entered the house. In accordance with his command, Hark yoked in the oxen (tethered near by under a mesquit, peacefully chewing the cud, indifferent to the passions raging so near them), drove up the wagon, and, with the assistance of the silent Dutchman, lifted up the ruffian and laid him, bound hand and foot, and never ceasing to complain of his treatment, in the bottom of the wagon.

"Handled by a nigger and a Dutchman!" he exclaimed with disgust; "well, that *is* hard to bear. But I'll pay you."

At a word from the Dutchman, his wife, accompanied by her children, climbed in beside him—shrinking to the front, as far as possible from their passenger — and so they drove off. The yard was full of men, yet not a word was spoken. Some were whittling sticks, others were getting up their horses or buggies; none paid any attention to the wagon as it rolled away out of the yard and along the road leading up into the brake. The profound indifference manifested seemed to appall the ruffian — at least he lay silent, saying not a word. Hark walked behind all the way, and it was late in the afternoon when they reached the door of the Dutchman's cabin, far away up among the rocks on the side of the mountain. As they lifted the ruffian out, he made a violent effort to escape; but it was hopeless, the knots had been tied too tightly. It was a heavy load for the two as they bore him, ox-chain and all, into the cabin and laid him down like some loathsome red reptile, filthy and dangerous, on the bed on one side of the room. In answer to his request, Hark gave him a gourd of water, holding it to his lips as he sat up to drink.

"Fifty dollars in gold," he whispered to the negro, "if you'll only cut one place in the rope. Nobody will see. One hundred — two hundred—three hundred!"

The negro, deaf as a post, carried the gourd back to the water-bucket. He did not look once into the eager face and hungry eyes, but silently took his leave. The ruffian turned on his side with a curse and looked at the Dutchman. He had first taken off his Sabbath coat and hung it carefully behind a calico curtain on the wall. One side of the room was covered with shelves crowded with books from floor to ceiling, and a German student-lamp stood on the mantel, but he did not seem disposed to read or talk. With his huge wool hat drawn over his head, he then sat down in his old arm-chair with his side to the prisoner and his meerschaum in his hand. The captive watched him as he slowly and methodically filled his pipe, raked a coal out of the ashes on the hearth, lighted it, and began to smoke, his dog Schlick, yellow and hairless, lying beside him with its eyes on the stranger. The wife had gone with her children into the little shed adjoining to put off her best clothes and to prepare supper. The eyes of the prisoner brightened.

"Mister, I beg your pardon, I haven't hearn your name yet," he said, in a conciliatory manner.

"Hoogenboom," said his host, removing the pipe from his lips and replacing it immediately.

"Hoogenboom!" said his guest— "you don't mean Hoogenboom? Why, I've a cousin of that name. A cousin? Hah! that was my *wife's* maiden name. Say! we are relations. I'm glad to make your acquaintance!"

The Dutchman smoked on placidly in silent attention.

"Yes," continued the man, "a Hoogenboom she was. She has told me five hundred times of a brother she had in Texas—let's see —a brother?—I think, or an uncle, was it? A cousin—something. She used to be talking about you forever."

The Dutchman listened with grave countenance.

"I say, you, look here," continued the man, after a long pause, "I wish you would just loosen this rope a little—it hurts a fellow. I can't talk."

A silent puff of smoke was the only reply.

"You're a steady-going business man; I can see that with half an eye," continued the ruffian, after another and longer silence still. "A solid, substantial business man, and no mistake. You're not very rich, I know. I'm a plain, straightforward fellow. You let me go, and I've got three hundred dollars in a belt here around me—they are yours. Heh?"

Not a syllable of reply.

"You can get it off me yourself, and lock it up in your chest there before you loose me, man. I'll tell you what — you won't believe me, perhaps, but there's five hundred — five *hundred* did I say? I mean five *thousand* dollars in gold in my saddle-bags down where my horse fell;" and here he broke into a torrent of curses upon the Texan who had disabled his horse. "You let me go, and you may have them every cent."

Had Hoogenboom been sitting for his portrait, he could not have been more dignified and severe in his repose of manner.

"Five thousand *dollars*, man," said his prisoner. "What do you care for that pale-faced preacher? Who would have dreamed that you people out here would have cared so much for a *preacher?* I never was more disappointed in a set of men in my life!" This was said with strong disgust.

The Dutchman here filled his pipe afresh, and resumed his repose of manner.

"Look here, man," said his prisoner, after another silence, with the sudden ferocity of a wolf at bay—"you let me go, now, straight away. You'd better. As sure as you don't I'll murder you and every child you have! I'm Buck Dyson. 'Tain't the first time I've been a prisoner and got off; and I always kill the men that take me—*always!*—after I get out. I've plenty of dimes to pay the lawyers—plenty of friends to slip a file in through the bars. It isn't wholesome—it's worst sort for

your health to keep me here!" and he wound up with a perfect fury of execrations. But Mount Hoogenboom itself was not more unmoved under the blowing of a norther than was the Dutchman now. He seemed rather to be listening as to something from without, and smoked silently on. And so for an hour the prisoner wasted threatening, entreaty, bribery, alternately — used every art known to him in a long experience— only paused from exhaustion—it was like wind against granite.

As the shades of night darkened, the wife of the Dutchman, white and silent, came in, set the table, spread the supper of bread, fried bacon, and buttermilk upon it. The father, mother, and children then gathered around. The Dutchman, laying aside his hat and pipe, asked a blessing in German, and the family proceeded with their supper silently, the children eating with frightened side glances at the prisoner.

"You surely won't let a man lay under your roof a-starvin' to death, and you eatin' before his very eyes, madam?" said the prisoner. "Jest loose one arm enough to eat a bite; I haven't had anything for six days — nine at least. I'll pay you for it."

The woman stole a glance at her husband. He replied in one syllable, and the family proceeded with their meal — finished it. The table was removed, the hearth swept, the father again resumed his chair, his pipe, his placid repose—listening, though, all the time, as for something.

"Won't you come here, little buddy ? — come here, sis — come here a moment, and I'll give you a pretty," whispered the man to the children. But at a half-word from the mother they only clustered more closely about their parents near the empty fireplace. The family seemed to be expecting something or somebody. At every sound without each gave a perceptible start, except the father, who sat immovable, with his eye upon the door, enveloped in the smoke from his pipe. Suddenly a new thought seemed to flash upon the Dutchman. At a quick word from him, his wife laid a large book in his lap, lighted and put on the table the student-lamp beside her husband, for it was now quite dark.

"Mine friend, mine friend," said the Dutchman, putting on his spectacles eagerly, and addressing his captive for the first time, "dis is de goot Book; let me read you one, two, dree lines about Christ and your soul. You in great danger—let me read, let me pray wid you." And he spoke in an earnest and hurried way, in singular contrast with his manner before. The man regarded him at first with astonishment, and then repelled the offer with a paroxysm of oaths. Again and again, with greater and greater earnestness, and as if in a hurry to do it as soon as possible, the German urged the matter, but in vain. He even attempted to read and then to pray, in spite of the man's resistance, but it was impossible. The ruffian broke out into a vile song, at the top of his voice, as he lay, drowning every other sound.

Silently, at last, the Dutchman resumed his chair and his pipe, more phlegmatic, if possible, than before —his children and wife seated beside him before the fireplace, their backs to the bed—waiting, listening.

As there came a sound of footsteps without, the woman drew up her wondering children about her, and bowed her head down among them, weeping and praying, her husband giving no sign of intelligence. He well knew that there were no jails to hold the man within fifty miles; plenty of friends to rescue him if they had time to hear of his arrest; in any case, plenty of lawyers to quibble and put off trial. In a word, the man knew that if the legal course were followed, the escape of the desperado, and his unchecked, exasperated course of future crime were a certainty. In any case, he was helpless to defend his prisoner without bloodshed, and he sat and smoked in silence, awaiting what he knew was coming, though not a syllable or a gesture from any one had intimated it.

As his wife bowed her head, there was a blow on the door and the little cabin was full of men. The children stared in terror, the yellow dog cowering under their feet, snarling and barking; neither the Dutchman nor his wife even looked around. Without a word spoken, or a sound, save the yells and curses of the prisoner, twenty hands were in an instant upon the man, and twenty arms lifted him off the bed and hurried him out. It seemed but a moment more, and the woman was weeping aloud convulsively on her knees beside her husband, and the sound of many rapid footsteps had died away outside, leaving the cabin in a silence and solitude appalling from the suddenness thereof. All night long the family sat cowering about the cold hearth-stone, the father smoking steadily and silently in the centre. When the morning sun dawned, its beams fell upon a stunted live-oak, miles away from any home, in an obscure ravine among the mountains; and the rays, flickering through its scanty foliage, fell upon a new-made grave beneath its largest limb. The mesquit grass had been trampled down around, as by the tread of many feet, and a close observer might have detected the bark rubbed away in places upon the limb overhead, as by the friction of a rope. At least, never again was the desperado seen by man in Texas, Alabama, or elsewhere. Very rarely was his name mentioned in the neighborhood, and soon the whole event had sunk into the Past under the current of fresher things.

CHAPTER XIX.

A LITTLE REST.

"When I have become immensely rich, and have ten or twenty thousand head of cattle grazing in the prairies around, and a magnificent two-story frame house on my ranch, with a cupola on top, and a splendid coach and four, and a sideboard loaded down with silver plate, I was just deciding what ought I to have as my coat of arms to paint upon the carriage-panels, and stamp upon the plate, and have worked upon the linen, and embossed upon all the letter-paper." Two months had passed since the events last recorded, and it was Uncle Frank who spoke, rocking at ease, in the capacious arm-chair upon the front porch of the house on the San Hieronymo, with the family grouped around.

"It must be this delicious moonlight which makes you so romantic, Frank," said his sister-in-law. "But do let us hear what you have selected as your coat of arms. Two revolvers crossed? or a bear and a hunter rampant? or what?"

"No, I would have a Spanish dagger-tree in full bloom, with the motto, 'Joy after Sorrow.' It's an idea that struck me the first time we visited this spot together a day or two after your arrival. Yonder is the very plant that I then pointed out to you when I made the remark. The plant, you see, is found only, or mainly, in Texas: that would show that I'm a Texan, heart and soul. It's an evergreen, needs no rain, seems to enjoy perpetual summer, and defies the bitterest blast of winter: that, too, would be emblematic of Texas and a genuine Texan. There it is, a perfect mass, from the hardy root up, of bristling spikes, not to be trampled down, even touched safely, by anything, beast or man. But the whole bristling tree ends in and is crowned by the towering, fragrant, splendid flower. Yes, Joy after Sorrow — joy growing out of sorrow; trouble, pain, anguish, trial, all ending superbly in happiness. It's a splendid crest, a noble emblem!"

"Yes," replied his sister-in-law; "but you should let *us* have it. Remember how our great trouble in Virginia has ended in the happiness we, as a family, possess this night on the San Hieronymo."

"No, madam, you must hunt up your own coat of arms," said the Texan, smiling. "You forget that I was a good-for-nothing runaway youth from Virginia. You do not know half the troubles and trials I have seen out here in Texas long before you came, and since, too, if you only knew them. It was that Communion Sabbath I began to flower— sterile, barren, rough, dangerous backwoodsman that I was—there is not a more worthless plant rooted in the prairie than I was. From that Sabbath I began, in my poor way, to flower, and just out of the darkest of moments."

"Let me decide the dispute," said Agnes, who sat beside him. "You will both of you yield to *me*. Think of my long and bitter sorrow before coming to Texas. And think of that hour father fell, shot down before my eyes. Only remember that dreadful, dreadful day I sat there on the floor, in the confusion of shrieking women and children, his white head on my lap, his dear life flowing swiftly away, deprived in one hour of my home, my father—it almost seemed to me, of my God. And then in that same hour—of all the hours of my life—to find so much in Frank—that darkest hour the beginning of the happiest days I have ever known. At least, not your coat of arms alone, Frank, *our* coat of arms, say." And she laid her little hand in his.

"I never rode so fast in my life," said Madison, speaking rapidly as if to relieve his uncle. "When you hurried out to me from the house, told me I was the only one there you could trust, and how important it was I should go and return as soon as possible, I felt as if I had wings. And I was not *very* long in getting to town and to the county courthouse, I know. The clerk had gone to bed and wouldn't get up; but I sent in word to his wife, and she made him do so, knowing what I was after. When I got him to the courthouse, he said that he had lost the office key and wanted to stop and look for it. I gave one jump against the door and stood, or rather lay, on the floor in the centre of the office. Then I got a newspaper ready, and the instant the old clerk had written out and stamped the license I had pressed it on the newspaper to dry it. Next I had folded it up, put it in my breast-pocket, paid the clerk for it and the broken lock, and was on my horse again in double-quick time.

10

'You'll do for Texas, do for Texas!' said the white-haired old clerk, and he came out. He wanted to shake hands with me, as well as tell me good-bye, when I mounted; I was sorry I had no time for it. Do all I could, it was daybreak before I got back."

"I remember so well," said Agnes, in a low, soft voice, "all that father said as he lay there so calm, and happy even. 'It was an angry blow—one angry blow Moses gave the rock that offended God,' he said. 'For that one blow, after all his long, weary wandering in the desert, he was not permitted to enter the promised land—only saw it at a distance and died. I was just entering on success in this wide, rich field of labor,' he said, 'and now I die, for that one wicked, wicked blow.' And yet how willing he was to die! 'Since my great sin God has in mercy permitted me to do some good in Texas,' he said. 'But oh! how I would like, if it pleased God, to live a few years —only a few Sabbaths even! I never knew how to preach at all before my great sorrow. Now I am just beginning to learn. Heaven is a bright and happy place; but if I only could stay here a little longer, to do a little more good—only to make up in some degree for the reproach I have brought on the Gospel!'"

"'Tis strange," said the Texan. "That night I carried him over to the ranch from Hark's cabin, and a hundred times since, I told him he did right in killing Bob Dyson. It was no use. 'I needn't have killed him,' he would always say. 'I might have entreated him; or I might have taken him in my arms and put him out of the house. It's the death of his *soul* I look at. To see my wife pale and trembling there was the sight that maddened me. But the instant after, when I saw that man lying dead on the carpet by the fireplace, so red and bloated and brutal, gone in the very instant of blasphemy and violence and desperate wickedness, not a moment for thought and repentance allowed him—it was the ghastly dead *soul* lying at my feet, and I a minister of the Gospel, whose business is to *save* souls, and to be an example of all meekness—it was this that overwhelmed me.'"

"And you remember," said Mrs. Morton McRobert, her eyes filling with tears as she spoke, "what he said about saving little Will's life. 'It was God,' he said, 'who ordered it that I should be on the river bank just at the right instant. When I snatched the little fellow out of the jaws of death, and had him warm and living again in my arms, it was the first flash of light on my darkness. I took a life,' he said, 'and now God has so wonderfully permitted me to save a life. Surely it is a token of forgiveness. And who knows, dear madam,' he said to me, 'but that I then saved from death a life that is to be of use to the world? I do believe so! Train him for it, madam,' he said." As she spoke the mother drew her boy nearer to her side, her arm around him.

"There was one thing that strikes me now with awe as I think of it," said Agnes, sinking her voice still lower in the hushed silence of the group around. "It was half an hour before Madison got back that morning. He had been talking of other things. Suddenly he thought for the first time of his murderer. He had said nothing about him—supposed him to have escaped safely. Yet suddenly he began to pray for him as he lay. His eyes were shut, his face deadly pale, but he clasped his hands together over the wound in his side, and seemed in an agony of prayer. 'Father, forgive him; he knew not what he did!' he said. 'Spare me, spare me *this* soul! Open his eyes now, now! Let him not die in sin!' He prayed as if by the bedside of a dying sinner, it must have been near half an hour. And then he opened his eyes and smiled upon me as if he felt entirely relieved. 'I do believe, Agnes,' he said, his face full of joy—'I do believe that my prayer for Dyson is heard.' Was it not strange?"

"Ah, that may account for what Lem Johnson told me," said the Texan, in a tone that thrilled every heart. "I don't like to refer to the thing but for this. All the way from Hoogenboom's he was struggling and yelling and blaspheming like a fiend. But just before he got to the spot he became still, on a sudden, as death. When they laid him on the ground under the tree, he begged them, in tones altogether changed, to wait with him a moment. It wasn't fright either, nor fawning, for he knew his men too well for that. The men halted from their work while he confessed all he had ever done; it was a terrible tale of crime—ten times worse than any one had ever suspected. Lem told me it made his blood curdle there in the moonlight to hear that man, sitting on the ground in the centre of them, telling the whole story like a little child. He seemed sorry from his very heart—and Lem isn't a man to be easily deceived; he's been present at too many such things. 'I don't know why it is, men,' Dyson said, 'but up to a few moments ago I was Buck Dyson to the core. Now a something has come over me—a power, a force, a something awful, men, and I ain't the same man. I've been as near death as this before,' he said; ''tain't that. A something has got at, got *into*, my heart. Now, from my soul I'm sorry for what I've done. God sees it; you can't. He sees it, and that's enough for me. Sorry, sorry, all through and through and through. I've heard Crittenden—the man I killed to-day—say that a man must repent—that means be sorry for his rascalities—and believe in Christ, who died to save sinners. Now I *do* repent. I *know* that certain, sure. And I'm a-trying now, men, to believe in Christ *hard!* I heard tell once of a rough that was crucified next Christ, and *he* believed in Christ there. If *he* could, I'll try.' Lem told me he never heard such a prayer as that man prayed then and there, kneeling among the rocks, so low— not loud like—so fervent, catching hold on God with desperate hands, pleading for mercy. Some of the men actually cried, he said. 'Suppose we let him go,' said Lem; 'at least let's hold on to him till he can be tried and hung all regular.' Dyson stood straight up on his feet at that. 'No, men,' he said—'no, not at all, not a bit of it. I've deserved to die just this death fifty times. Better die now, here this quiet night, off alone here by ourselves. And I do hope, trust, ac'lly believe, I'm a pardoned man! I've got God's pardon, men; yours is no account—that is, in comparison. Let me die, gentlemen. I've got a poor crippled sister at home; father threw her out of the window when he was drunk, and I killed him for it. Please send her what I leave in this belt and the saddle-bags.' And he told them where to send. 'Write her I died repentant,' he said. Lem says he stood there that midnight another man from Buck Dyson altogether; it almost seemed wrong to hang him. But they did it. I never would have told all this but for what you said about Mr. Crittenden's praying just at that same hour for him."

There was a long silence after this. No one on the porch seemed inclined to speak or even move. At last, and to give a turn to the tide of thought, Mrs. Morton McRobert said,

"Next to that belief in his prayer being answered, I believe it was your marriage, Agnes, that did most to soothe his dying hour."

"And it was so strange," said Agnes. "Not a word, hardly a look, had ever passed between Frank and myself about even the possibility of such a thing. I didn't know — that is, I was not sure—that he loved me.

At least — yes, I knew well enough that I loved *him*," she added, smiling.

"It was the boldest, coolest thing, I *do* think, I ever did," said the Texan. "I whispered to you to come out for one moment—only one. I don't know what I said to you when I tried to ask you about it. I haven't the least recollection what you said to me—I don't really believe you said anything at all. But Madison was off and back again with the license, and sister here prepared your father for it, and he married us as we knelt down beside his pallet on the floor. It was just after his prayer for Dyson. This, taken with that, seemed to fill the measure of his peace, and he was gone."

Another long and happy silence. A deep and holy calm had settled upon all. The breeze sighed gently among the trees, the moonbeams sparkled brightly upon the San Hieronymo, and the rapids of the Colorado were heard in the distance.

"How much we all have learned since we have been in Texas!" said Mr. Morton McRobert, at last. "The old prophets, and John the Baptist, and our Saviour taught their most precious lessons to people who came out to them, away from the cities and villages, into the wilderness to learn. And Christ never fed the multitude except in "a desert place." I think *I* at least have learned something since I reached this spot—that is to do the best I can through the darkest hour, trusting quietly in God."

"And I hope I have shared the lesson with you," said his wife, laying her hand in his. "How many dangers and privations have we been threatened with, and yet how happy our home has been all the time!"

"I ought to have learned the same too," said Madison, "that night out on the burning prairie, and at the springs when Dyson had hold of me, and up among the Indians. I've got that quiver, bow, arrows, paint-bag, Iron-Jacket's armor, and the powder-horn that burst by me in the fire that night, all hanging up in a row against the wall of my room, as reminders of it all. It beats Will's museum of bugs and snakes and things, big as that is, all to pieces. I need them, for I'm very apt to forget."

"As to us," said the Texan, drawing the head of his wife upon his bosom, "till Agnes and I get rich enough to have the coat of arms on our silver and carriage, we'll plant a perfect hedge of the yuca—the dagger-plant—about our ranch to remind *us* of the same thing. We have all learned the same lesson in common, being here in the same school together."

How little they knew the future! While they spoke, the most terrible catastrophe was impending over them. It was to be as if the dagger-plant had suddenly grown to heaven, its terrible points overshadowing the whole land, and transfixed upon every one of them a human heart, quivering, bleeding, perishing!

CHAPTER XX.

TWO YEARS AFTER.

We must take—like one of Madison's deer—a leap, and a long one.

"It is only two years since that night the prairie was on fire—two years this morning! Hah! perhaps so. But it seems to me more like ten; for since then the South has seceded, and all the world has gone to smash."

It is Uncle Frank who says it. His beard is more luxuriant, his eye is brighter, his face, if possible, more browned by the sun and the never-ending winds; certainly he is a stouter, comelier Texan than we left him in our last chapter. For probably the ten-thousandth time in his life he is engaged in cleaning out his favorite rifle at a stump, the broad top of which has been neatly levelled off to make a table, in his brother's front yard. Upon the stump lie his revolvers, with which he has just got through. No children in the neatest household in Christendom are more regularly and thoroughly washed than they. You can see at a glance that his bowie-knife, which he has stuck into a tree beside him, out of Bessie's ever-curious reach, has a new edge from whetstone and strap. He is refreshed, as he works, by having, every ten minutes or so, his rosy-cheeked and very plump baby brought to him to be kissed by his pretty wife, who generally seizes the same opportunity of kissing both of them herself, in view of the event for which all the preparation is on foot.

Near by sits Madison at work, cross-legged, upon the straps and buckles of his uncle's Mexican saddle. Dodles can be heard chopping and hammering at some one of his manifold "contraptions," Will calls them, in the back yard. Will is manufacturing a leather satchel. Mr. Morton McRobert is in the house writing vigorously at his desk. The ladies and servants are grinding coffee and baking bushels of biscuits and hard cakes, as if for an army about to march. Bessie is eagerly supplying all her friends with water for the washing, thread and wax for the sewing, chips for the baking, and innumerable questions for the answering. But it is very evident that all the unusual activity of the hour has reference to Uncle Frank.

"Two years!" And the Texan pushed back the brim of his great wool hat from his brow with the left hand, holding his rifle, end down for the water to run out, with his right.

"We lived so quietly, uncle, up here, all among ourselves—so happily, too—that we hardly knew or cared what was going on in the world. Why," continued Madison, looking up from his saddle, "my father always taught me the Union was patterned after the solar system, each separate star having its own independent axis and orbit, yet each and all revolving about a great centre. I no more dreamed of the Union being broken up than I did of all the planets tumbling apart. It looks to me like trying to upset nature itself. We've been too busy up here to study such matters as closely as we might; but, for my part, I can't believe it, I *won't* believe it, at least not yet."

"I never believed they even meant to *try* such a foolish thing till that day I went down to Austin," replied his uncle. "There was a fellow in the Convention, just below where I sat in the gallery, with their Ordinance of Secession spread out on his desk. Leaning a little over the railing, I could have spit right in the centre of it, and it was all I could do not to do it. I told you about what Agnes sitting next to me said. 'Just do it,' she whispered to me—she must have seen it all in my face—'do it, do it! I'll say it was *me!* If I could only get my hands on it, I would tear it up. *I* ain't afraid,' she said. But they passed it, and signed it, and put it in a long tin case, and labelled it, and put it on a shelf behind the glass doors of the book-case in the State Department there in the Capitol. I've seen it often since.

"And that day they summoned Sam Houston to the bar to take their new oath," continued the Texan. "Yes, I was there. I never will forget that Lieutenant-Governor Clarke stepping up to the desk, so spry and pert, to take it instead, when no Sam Houston answered. Sam was like a big bear retreating slowly before a pack of curs—giving way, but his eyes and teeth towards them all the time. Despising them, growling at them, striking at them right and left with his paws when they pressed on him too near. I wonder," added the speaker, pausing with his oiled rag over the lock of his rifle as he spoke —"I do wonder what would have been the upshot of the business if old Sam *had* listened to some of us. There were enough of us to do it. He had only to say the word, and we would have sent that Convention whirling soon enough! 'No, no, gentlemen,' he said, in that slow way of his—I can see him now sitting in his large chair, whittling crosses and hearts and such like out of white pine while he talked —'no, no, my friends; those fools up-stairs'—we were talking to him in his room in the basement of the Capitol—'are going head-foremost to ruin; but no, I cannot imbrue my hands in the blood of my fellow-citizens. Won't you take some of these trifles to remember me by?' he said, as we were leaving, holding out an old cigar-box on the table by him, brimful of his tobacco-stoppers, crosses, and things. Not a man of us took one! He was a wise man, a great man, a good man—that is, of late years; he had his good wife to thank for that. But he was old, that was the trouble — too old. There he lives this moment at his place on the Bay, making a hard living, by boating wood to Galveston for sale, growling at the madmen who have *got* us, prophesying, as he always did, only ruin, ruin as the end of it all. What I say—"

"Better take the sober, sensible view of matters which I do, Frank," interrupted his brother, who had come out from his writing during the last few moments, and was tossing Bessie in the air by way of exercise. "We are Union men. Yes; but why? Because our father was so before us. No one was more devoted to the Union than our mother, too, for that matter. Then, all our nearest associates in Virginia held the same opinions. I am sure we never permitted a newspaper to come into the house that did not teach the same. So, ever since we were born. I believe we have been right in our opinions; but no merit in you or in me for that. We couldn't *help* thinking and feeling as we do—it's part of our very nature. And isn't it exactly so with the other side? In almost every case their parents, associates, reading, have been exactly the opposite from ours, and they are, in consequence, just what they are to-day. Mind," added he, with a species of calm warmth, "not that I do not hate their course as much as any man can; not that I do not pray it may be an utter failure; not that I would not fight against it, however sorrowfully, if I could; yet all my feeling for the men themselves is chiefly pity —pity—not hatred!"

"Oh, these ladies, these ladies!" groaned the younger brother, as he proceeded to put his rifle lock on again, dipping each screw in the saucer of oil before him as he placed it in its hole.

"You never were more mistaken, Frank," replied his brother, coloring a little, "Mrs. McRobert naturally feels for her native state—is indignant at the outrages committed by the Federals. I have often explained to her the principles involved. The feelings of the other sex are stronger and deeper than ours."

"And those Yankees up North are talking about giving the women the right of voting—as if they didn't rule the land already, at the South at least! I don't know how about it at the North," said Uncle Frank, mournfully. "Not but what I respect and esteem and love them as much as any man doing his level best can," he added, earnestly; "only I do wish with all my soul they would, here in the South—"

But what he desired of the sex was lost upon the ears of all by the sudden ringing of the dinner-bell, accompanied by the joyful cries of Bessie, whose feelings, being of that gender, were excitable, even in reference to a meal, especially when, as is the case to-day, there was to be a pudding.

At dinner there were a hundred things to be said, for there was no telling how long it might be before they would see Uncle Frank again. For so many weeks, now, they have had his trip in contemplation as to wear off a good deal of the eager interest in it they might otherwise have had. Near a dozen times before has he been ready to start for Mexico—his provisions packed, his horse saddled at the gate—when something would arise to make it barely possible for him to stay a little longer.

"You see, this is the way I put it up," he had announced to all under that roof long before, and very often indeed; "there's some things I can do; some things I can't do. I *can* make a break for Mexico; but I cannot go into the Confederate ranks —cannot! For two reasons: first, I would be mighty apt to shoot, in the first battle, my own officers who dragged me, against my conscience, into the fight by the ears like a dog. Second, in any battle I might accidentally kill some Federal or other; and that, with my views, would be worse murder still. Moreover, suppose I did pester and beg and beseech until I got a detail to do something so as to stay at home, wouldn't I have to take that oath, eh? I'd die first!—at any rate, what is about as bad, leave wife and baby here. Yes," the Texan continued, doggedly, "I'll go to Mexico first!"

"This time you shall go, Frank, if I have to put you on your horse with my own hands, and give him a good cut with a switch to start him!" exclaimed the elder Mrs. McRobert, in a laughing tone, but with tears in her eyes; while his wife said nothing, only looked upon him with anxiety and speechless affection.

"You know how it was with Mr. Maginnis, uncle," said Madison, grown now nearly as large as uncle or father. "That Tuesday I was there, while we were spinning that *cabris* together—there it hangs—he said to me, 'Well, Madison, they've been here again.' 'The same men after the horses?' I asked. 'No, another set—three men. They said they had orders to seize my horses for use in the army. I only told them the first man who lariated a horse of mine, I would shoot on the spot. With that, off they went, saying they would see about it. I'm not afraid of them,' he went on to say; 'it is months ago they told me I must take the oath. I told them I wouldn't. "You must," they said; "I won't," I replied. "Why, they'll kill you if you don't," they told me. "I can *be* killed, then," I said.' The reason is, he was Scotch-Irish—obstinate as he could be," continued Madison.

"And I told him, when he rode home with you that night, how wicked it was to expose his life for the sake of a few horses," said Madison's father. "I reasoned with him for hours about it, you remember. He told me that he was the first man in his county to pay his Confederate taxes; that he always gave every Confederate soldier that came along board and bed; that while he couldn't and wouldn't voluntarily give any money to help the war, he gave as much as any man to the poor, the widows, and orphans. He made me a solemn promise that he would yield everything rather than resist and be killed—all except taking the oath."

"That was Wednesday," said Madison. "Thursday morning sixteen men rode up to the door of his ranch and demanded his horses. He told them there they were, pointing over the prairies, where hundreds of them were grazing. 'And I will drive them up, and let you take your pick,' he said. No, they wanted what he had up already. They went there only to kill him. He had only one horse up, his favorite horse, the only thing then in the corral to herd up the rest on the range. They said they'd take that horse! Then he got excited—he had been trampled upon so long. You remember he led the horse out of the stable by the halter wrapped around his arm. The captain of the men ordered them to seize the animal. Oh!" continued Madison, with enthusiasm, "was not Mr. Maginnis a true gentleman? gentle as a woman, kind, even refined, when you once knew the man, under his rough clothes and great beard and plain ways, living out from society among his horses so long: a Christian gentleman, if there ever was one — Mr. Maginnis drew his revolver and shot his horse through the head rather than they should have him. The next instant the captain gave the word to his men, and there he lay, in his own stable-yard, sixteen bullets through his body!"

"Yes, Madison," said Will, eagerly, "and you remember, while he was lying in his *jacal* gasping in death, the men who killed him were sauntering over the place, laughing and talking. One of them lounged into the room where he lay, and when Mr. Maginnis said, 'There's one of my murderers,' the man replied, 'Yes, you old scoundrel, and I'll just put another bullet through you if you say a word!' I only wish," continued the excited boy, "I could—"

"Silence!" interrupted his mother. "They were wicked men; God will surely punish them. Yet the Federals too have done a thousand things as bad, even worse, in Virginia. There are abandoned men everywhere."

"Yes, it *is* a terrible trial to the

women in the South," said Mr. Morton McRobert, sadly, as he walked up and down the porch, after they had come out from dinner again; "even those who had been trained from childhood to love the Union; who have brothers, fathers, husbands, devoted Union men; who as fully understand the principles involved in the war as anybody. Hearing and reading daily of Federal raids; of the desperate valor of the Confederate troops; of heavy losses among relatives at the South, if not enduring it in their own negro quarters and smoke-houses; of deaths in camp and battle from among relatives and from their own hearth; then all the ingrained, life-long prejudices of section— No one," he continued, "denies the existence of the beautiful and eternal stars, ever moving in their serene orbits above us all; but oh! let us make all gentle, ay, just allowance, for those between whom and these gather dense clouds, hanging low and heavy with tears, and for so long! Even while his awful hand accomplishes his will on earth, the Heavenly Father bends pityingly over those bleeding on both sides, bends far more pityingly than we whom little merit of our own has cast on the right and, I hope, victorious side — he, as much greater than we in love as he is in justice and might."

But the family have a hundred things to do in case Uncle Frank really *does* have to be off to-night for Mexico. Duke and Snap, evidently wide awake to something unusual going on, and frequently conferring together as to what it is, have to be securely chained up, lest they should follow the one departing. Bullets have to be moulded; clothes repaired and packed into the smallest space; the horse shod; nothing forgotten of sugar, salt, pepper, a little medicine, and a vast deal of coffee, for the haversack. There are a thousand things to do, and every soul is as busy as possible, in order to avoid thinking of the actual leaving of Uncle Frank, whose broad, free, wholesome, hearty nature makes perpetual summer on the San Hieronymo. He, in bosom and wide-brimmed hat, is himself a sort of Texas, with all its prairie and genial clime— "worth," Madison says, "precisely nineteen million nine hundred and ninety-nine thousand city dandies!" One woman who followed him in his every motion that afternoon would have added to that the population of London, Paris, Pekin, and Jeddo—yes, even Charley, the baby, too—and not find his side of the scale even quiver therefrom. Only, in such times as these, you see, we all get used to such things. If the keen edge remained all the years through, it would cut the heart to pieces.

And so, before we know it, we have the yard filled with rough men, all garbed, like Uncle Frank, for travel. They came in, somehow, one by one—very quietly, too. Although they have stationed pickets all about the place to guard against surprise, every Union man of the twenty-eight met there by appointment is very silent. Their horses are ready for the long ride—some of them, it is greatly to be feared, abstracted from Confederate *caballados* on account of points of wind, bone, build, bottom, too tempting to be resisted. The men eat without alighting, for they must make a forced march tonight. The quantity of bread and meat handed to them by every member of the family, now hard at work, is wonderful; but the number of tin cups of strong black coffee drunk by those seated in the saddle is something absolutely astonishing. Each man, with the rapid run to Mexico—two hundred miles and over—before him, almost seems to have all the stomachs—seven, are there not?—of a camel to store for the trip.

The motive with each is the one motive with all alike. As long as possible they have "held on" to home, hoping in some way to escape going into the Confederate service. But Provost Marshal and Conscripting Officer are after them just now to that degree that they can hesitate no longer. And these officials will be "after them" on fleet horses and in good earnest by to-morrow night, when it is known that they have "broken for Mexico." There is not a moment for anything now but—a few more pints of coffee!

The family can hardly realize it. An instant more, and the place is empty of them; Uncle Frank gone with them, too, from out of a whirlwind of kissing—in which baby is tossed about like a straw—and hand-shaking, none more demonstrative than Hark, Rohamma, 'Markable; Duke and Snap tugging at their chains, and protesting vehemently.

Gone to Mexico! But for every touch of his horse's hoofs upon the prairie hurrying him away there is a heart-throb on the San Hieronymo bearing him steadily upward in fervent prayer. At the same moment there are many hundreds of like kinds of men—not the least valuable to Texas either—riding in the same direction from the same cause. And for a long time it seemed the oddest thing in the world to people in Texas slow to realize things, the idea of running away for life and freedom from the United States to—Mexico! *Mexico?*

CHAPTER XXI.

THE END AT HAND.

It is a beautiful evening, many, many long months after that eventful night. Both households have been long living together in the now thoroughly comfortable house on the San Hieronymo, bound a hundred-fold more closely together by the terrible times which have howled and foamed and broken about them like the waves upon an island. Supper has been ready and waiting an hour now, cooling, in fact, in the kitchen, while Rohamma has grown warmer in the expression, to Hark and 'Markable, of her sentiments in reference to Mass Madison, who is keeping them waiting. Not that she does not love Madison dearly; only it is a trial to her feelings to see so nice a supper "act'ly spilin' here, an he knows it, an he a sittin' on a log dar at de poss-ofiis listin' to de fool talk of dem poor 'stracted white folks. May de Yankees make dem scatter!"

"You better hold your tongue, woman," says her husband, fitting a new helve to his axe amid a pile of litter at the cabin door. "Fur what we know, Mass Madison been hangin' two hours by de neck to a live-oak. Nothin' more common dese last four years to people of *our* sort, an' you know it!"

Which effectually silences his wife.

It is getting darker every moment, and the family in the house have become thoroughly uneasy about the absent one. Long ago Mr. McRobert has walked to the bluff which commands a view of the road, Bessie beside him. The ladies, standing with Will and Dodles on the front porch, can see Bessie and her father shading their eyes with their hands, and looking down the road into the deepening twilight.

"We have been so wonderfully preserved, and for so long, may God forbid anything should have happened at last!" says the elder of the ladies.

"I have no fear at all," replies the other. "Frank has been so amazingly protected through all the peril *he* has passed that I have almost lost all apprehension, and you know how foolish Charley and I once were. Were we not, Charley?" And she kisses the curly-headed little boy, who is altogether too old and too fat and too restless to be in her arms as he is, only she has to lavish upon him not only all the affection due him, but his absent and imperilled father also. "Frank has come and gone so often between home and Mexico unhurt that I have hardly any fear at all now," she adds. "And then what a blessed thing it is that Madison is too young to be conscripted. There was your husband, you know how impossible it seemed for *him* to escape having to take the oath when he was conscripted, how we had everything ready for him to leave by himself for Mexico, and how they actually forgot to make him swear. And when he got his detail to collect saltpetre in the caves, we all said, surely they will not forget *this* time—and yet they forgot it again! Yes, I'm a firm believer in Providence; both of us are, ain't we, Charley?"

"Yes, but Providence very often permits— Bless me, Madison must be crazy!" remarks Mrs. McRobert. Not so incoherently as you might imagine either. For in the moment it is said they can see that the young gentleman so apostrophized has galloped up to his father, jumped off his foaming mustang almost before it has been reined in; has given his father a good hug; has seized his father's hat, and waved it and his own over his head with a shout; has caught up Bessie, thrown her, a heavy weight, higher by a yard in the air than he ever dared do before. Placing her on the ground any way, he has started on a run for the house; has seized Will, hastening to meet him, by the shoulders, and, placing one leg behind his brother for the purpose, has laid him flat upon his back on the ground; he would do it with Dodles, but he has a saw in his hand, and so saws at him as he tries it that he gives it up. It is as when he came back after his escape from the Indians, so long before.

"Oh, mother!" he shouts, "oh, aunt! at last! at last! Great news! Glorious news! Best news!" And he makes a clutch at Charley, evidently for the purpose of waving him over his head like a flag, his hat being dropped far behind. Prevented from this by the mother's redoubled embrace of the child, laughing and kicking to get to him, he hugs first his mother and then his aunt in his arms, his brown and handsome face sparkling with excitement.

"Why, Madison, I never knew you to do so," exclaims his astonished parent; and with real alarm, she adds, "Is it possible—?" ("You have been drinking," she would have added, only it is too absurdly impossible a thing to say.)

"Oh, news, mother—news, aunty—the best news in the world!" exclaims the excited youth. Hark, Rohamma, and 'Markable have joined the party on the porch, increased now by the coming-up of Mr. McRobert, Bessie, and Will, and all are eager to know what has crazed Madison, ordinarily sedate, and specially sobered by the severe experiences of the last few years—experiences which have whitened prematurely many a head and broken many a heart even among those far from actual fields of battle.

"But what is the news?" asks his father, and the question is repeated in the eager eyes of the rest crowding about him.

"Mr. Lincoln has been killed—assassinated. The news is certainly true!"

There is a sharp cry of intense anguish from the negroes. Even in the shock of their own surprise, the white family observe and are struck by it. In his eagerness, Madison had not noticed that they were present, or he would not have said it. During the whole war the whites in all families, Union or Secession, imparted no information, in reference to the progress of the war, to the blacks. Stranger still, these never asked any questions in regard to it of the whites; they seemed, so far as any manifestation in the presence of master, mistress, or the white children could evidence it, utterly unconcerned, uninterested. Among themselves, however, hoeing together in the field apart from white ears, or around their cabin fires at night, the case was very different.

"And do you call *that* glorious news?" exclaimed Mr. McRobert.

"Oh no, sir! no, no!" Madison hastened to explain. "Only the news has all come at once. You know not a soul of us has been off the place for a week. Oh, father, Richmond has fallen! General Lee's army has been captured! The Confederacy is gone! The war is over!"

"Thank God!" Mr. McRobert said it from the depth of his soul, giving expression to the feeling of every heart.

"And yet I cannot say that I do not also have a sense of humiliation, a regret at it, too," said his wife. "It is the defeat of our own, own people. I cannot endure the thought of their mortification and overthrow," she added, almost in tears; and her feelings were shared by all present, as they sat at the supper-table. "I do hope, Madison, you were prudent enough not to show any feeling at the post-office when you heard the news," she added, with sudden anxiety.

"As mum as a mouse, mother," said her son. "By this time I have had experience enough in all that. Don't you remember how it was when I was down at the Port last Christmas? That Monday news came there that Hood had captured Nashville, and that Sherman had been cut to pieces west of Savannah. Everybody believed it, and oh, how terribly sad I was! I told you how, at the first depot, on my way home, as I was sitting there so very blue, waiting for the cars to start again, a Confederate officer came in and sank upon the seat near me, his face a picture of distress, exclaiming, 'It is terrible! —terrible!' and told me of the telegram, just arrived at the depot, of Hood's defeat instead, and Sherman's safe arrival at the sea. My face was like wood, but my heart began beating, Thank God! thank God! thank God! like the ticking of a watch. While the cars were filling with people discussing the news, scoffing at it, General Hébert among them exclaimed with dignity, 'Evidently false, gentlemen — unworthy your least attention! As a military man, I *know* it to be impossible and untrue!' All the time — yes, and for hours after — I kept saying to myself, 'Oh, thank God! thank God! thank God!' My face was cold and hard as a mask, but a regular jubilee was going on inside. Never fear me; even Will here, and Bessie — Charley, too — we've all learned to be prudent; as to Doodle-bug, he was born as prudent as Solomon. We've been four years at school—are all of us ready to graduate in Prudence now."

"It seems to me like a long, feverish dream," said his mother, an hour later, after the news had been thoroughly read and discussed with the aid of the map, worn to tatters by perpetual use for so long a time.

"All your and aunt's puzzling how to make new shoes for us children and yourselves out of old ones," said Dodles; "how to get make-believes for coffee and tea and saleratus and bluing and soap, and all that; how to twist and pinch your bonnets so as to last a little longer, we mustn't forget that. And what a trouble we had having the spinning-wheel and loom made — such a spinning and weaving!"

"And moulding of candles, and making starch out of potatoes and wheat bran!" added Will. "What a time we had!"

"An' spoilin' my aprons an' things tryin' to dye them with pecan-tree bark! An'—oh yes!—an' the saddles an' bridles, Dodles, you an' Will were always tryin' to make, so ugly, an' always comin' to pieces again as soon as you tried them," said Bessie, who was getting over her lisp.

"Oh, what a sto-ry! They didn't!" replied Will.

"Yes they did, Will," persisted Bessie. "So did the shoes you an' Madison made, the ugly hats an' caps! How we all laughed at Hark that day he first wore the clothes ma made him out of our parlor carpet! An' my funny little bonnet ma made out of my doll's cloak! An', aunty, how we had to cut up the counterpane into frocks for Charlie, until Uncle Frank brought us those nice things from Mexico. An' oh, what times, aunty, we had twistin' an' hammerin' at our old hoops—ma an' me an' you!"

"And we all remember—hush, Bessie!—the sleepless nights we had lest Madison should be forced into the ranks," said Mr. McRobert.

"I remember," Madison said, "very well your not allowing me to go outside the house during the day for weeks and weeks, as I was too young to be conscripted—*barely* too young!—for fear some one passing by should see me. And how glad we were, as if we had inherited a fortune, that day I got my contract to furnish so much saltpetre a month, so as to keep out of the army."

"You must not forget the newspapers, printed on brown paper and wall-paper and the backs of court-house blanks, which we used to get — it seems already as if it all were ages ago," continued Mrs. Frank McRobert. "They were full of great Confederate victories; and how miserable you used to look, Brother Morton, over them; how you couldn't eat any dinner, nor play with the children; and how I could hear you from my room turning and groaning in your bed, or walking all night up and down, up and down!"

"Don't you remember, aunty, how very sad father was that night after Grant had besieged Vicksburg so long, and the paper proved that it was provisioned for two years longer, and could never be taken—never, never!" contributed Will.

"An'—oh yes!—how pa said in prayers that night, so often, Thy will be done! as if he was sick an' dyin'; yes, I remember it," added Bessie.

"Yes, and that very night, sitting right there at supper-table, you remember what *you* said, mother!" exclaimed Dodles. "You said, 'I've always thought they could never conquer the South, Morton. I've listened, my dear husband, faithfully to all' (mimicking his mother's tones as nearly as he dared); 'you can tell me of the wrong of secession. You may be right in the abstract'—I remember as if it were last night, mother— 'you *may* be right, Morton,' you said; 'but, for one, I cannot help wanting old Virginia to conquer the Federals. They are all of them Abolitionists, Morton—*Ab-o-li-tion-ists!*'"

"Oh yes," chorused Will and Bessie in a breath, "that was the very night Uncle Frank—"

"Came home from Mexico, crept into the window of my room so quietly after you were all asleep," said their aunt, promptly, and with a blush.

"But oh, aunty, what a fib it was!" exclaimed plain-spoken Bessie. "You told ma nothing was the matter with Charley when she heard him cry, and went to your door to ask."

"Nothing was the matter—he was only a little frightened at his pa with his long beard. You know I wouldn't let Frank disturb you all, sleeping so. And how we astonished you with Uncle Frank next morning! And," continued Charley's mother, "you remember how Frank laughed at you, Morton, for being so blue, and told you how the victory at Gettysburg was just the other way from what our news had made it, and all about the surrender of Vicksburg the very next day."

"An' oh, the good coffee uncle brought us from Mexico!" said Bessie, clapping her hands at the memory. "That was why I wasn't a bit sorry when he ran away again to Mexico, because I knew what beautiful, beautiful combs an' shoes an' things he would bring when he came back again."

"I wonder who it was kept Frank in the house, as if he had the measles, all the time he was here? And who—?" began Mr. McRobert, wonderfully brightened up.

"Of course I did," said the young wife, stoutly, "after his guiding that Union party to Mexico. And to think of his having come and gone twice between us and Mexico safely! and that he can actually come home *now*, come in broad day, come to stay, to live all the rest of his dear life with Charley and me!" And the joyful wife can say no more, but hides her face on Charley's fat shoulders and weeps silently; only she cannot realize that the war is indeed over—it is too good to be true; none of them can.

"But I wonder," says Madison, at last, to relieve the almost painful happiness of the moment, "if we ever will enjoy anything again as we did the magazines and picture papers from the North Uncle Frank used to send or bring us. I do believe we got to know each of them by heart. And 'don't you remember, father," he continued, in the restless joy of the occasion, shifting yet again the kaleidoscope of the wondrous period just expiring, "how often we expected the Federals to arrive—no doubt on earth about it *this* time—dozens of times?"

"And that afternoon," broke in Will, "I came tearing in nearly crazy, and told you I knew they were coming this time, for I had heard their cannon down south, and how I hurried out my flag from where I had hidden it under the floor—"

"Only thunder at last!" interrupted his brother. "Yes, and how you had barely time to hurry your flag under the floor again as Mr. Barker came in to tell us of the Federal repulse at the Sabine."

"The only people in this world," said Mr. McRobert, after a long silence among the excited group, "who thoroughly understand and appreciate our national deliverance, who come nearest thanking God for it as he ought to be thanked, are the Union people at the South. And their feeling is—unutterable," he added, with quivering lip and fast-filling eyes.

"And to think that we will see the old, old flag again after so many years! I feel as if I could hug and kiss it over and over again a thousand times!" exclaimed Mrs. Frank McRobert.

"Why, I thought it was Frank you loved most," began her brother-in-law.

"No, we love pa; but we love pa's flag a hundred times most; don't we, Charley?" she replied, Charley yielding only a sleepy assent thereto.

"And now," remarks the other Mrs. McRobert, as, at a late hour, they reluctantly separated for the night, "for one, I am glad the war is over, yet I *cannot* say I'm glad Virginia is subdued! I never want to see it again. Never mind. We won't speak about it. Now the war is over, there is this, at least—Madison can go on with his studies."

"And I can get some new books—bran-new picture-books—I feel as if I hadn't seen one for a hundred years!" said Will.

"An' I can get a new doll an' some real rock-candy! Oh yes, an' some new dresses an' hoops an' round combs, to break just as many as I please," cries Bessie, "now the bad, bad war is over!"

"All I want is to be sent to school to learn engineering," said Josie, gravely.

"An' we's free!" says Hark, in his cabin, at the same moment, but only to his wife, and in strictest confidence.

"Free? What you think *I* want wid freedom? Don't understand nothin' about it!" was her reply. "It's some mis'able *Texas* notion," she added.

But, except Charley and Bessie, no one could be truthfully said to have slept under that roof that night. No, nor under hundreds of thousands of other roofs that same night, either.

CHAPTER XXII.

IN WHICH OUR STORY ENDS AT LAST.

"YES, home at last, home, home! For the next year or so I don't expect to be outside my fence; for all the rest of my life I intend to whistle but one tune, except 'Hail Columbia,' 'Star-Spangled Banner,' and 'Yankee Doodle'—it's about the only other one I know—and that is 'Home, Sweet Home!'"

You have guessed aright as to who said it: it is Uncle Frank back again. He arrived last night—just three months and a half, to a day, since the events recorded in the last chapter. The returned Texan was in magnificent health. "If all the world over there is a nobler specimen of a man," his wife says to herself, as she sits there looking at his open, generous, though bronzed and bearded face, herself blushing at one moment, and pale the next with excessive joy—"all the wide world over a husband to be prouder of, or a happier wife, why, then—yes, Charley, you are right—get as close as you can—hold on with both hands!"

Which advice is not needed by Charley, who has coiled himself in a fat circle about his father's neck, and has hold upon his father's luxuriant beard with both of his chub-by hands, evidently intending never again to let go as long as he lives. But he is not a bit worse than his mother, who has tight hold upon her husband's hand, kissing, when she deceives herself into believing nobody sees her, such parts of the beaming face as Charlie for the moment leaves open to approach.

"And you have improved, Frank!" she says, for the hundredth time. "Hasn't he, Morton?"

"Amazingly! And this is the reason," says the one appealed to, who dearly loves to trace all events to their causes—"Frank has been exposed to incessant dangers for years now, day and night, and nothing quickens a man more. Then, he has travelled over the Union, seen all its cities, associated with its leading men, made thrilling appeals to vast audiences everywhere — you see, Frank, we have been reading about you in the papers. Most of all, you have gone heart, soul, and body into the grandest cause the world ever knew. Of course he is improved! No merit in him for it, I'm sure. Only I am afraid, afraid—" adds didactic Mr. Morton McRobert.

"He won't be contented to settle down to our quiet life at the ranch," adds the wife, with a flash of anxiety over her eager face. "Yes, I've thought of that," she says. "But do as you please, dear—you may do as you *please;* if you will only keep Charley and me with you, you may live in a whirlwind if you wish; we will hold to you only the closer, won't we, Charley?"

"And after I have just said I won't leave home soon again!" exclaims the aggrieved Texan. "There is plenty to do on the ranch. Plenty to do besides the looking - up and branding of stock — so many years' arrears to be done; a little hunting between times. Game has had its own way all these years; we will have to fight it a little to keep it out of doors. Most of all, after a while, not now, not for years perhaps, but some day, certain, I intend to go on the stump!"

"On the stump!" ejaculate those present. Uncle Frank is seated in the midst of a good deal of confusion, himself the radiant centre. He has known very well during his absence, and the last has been the longest by far, of the privations of the family in reference even to the most necessary articles of clothing. And during his long absence it has been a chief pleasure with him to buy continually, while in the cities, such things as he supposed were needed. Four large trunks are standing open around him—Madison, Will, Dodles, Bessie, Rohamma, and Mrs. Morton McRobert have been at work an hour now unpacking them. As to Mrs. Frank, all she cares for is her husband; she hardly looks at any-

thing else. And a noisy time it is, as one after another of the exceedingly miscellaneous assortment is brought to light. Bessie has already come upon three dolls, beautiful beyond her wildest dreams, and, fortified from interruption behind a bulwark of dresses and shoes, rock-candy, hoops, and flaming picture-books, is in unsatiated search for more, with incessant screams of delight. Will is not much more silent than his sister, as he, too, comes upon articles evidently purchased for Madison, Dodles, and himself. There is a new book for Dodles, full of pictures of machinery; but the incipient machinist almost loses his wits when he comes at last upon a small but costly steam-engine, all of brass and steel, ready for working—"one calf-power," his uncle tells him. Every now and then Mrs. Morton McRobert finds and unrolls some shawl or dress altogether too costly for country life, or of a wrong shade or fabric.

"Bless my soul, Frank, what *did* you buy —?" she begins. But Frank's wife shakes her head at her with laughing but earnest rebuke. If he had brought in the trunks a diamond crown, a complete bridal outfit, or a small crocodile, it would have been exactly right in her eyes.

"Well, you know," Uncle Frank has replied to any special remonstrance of the kind, with a rueful glance at the article in question, "you ladies understand shopping; I don't. I saw that roll of lace, for instance, in the window of a milliner, or something of the kind, on Broadway, New York. I went in, and told the lady behind the counter—she had the freshest complexion I ever knew—that it was one of the prettiest things I ever saw, and asked her if it wasn't the kind of thing ladies sewed around the edges of their bonnets, or frocks, or sleeves—somewhere or other. She said yes, it was exactly that. I remember I paid a tremendous price for it. She was so kind as to show me those other things there. Yes, I bought them all. When I paid her bill, she said I was a gentleman of excellent taste in such things, hoped I would call again. You see I always had one trunk on hand at my hotel. It was so convenient to buy things as I came on them along the streets, to pack them in when I came home at night; it made me feel so pleasant, doing something for you all far away."

And so good Mrs. McRobert could only groan as she brought up article after article, holding it up in mute appeal for her sister-in-law to see, who would only assent to her dismay with a merry nod, but not for an instant permit her husband to be called in question therefor.

"The stump! Why, uncle, unless there was a Federal force right there, they would shoot or hang you!" says Madison, returning to what his uncle had said about it.

"They would *now*, of course," Uncle Frank cheerfully acquiesces. "I think I ought to know that. But they won't after a while. I can wait. The day will come when I can—yes, and will—take the stump in any part of Texas. Two parties in this land are grinding away upon each other, in opposite directions, like mill-stones, turning tremendously—"

"Why, uncle, in a mill it's only *one* stone that turns—the upper one; the lower stone never stirs a hair—" begins Dodles.

"Never mind," says the Texan, with a smile. "What I mean is, the questions before this nation are being steadily, if slowly, ground out. We'll get the fine flour at last! As if the sublimest revolution in all history could be completed in a year or two! No, sir! There are few men who understand how vast are the results we are arriving at. Arriving at, not for this great republic only and for all generations after us, but for every other nation in the world besides. I tell you—"

"Law, Mass Frank," breaks in Rohamma, a gorgeous package in hand, which her mistress had just thrust therein in mute despair, "dis here dress for *me!* It's mighty splendid; but it's stuff for parlor windows like we used to have in ole Virgin—"

"Hush!" says Mrs. Frank, with warning hand; and Rohamma pours the rest of her remark into the sympathizing ear of Mrs. McRobert, kneeling beside her among the open trunks.

"Never mind. Wait till you hear me on the stump. Wait; that's all; wait a while. If I don't know the people of Texas," continues the Texan, almost pathetically, "I would like to know who does; and I tell you—" and here he rises in his enthusiasm from his seat and stands erect, Charley cleaving with both arms, like a crab, about his neck—"the Texans are the noblest people on this earth.

Intelligent, energetic, truthful, ardent, wholesome, healthy, whole-souled! I tell you," continued the speaker, himself a fit specimen thereof, "Texas is in the ore yet, but it's the richest ore the sun ever shone on. Wait; that's what I say; wait. As to the New-Englanders, no one can admire them more than I do for their wonderful traits of character. Like the rest of us, they have defects, of course. I have been up among them, off and on, for years now. They are bright, keen, cold, sharp — too sharp, *over-whet* by eternal sharpening. There is more breadth, depth, warmth about us of the South and the West. It is like an axe. The Yankees are the edge—steel, blue, and razorish; we are the rest of the axe, thicker, stronger, more lasting. The edge must go first, but the rest of the axe follows. Just wait," he adds, wincing a little at Charley's clutch upon his beard, and laying his hand upon the head of his wife, seated beside him; "Texas is at school just now; the lesson is awfully hard to learn, but the discipline is tremendous, and the scholars are smart. It'll be with us like that poor Pete Hoogenboom — Hoogenboom's oldest son, you know; I saw him yesterday—"

"Pete Hoogenboom!" exclaimed Will and Madison in a breath.

"Yes, I know all about his conscription," says Uncle Frank, "and desertion. You thought here he had been hung, or had escaped to Mexico. Not a bit of it. He has been lying in the brake afraid to come in, till he is a perfect savage. He came upon me as I was riding home yesterday. I've learned a way of looking around very sharp for game as I go, especially sharp for bushwhackers these last few years. As I was riding, I saw one eye of the man peeping at me from an old dead cedar-top pile fifty yards off the road to the right. Somehow I felt it was Pete. I halted, called out to him who I was, ordered him, in a cheery way, to come to me. It was a long time before he would. In fact, I went up to him. He was almost stark-naked. What with hair and beard and finger-nails uncut, starvation, sleeping on the earth, and miserable watching for his life, he had become a wild animal. He sat there on the ground, crouched together like a dying brute.

"'Colonel, what *is* the news?' he said at last, glancing up at me like a wild thing fastened in a trap—keen, but shaking all over. 'Why, don't you know, Pete? Where have you been all this time not to have heard?' I said. 'In the brake up here, Colonel. I haven't seen a soul to speak to for months — been so hunted, you know. Colonel, what *is* the news?' he said, like a wounded man begging for water. I told him. Told him the Confederacy was gone to final smash; told him the old flag was over us again; told him all—*all!*" The Texan added, with kindling eye and cheek, "He was, yes, drawn together like a dying panther at my feet, looking up with glittering eyes, though, as I talked. As soon as I told him the war was over, he gave a sort of bound. I tell you he left the earth a brute, on his back at that; he landed on his feet a man; yes, lighted on his feet erect as an arrow, strong as an oak, a man again! And so Texas will land on its feet again, the grandest state in all the Union. Just wait."

"This wretched abolition of slavery has to be settled first. Just to think, Frank," exclaims Mrs. Morton McRobert, turning, in the energy of her vexation, from the open trunks to say it, "Hark and Rohamma here, born in the family, raised with us from children, indulged, and even petted all their lives—look at them! As soon as General Granger landed at Galveston, he issued a proclamation freeing the negroes. There wasn't a family in Texas but called all their people in the house the day they got the proclamation, and read it to them, just as we did!"

"And how did Hark and Rohamma here take it?" inquired her brother-in-law, with interest, and resuming his seat by his wife.

"Well, for a long time they seemed bewildered, couldn't work, would neither stand nor sit nor lie down—they were in a joyful maze, perfectly crazy I called it. Then they, and all the negroes in the country, took a sudden notion to leave—couldn't realize they were free except by going off the place and living to themselves. Going to housekeeping! That was the cry among them all. Morton fixed up a cabin for Hark and his family on the south field; we gave them everything we could possibly spare—all owners did—towards their housekeeping, as they called it, poor things! You ought to have seen how solemn

and important they were, but they soon got tired of it, begged to come back. We ha... them, of course, and they are... again on wages. And now I d... you foolish creature, you"—thi... Rohamma, folding and unfolding... very miscellaneous goods, with a... ure face, beside her former mistress—"you will have sense to *stay* where you are!"

"You see, I'm teaching 'Markable to read and write and cipher, uncle, and you have no idea how fast he is learning," Will, ceasing from pulling on a pair of new boots just drawn from a trunk, eagerly remarks. "And oh! I want so much to tell you about the break-up of the Confederate army at Austin; it was so funny the way they seized all the government stores they could lay their hands on, every man riding off with a sack of coffee, or a dozen boots, or ever so many bottles of quinine! Madison and I were down there, and saw it all."

"But it was not so funny to see the powder-house thrown open to everybody," added Madison, "men and children, wading in among the powder, inches deep on the floor, helping themselves, carrying it off in hats and wash-basins. No wonder there were so many boys burned or blown up, experimenting with their powder."

"And, oh yes, uncle," breaks in Will again, "Madison and I saw General Shelby ride through Austin, at the head of his men, on their way to Mexico—more than three hundred of them, almost all of them officers— such noble-looking men! Everybody said they were going to sack the towns as they passed through, but

they ... ...ey kept the best
disc... ... e world until they
got ... Antonio, at least."
" ... time they will have
in ... added Uncle Frank.
" ... concern it is, tumbling
al ... rs of all who go near
it ... g I do most earnestly
h ... earnestly hope," he con-
t ... considerable emphasis,
... s, that our own govern-
have the sense to keep
ico — to keep away from
shape, fashion, and form!
...xico well; have been over
...es, in every direction, buy-
before the war, and travel-
during the war. Our one
to leave the Mexicans to
...es, keep away from them, let
...ne! In a few years or so
..... will be in the Union; but it
must drop into it of itself, after having utterly used itself up. With its
mines and its rich lands and its delightful climate, it *is* worth having,
but not till the people who are such
a curse to it have mutually pronun-
ciamentoed themselves from the face
of the earth! Providence? Any
man is stone-blind, a born fool into
the bargain"—and the Texan is compelled to rise again to his feet suit-
ably to express himself—"who cannot see what a glorious republic God
intends ours to be. Look at our Texas boys! Did ever men fight so, endure so, if it *was* under the wrong
flag? And Texas never was whipped
yet. Half a dozen times the Federals tried it, but we know how they
succeeded! Texas was the only state
in the Confederacy that wasn't whip-

ped—that yielded only because the
others were. Get these same men
under the old and the true flag and
see! Just wait, that's all—wait!
Those little bits of half-acres they
call states in New England *have*
been ahead of us all along in some
things—settled first, you know—but
their work is about done; ours is
coming on. Only you wait until
Texas comes fairly on the stage, all
its obsolete follies sloughed off, its
rich lands under cultivation, stock
grazing by millions on its prairies,
its quarries and mines worked; railroads, manufactories, churches, public
schools, everywhere; law supreme
upon every league of land; absolute
and equal justice and freedom as uni-
versal over it as its glorious climate!
Then our time will have come! It
will be like Franklin's little old
printing-press as compared with
one of Hoe's cylinder machines.
We'll put New England on a shelf,
with a glass case over it, for the sake
of what it has been; but we—we are
the People of the Future!—ain't we,
Will? ain't we, Dodles? ain't we,
Madison? ain't we, Charley? Things
move fast these days. God knows
there's too much bitterness yet; many
of our best people shut their eyes
tight, and *won't* see the certain future! Only wait. Ten years from
this time we will all have agreed to
forget the bloody past; will be a
peaceful and united people. God
Almighty wills it, and, in his own
way, he is powerful enough to bring
it about—yes, and wise enough and
loving enough. See if I'm not a
true prophet!"

"I don't think I have half done learning all Texas has got to teach me," said Madison. "There's a great deal to be seen and to be done here yet."

"Oh yes," said Will, who had been silent in his chair so long that they supposed him asleep, "plenty to do: there's the bathing-house to put up, and that splendid pleasure-boat we've all been intending so long to build, too. And I've got to finish my collection of bugs and reptiles and things—as you call them, petrifactions and the like. I find something new for it every day. And there's budding and grafting of choice varieties on mustang grape-stock; and apples on the haws. Then there's a collection of cactus to make; and a honey-palace for the bees to build; and—oh yes! a hundred thousand things to do."

"Oh, as to that," said his brother, "you haven't mentioned half. There's a fish-trap to make in the spring, and a seine to knit for the river. And there's New Braunsfels, the German town, to visit; and San Antonio, the wonderful Mexican city, with the ruins of grand old missions around it, to see. Yes, I want to visit the Enchanted Rock I've heard so much about, that glitters like a mountain of diamonds—it's not two hundred miles from here. And, then, I've heard of wonderful caves all around. Oh yes, there's that one-eyed panther uncle has fought so often—if he is alive still—*he* has to be shot!"

"And there's the new church to build," suggested the father; "and a nice one it shall be. And Frank and myself must both erect better houses soon, and take in a great deal more prairie under fence."

"Yes, father," said Madison; "and I've set my heart on going out on a buffalo-hunt with uncle. And I want to learn German of Hoogenboom, and how to draw of Aunt Agnes."

"And I'm going to make a better electrical machine," said Dolles. "Besides, I am sure I can fix to grind our hominy mill with the engine uncle brought me. Then, Bessie and I have our 'elephants' to look after. Yes, and—"

"And there's the silver-mines we've got to visit," added Uncle Frank, in a lower tone, to Madison. "If necessary, we'll go to the Santa Rita mines of Arizona, the richest beds of silver in the world. Oh, as to Texas, it is a grand country!" he continued, in a louder voice—"it's so tremendously large—old Virginia multiplied by fifty, I believe—that it'll take years to hunt out all there is to see in it. I believe new insects and flowers and the like are created every year—new kinds, I mean. There isn't a week hardly but what I come upon something bran-new to me. As to adventures of all kinds, they spring up, like everything else on Texas soil, abundant, innumerable. We haven't learned more than the A B C of Texas yet—we have only made a little start in knowing about it. But it's time for us, Agnes, darling, to be walking over home," he said, rising from his seat. "I'll tell what we'll do. Will, you go ahead collecting for your museum as fast as you can: we'll all add to it everything we happen upon. Hark and Hoogenboom will do what they can to help us. So will the rest. Next time I'm in Austin, I'll buy Madison a writing-desk, several reams of the best paper I can find, a big bottle of ink, and a gold pen, and let him keep a history of everything for us. He can make a fair start from the first of next month, and by the end of a year I'll be bound his book will be worth reading. All in favor of my proposition will please to say Ay!" And, with the laughing and unanimous assent that followed, the group separated for the night.

THE END.

HARPER & BROTHERS'

OCTOBER BOOK-LIST.

☞ HARPER & BROTHERS *will send any of the following books by mail (excepting the larger works whose weight excludes them from the mail), postage prepaid, to any part of the United States, on receipt of the price.*

☞ HARPER'S NEW CATALOGUE, 532 *pp., 8vo, being a descriptive list of about 3000 volumes, with a* COMPLETE ANALYTICAL INDEX, *and a* VISITORS' GUIDE TO HARPER & BROTHERS' ESTABLISHMENT *giving an interesting description of the buildings in which their business is carried on, and of the various processes in the manufacture of their books, sent by mail on receipt of Nine Cents in Postage Stamps.*

Just Published or Nearly Ready:

SCIENTIFIC MEMOIRS. By Dr. J. W. DRAPER.
THE STORY OF LIBERTY. By C. C. COFFIN.
ILLUSTRATED HISTORY OF ANCIENT LITERATURE. By J. D. QUACKENBOS.
LIKE UNTO LIKE.

PRIMER OF ENGLISH LITERATURE: CLASSICAL PERIOD. By EUGENE LAWRENCE.
THE BUBBLE REPUTATION. By KATHARINE KING.
SELECTED POEMS OF MATTHEW ARNOLD.

THE ROMANCE OF A BACK STREET.

The Ceramic Art.

A Compendium of the History and Manufacture of Pottery and Porcelain. By JENNIE J. YOUNG. With 464 Illustrations. 8vo, Cloth, $5 00. (*Just Ready.*)

This work has been arranged upon so comprehensive a plan that it must meet the requirements of every one interested in ceramic art or any of its branches. An unusually full and carefully compiled index makes it invaluable as a book of reference. Potters, artists, and all who are attracted by the technology and methods of the ceramic art, will be amply gratified by the section devoted to materials, and to the many processes by which vases and table wares become in form and decoration entitled to be ranked with works of art. The general principles of the art, as they can be gathered from a comparative review of distinctive national styles, are fully explained. Their application to a critical estimate of the works of the potter is also pointed out.

The historical part of the book covers more ground than any previous work. While the earliest relics of the potters of Egypt and the East, the famous old wares of China and Japan, the mediæval wonders of Spain, Italy, and France, are described at length, due space is also given to the modern European factories, manufacturers, and artists. Many new points have been made in writing of China, and the chapter devoted to Japan throws over that country a flood of light which will be welcome to all who have felt the fascination of Oriental art. The narrative throughout is enlivened by biographical sketches of eminent potters and incidents in their lives, and by many historical episodes in the careers of famous men and women who exercised an influence upon the development of the art.

The section devoted to America contains full details of the potteries of the Peruvians, Brazilians, Central Americans, Mound-builders, Pueblos, and Indians, and also of the modern potters and artists of the United States, down to the present year.

The Story of Liberty.

By CHARLES CARLETON COFFIN, Author of "The Boys of '76." Illustrated. 8vo, Cloth. (*Nearly Ready.*)

Villages and Village Life.

With Hints for their Improvement. By NATHANIEL HILLYER EGLESTON. Post 8vo, Cloth, $1 75.

"This is the work of a man who possesses a genuine love of the country and of country life, and who writes from personal experience of the rural enjoyments he describes. But while he writes with a truly poetic sense of the beauties and pleasures of the country, he gives due weight to the practical side of rural life, and treats of 'village improvements,' 'trees and tree-planting,' 'country dwelling-houses,' 'drainage,' 'ventilation,' 'roads and bridges,' 'the preservation of woodlands,' 'the village library,' and kindred topics; so that, besides being a most delightful book, it is a practical guide for those who wish to adorn or improve a country residence, or assist in making a village at once beautiful and healthful."

Draper's Scientific Memoirs.

Scientific Memoirs, being Experimental Contributions to a Knowledge of Radiant Energy. By JOHN WILLIAM DRAPER, M.D., LL.D., President of the Faculty of Science in the University of New York, Author of "A Treatise on Human Physiology," "History of the Intellectual Development of Europe," "History of the American Civil War," &c. With a Portrait. 8vo, Cloth, $3 00. (*Just Ready.*)

The Primrose Path.

A Chapter in the Annals of the Kingdom of Fife. By Mrs. OLIPHANT, Author of "The Chronicles of Carlingford," "Agnes," &c. 8vo, Paper, 50 cents.

The refinement of its humor and the picturesqueness of its descriptive setting cannot fail to be appreciated. * * * There is not a character without individuality from one end of the book to the other.—*Athenæum, London.*

Very few modern novelists have written more or better than Mrs. Oliphant. Her plots are always well matured and artistically developed. There is not a poor character nor a dull chapter in this story.—*Albany Journal.*

A charming novel from the pen of Mrs. Oliphant, to whom thanks are due for some of the most finished, refined, and agreeable novels of the day.—*Portland Press.*

The Atlantic Islands.

The Atlantic Islands as Resorts of Health and Pleasure. By S. G. W. BENJAMIN, Author of "Contemporary Art in Europe," &c. Illustrated. 8vo, Cloth, $3 00.

The author has given us some of the liveliest and most interesting descriptions of island scenery and island life that have recently appeared in print. * * * His pages abound with bits of local history, and there are numerous amusing anecdotes of his adventures with the islanders which make his narrative interesting even to those who never expect to make the journeys he recommends. * * * The abundant information it offers regarding the islands which it mentions, their history, the peculiar features of their scenery, the various statistics of population, and the condition of the industries carried on upon their shores, will have an interest for many, while the illustrations profusely distributed through each chapter add much to the general attractiveness of the text.—*N. Y. Times.*

Mr. Benjamin has the instincts of a true traveller. He sees everything, and he remembers everything.—*Boston Transcript.*

It gives very vivid and entertaining descriptions of the scenery, social life, business and commerce, climate and accommodations for visitors, in all the chief groups of islands on both the eastern and western side of the Atlantic.—*Zion's Herald, Boston.*

Very intelligently and pleasingly written, and affords valuable information to the invalid or the pleasure seeker.—*Saturday Evening Gazette, Boston.*

A Legacy. Written and Edited by the Author of "John Halifax."

A Legacy: Being the Life and Remains of John Martin, Written and Edited by the Author of "John Halifax, Gentleman." 12mo, Cloth, $1 50.

Among the many tributes that are offered to success, it is instructive to find one like this volume of Miss Mulock laid at the feet of failure. It is impossible to read such a history as that of John Martin without feeling drawn into deeper sympathy with that immense class of men and women whom we see everywhere about us toiling, suffering, struggling, and hoping, those whose lives go to make up the truth of the bitter proverb, "The many fail, the one succeeds."—*N. Y. Times.*

The China Hunters Club.

By the Youngest Member. Illustrated. Post 8vo, Cloth, $1 75.

Gives a vast deal of information about the kinds of pottery used by the American forefathers and foremothers. * * * The chapters are a succession of stories connected with old pottery, discussions that abound in pleasant information and amusement; and the book, a pleasant summer or winter companion, gives just the sort of information many want about ceramic art without being technical.—*Journal of Commerce, N. Y.*

A fascinating book.—*Hartford Daily Times.*

The writer has so skilfully used her technical information that the ordinary reader will need to be told that he is engaged in obtaining new and valuable information instead of loitering about in quaint New England homes for the mere pleasure of studying the people and their ways. * * * It is a volume of the first importance to all American collectors.—*Hartford Courant.*

The grace and liveliness of the author's style are qualities which lie upon the surface, and we are not a little impressed by her exhaustive acquaintance with what may be called the anecdotical record of the potter's art. Under the guise of recounting the proceedings and discussions of a club of amateurs, she has managed to infuse a good deal of human interest into a somewhat didactic theme. * * * The capital merit of the book is the effective exhibition of the historical and literary aspects of ceramics.—*N. Y. Sun.*

The Student's Ecclesiastical History.

The History of the Christian Church during the First Ten Centuries: from its Foundation to the Full Establishment of the Holy Roman Empire and the Papal Power. By PHILIP SMITH, B.A., Author of the "Student's Old Testament History," and the "Student's New Testament History." With Illustrations. 12mo, Cloth, $1 75. Uniform with the *Student's Series.*

This valuable work should be in the hands of all who are interested in the subject. The reader's interest is fully maintained by the pleasing and unaffected manner adopted.—*Rock, London.*